"I'm sorry," Sarah said quietly.

"They had no right to talk to you that way."

Connor shrugged, a tight, bitter smile thinning his lips. "It's no less than I expected. They're just picking up where they left off twelve years ago."

"What do you mean?"

"Don't tell me you've forgotten, Sarah. Every town needs a bad boy, and I was nominated real early. Don't tell me that the citizens of Pine Butte haven't filled your ears with a catalog of my sins, past and present."

"Yes, but that's because..." She hesitated.

"It doesn't matter anymore. Actually, I should thank them. If it wasn't for the way I was treated here in Pine Butte, I wouldn't be what I am today."

"And what is that, Connor?" she asked softly.

"A man who gets what he wants. Remember that, Sarah."

Sarah shivered. She had a feeling she knew what Connor MacCormac wanted....

Dear Reader,

We've got one of our most irresistible lineups ever for you this month, and you'll know why as soon as I start talking about the very first book. With *The Return of Rafe MacKade, New York Times* bestseller Nora Roberts begins a new miniseries, The MacKade Brothers, that will move back and forth between Intimate Moments and Special Edition. Rafe is also our Heartbreaker for the month, so don't get your heart broken by missing this very special book!

Romantic Traditions continues with Patricia Coughlin's *Love in the First Degree,* a compelling spin on the "wrongly convicted" story line. For fans of our Spellbound titles, there's *Out-Of-This-World Marriage* by Maggie Shayne, a marriage-of-convenience story with a star-crossed—and I mean that literally!— twist. Finish the month with new titles from popular authors Terese Ramin with *A Certain Slant of Light,* Alexandra Sellers with *Dearest Enemy,* as well as *An Innocent Man* by an exciting new writer, Margaret Watson.

This month, and every month, when you're looking for exciting romantic reading, come to Silhouette Intimate Moments—and enjoy!

Yours,

Leslie J. Wainger
Senior Editor and Editorial Coordinator

Please address questions and book requests to:
Silhouette Reader Service
U.S.: 3010 Walden Ave., P.O. Box 1325, Buffalo, NY 14269
Canadian: P.O. Box 609, Fort Erie, Ont. L2A 5X3

AN INNOCENT MAN

MARGARET WATSON

Silhouette

INTIMATE MOMENTS®

Published by Silhouette Books

America's Publisher of Contemporary Romance

SILHOUETTE BOOKS

ISBN 0-373-07636-3

AN INNOCENT MAN

MARGARET WATSON

says that from the time she learned to read, she could usually be found with her nose in a book. Her lifelong passion for reading led to her interest in writing, and now she's happily writing exactly the kind of stories she likes to read. Margaret is a veterinarian who lives in the Chicago suburbs with her husband and their three daughters. In her spare time she enjoys in-line skating, birding and spending time with her family.

For Bill,
with all my love

Chapter 1

The motorcycle skidded to a halt at the edge of the hard-packed dirt road. Connor MacCormac slowly loosened his grip on the handlebars and raised the dusty visor of his helmet, never taking his eyes off the town nestled in the valley below.

He didn't need a map to tell him it was Pine Butte, Colorado. The pattern of houses, the weathered sign proclaiming it as the home of Wesley Mining Inc., the shape of the road twisting down the mountain were all burned into his memory. No, he couldn't forget Pine Butte.

Snapping the visor into place, he jump started the motorcycle and pressed the accelerator just a little too hard. The bike slid to the side, then righted itself and roared toward the next switchback. Pine Butte was fifteen minutes away.

A pair of eagles soared in the turquoise sky, and the tree-covered mountain next to him dappled the road with shadows. He barely noticed. All his attention was focused on the town that drew steadily closer. Anticipation, anger and the memory of old shame curled through him as he looked down on the houses, still no larger than tiny pebbles below him.

This time would be different, he told himself. The motorcycle shot forward. He wasn't a boy anymore. This time he was a man, and justice would be done.

He spared only a glance for the car that approached around the curve of the next switchback. It was going too fast, judging by the plume of dust that trailed behind it. But hell, if some fool wanted to throw himself off the side of the mountain, it wasn't his business.

As the car approached, he instinctively moved to the far side of the road. He'd give the idiot all the room he wanted. The car seemed to accelerate as it got closer, and Connor moved over a hair farther. Glancing at the edge of the road, he realized with a lick of uneasiness that there wasn't anywhere to go but down.

The car barreled toward him, going much too fast for the curving, narrow road. Connor stared at it, his hands clutching the brakes as he tried futilely to stop.

In a horrible kind of suspended motion, he saw the car swerve toward him. Searing pain ripped up his leg as the fender flashed past. As he fell, spinning through the air, he realized that Pine Butte had won, after all.

Sarah Wesley stepped back, dropped a kiss on the small blond head of the sobbing girl sitting on the examination table and pulled a brightly colored sticker out of her pocket with great ceremony. As she'd hoped it would, the appearance of the prize stopped the tears as if by magic.

"You don't have this one in your collection yet, do you, Jenny?" she teased gently, trying to distract the child from the pain of the injection.

Jenny shook her head vigorously and reached for the sticker. "No! Can I go show it to Tommy?"

"Go ahead, honey," Jenny's mother said. "Your brother's in the waiting room." As the child ran out the door, the woman turned to Sarah. "What now?" she asked with quiet desperation.

Sarah leaned against the counter and unwound the stethoscope from her neck with a sigh. "I don't think you have any choice, Mary. I think you need to get the surgery done."

The girl's mother paled. "She's so small, Sarah."

"I know." Reaching out, she took the other woman's hand. "But the heart specialist in Denver is wonderful. I wouldn't send you to him if I didn't think he was the best." After squeezing Mary's hand, she let it go and turned around, scribbling a name and phone number on a piece of paper. "At least call and talk to him. I'll write up a history for him and send it off today. If nothing else, go up to Denver and have him look at Jenny."

Mary rested her hands on the rounded swelling of her abdomen, as if protecting her unborn baby from the news. "I'm scared," she whispered.

"That's why I want you to talk to the specialist," Sarah replied firmly. "All this stress and worry isn't good for you or the baby." Pressing the slip of paper in her friend's hand, she said, "Call him today, Mary."

Sarah watched as her oldest friend turned and walked slowly out of the exam room, collected her two children and left the office. Mary looked as if she bore the weight of the world on her slender shoulders.

Wishing sadly that she could have given Mary good news, Sarah stared for a moment at the place where she had disappeared, then turned and walked into her little cubicle in the corner. Her desk was overflowing with papers, books and magazines. A stack of patient records stood in one corner, silently demanding her attention.

Throwing herself into her chair, she sat for a moment with her head cupped in both hands. A wisp of inadequacy and helplessness fluttered in her chest and was quickly banished. Useless wishes wouldn't help either Mary or Jenny. Writing this letter would.

Engrossed in her description of Jenny Johnson's medical history and symptoms, she didn't register the commotion in the waiting room of her clinic. Not until her assistant burst into her office, breathless, did she look up with a start.

"What's the matter, Josie?"

"An accident," the girl panted. "Up on Eagle Ridge Road. Someone on a motorcycle went off the edge."

Sarah jumped up and looked around for her emergency bag. "How long ago?"

Josie shrugged. "Sheriff just found him. All he said was the guy needs help, real bad."

Heart pounding, palms already beginning to sweat, Sarah tossed syringes and bottles of medication into her bag, grabbing anything she might conceivably need. "Get him on the radio and tell him I'm on my way."

Jumping into her ancient pickup truck, she threw the bag onto the seat next to her and looked down with disgust at her shaking hands. Clenching her teeth against the automatic reaction to the news of an accident on Eagle Ridge Road, she used both hands to insert the key into the ignition. With a cough and a sputter, the engine started up. A few seconds later she was on Main Street, heading toward the mountain.

Taking deep breaths, she banished from her mind the nightmare images of horribly tight curves and steep dropoffs. Running through all the different injuries a motorcycle-accident victim might have, she forced herself to think only about her job.

For about the millionth time she cursed the fact that she might not have enough training to save the victim. As a nurse practitioner, she could handle a lot of emergencies, but there were some things she just couldn't do. For the second time that day the old regret burned in her throat. If only she had been able to go to medical school.

Gripping the steering wheel more tightly, she steeled her mind against that useless thought. Regretting the path her life had taken wasn't going to do this accident victim any good. As she bumped along the dusty road, she prayed that she could help her patient until they could get the evacuation helicopter into Pine Butte.

Just around the next curve, she spotted the flashing lights of the sheriff's car. She jumped out of her truck almost before it had stopped and ran to the edge of the road.

The sheriff crouched beside a figure dressed all in black lying prone and very still among the rocks. Down the slope, sunlight reflected off the crumpled remains of a motorcycle. Scrambling around the scrub bushes and larger rocks, Sarah skidded to a stop next to the sheriff and knelt.

"Is he still alive?" she asked, her hand automatically reaching for a pulse on the body.

Tom Johnson nodded without looking at her. "He's breathing."

Her gaze swept quickly over the body that lay so still, stopping at the sight of her reflection in the visor of his helmet. Ignoring the sheriff kneeling next to her, she gently pulled away the blanket covering the unconscious man. A huge gash on his left thigh oozed blood steadily. The ground beneath it was soaked with blood, and she saw that the sheriff had placed a tourniquet just above the cut.

"Looks like you got here just in time, Tom. He could have bled to death without that tourniquet." She pulled open her bag, then fastened her stethoscope over her ears, unzipped his black leather jacket and listened to his chest. When she'd finished that, she examined him carefully from the tips of his toes to his neck. His muscles were hard and fit, his shoulders broad beneath the jacket. The visor on his helmet refused to budge when she tried to raise it to look at his face.

"He may have a few cracked ribs," she announced, dropping her stethoscope into her bag and reaching for a syringe. "Nothing else is broken, and I don't think he's bleeding internally. I'm afraid to take his helmet off right now. Stumbling around on this uneven ground could make any head or neck injury worse. It can wait until he's at the clinic."

"Okay, what next?"

"Run up to my truck and get the board."

As the sheriff struggled up the slope, Sarah sat back on her heels and looked at the man lying so still in front of her. He was long and lean, his muscles sleek rather than bulky. Even when he was unconscious, vitality radiated out of him with every beat of his heart beneath her fingers. Her hand tightened on the pulse in his wrist, then she gently laid his hand on the rocky ground. She would make sure all that life and vitality didn't slip away.

"You're going to be all right," she murmured. "Tom's getting the stretcher, and we'll get you into the clinic." He didn't stir or give any indication he'd heard her, but she kept talking, murmuring reassuring nothings to him.

She wondered who he was. Not anyone from Pine Butte, she knew that for a fact. This man wasn't one she would have forgotten, and as the only medical person in the town, she was sure she knew just about all of them. No, he was a stranger. "We'll take care of you," she whispered, again taking his hand in hers.

As she laid her other hand on his chest to monitor his breathing, the heat of his body burned into her fingers through the thin material of his T-shirt. She wondered where he'd been headed. Watching his motionless form intently, she beat down a whisper of envy. She couldn't even begin to imagine how free he must have felt, roaring up and down the mountains with the wind in his hair.

"Here's the board, Sarah," Tom Johnson panted, interrupting her thoughts. Laying it down carefully next to the faceless stranger, he squatted. "You lift, I shove?"

"You got it, Tom."

She stood and moved to the man's head. Slowly, carefully, trying not to shift the position of his neck at all, she raised his head and shoulders just enough for Tom to slide the board underneath. The feathery ends of his hair at the bottom of his helmet slipped through her fingers like silk. She kept up a soothing monologue, explaining every move to the faceless, motionless stranger. They repeated the process on his chest and finally his legs, until eventually his whole body was lying on the board.

Sarah quickly and efficiently strapped the man's helmet-covered head, chest, abdomen and legs to the board, completely immobilizing him. Then she turned to the sheriff. "Ready, Tom?"

He squatted next to the feet and grunted. Crouching in front of the man's head, she slipped her hands under the board and began to lift.

He was heavier than he looked. Arms straining, the muscles in her back tightening, she finally managed to stand upright. Inching backward over the uneven ground, she glanced anxiously at Tom Johnson. "Careful, Tom," she warned breathlessly. "Don't jostle him so much."

The sheriff shot her an exasperated look. "We got him strapped down, Sarah. We're not going to get him up this mountain without a little jostling."

"I know," she muttered. She tensed her arms, trying to absorb the bumps herself, reluctant to cause him any more pain. Glancing at the limp body again, she tried to walk a little faster. "Just a few more minutes," she whispered to the unconscious man.

By the time they reached the road, sweat poured off her, and her slender arms and legs burned from the strain. After shuffling to the truck, she and Tom eased the board into the makeshift support she'd built into the back of the pickup. They didn't often need an ambulance in Pine Butte, but she was fervently glad now that she'd planned ahead.

It took only a few moments to secure the man in the truck. "I'll meet you back in town, Sarah," said Tom tersely as he got into his car and drove off.

She raised a hand in answer, still staring at the faceless, nameless man in the back of her truck. None of his features was visible beneath the dark visor of his helmet. His black clothes blended into the dim light that filtered through the cap of the truck, making it look as if he was fading away.

"I won't let that happen," she vowed fiercely. Amazed at the conviction in her voice, she stepped closer to the unconscious man, staring for a moment at his motionless body.

Every patient was important to her, she told herself uneasily, gripping the truck more tightly. So why did she feel so strongly about this man? It was because he looked so alone, so helpless, lying in her truck without even a face or a name. It was only natural that she would feel protective of him. She was the only one he had right now.

She closed the door to the back of the truck with a quiet click, got into the cab, turned the truck around carefully and started toward town.

By the time she arrived at her storefront clinic, several people waited in front of the building to help her carry the man inside. She directed them to the largest exam room, and after they'd laid their burden on the table, she gently but firmly shooed them out the door.

"I promise I'll let you know how he is as soon as I know myself," she assured them.

After hurrying to the exam room, she stood staring at the still figure for a moment, feeling that same jolt of empathy, then turned and called, "Josie!"

"I'm right here," her assistant answered from behind her, carrying an armload of equipment.

"Let's start an IV first, then we'll get this helmet off."

As soon as the electrolyte solution began flowing into the patient's arm, Sarah turned her attention to the helmet. Carefully unfastening the buckle under his chin, she loosened the strap that held his head firmly to the board and slid one hand under his neck.

His skin was hot and somehow felt very much alive. Pausing for a moment, she imagined she could feel his life force pulsing just below the surface.

Wondering at her flight of fancy when she had a patient to treat, she muttered to herself, "Too much hot sun for you today." Sliding her other hand under the helmet so his head was supported, too, she said over her shoulder to Josie, "Okay, I've got his head and neck. You slide the helmet off. *Slowly.*"

As the helmet slipped upward, she saw a full mouth, an angular face that would never be called pretty and eyelashes that lay against his pale skin like brushes. A tiny gold hoop earring hung from one ear, and his too-long black hair was tousled and matted with sweat.

As she examined his scalp for signs of injury, she heard Josie inhale sharply behind her.

"What's wrong?" Her hands still supporting his head and neck, she glanced over her shoulder, dread gathering in her stomach. Had she missed something?

Her assistant's face looked almost as white as the victim's. "Do you know who this is?"

"Is it someone you know?" Sarah asked, quickly turning to look at the man. She'd been so preoccupied looking for injuries she hadn't even thought about his identity.

As she looked again, she felt the blood drain from her face. It was impossible. Her hands tightened momentarily on his head and she said faintly, "Josie, get the brace."

When the cloth-covered piece of wood had been fitted around his head and neck, she slowly withdrew her shaking hands and stuffed them in her pockets. "It can't be," she whispered.

"It is," Josie replied, staring at the unconscious man. "It's been a long time, but I'd know that face anywhere."

"Connor MacCormac," Sarah whispered. "What is he doing in Pine Butte?"

"I guess we'll just have to wait until he wakes up and find out, won't we?"

"He isn't going to be anywhere near Pine Butte when he wakes up." Sarah walked to the exam table and checked his IV line. "Call the evacuation helicopter and have them come pick him up right away."

She didn't wait for Josie to answer. Her gaze drifted over the long, lean form lying on her table, and she found herself studying Connor's face. It definitely wasn't that of the wild, sulky boy he'd been twelve years ago. This face was eons older and infinitely harder. Connor MacCormac had grown up.

And after twelve years, what could he possibly want in Pine Butte? His mother had died long ago, and her house had stood empty ever since. As far as Sarah knew, not one person in Pine Butte had heard from him since the summer day he'd taken off.

And now he was back. Not only back, but a patient on an exam table in her clinic. She took his blood pressure, telling herself that she had to be objective. No matter how she felt about him, he was still a patient.

As she stood next to him, urging herself to get busy, she saw his eyelids flutter. His hands twitched, his left hand straining against the restraints still wrapped around him. When he groaned and struggled to sit up, she put her hands on his shoulders and eased him gently back onto the board.

"You can't move. Lie still."

"Can, too. Gotta get going."

The muscles of his legs tensed as he threw his weight against the straps, and blood ran from his wound.

"You've been injured," she said clearly in her best impersonal nurse voice as she held onto him. "You have to hold still until we can take care of you."

"Gotta go," he mumbled, drifting into unconsciousness again.

"Very soon," she soothed. She hoped to God the helicopter was on its way.

Josie stuck her head around the corner. "Bad news. One of the copters is out of commission and the other one is picking up a critical newborn on the other side of the state. It'll be a while before they can get here."

Glancing at Connor MacCormac, Sarah took a deep breath. She would get through this. She'd patch him up, and by that time the chopper would be here. "Okay, let's get busy and suture that wound. We can't wait for the doctor or he'll lose too much blood. Come help me get his pants off."

The two women struggled to cut off his black jeans, now stiff and rust-colored with congealing blood. The cut on his thigh was deep, but as she cleaned it up Sarah stared at it, puzzled. It should have been ragged and uneven, the result of tumbling down that rock-covered slope. Instead, the edges looked almost surgically neat.

"Lucky guy," she muttered as she swabbed it with the yellow iodine solution. Trying to ignore his long, tightly muscled legs and the skimpy purple briefs he wore, she finally finished cleaning the wound and covered the lower half of his body in a green drape. The sooner she finished with Connor MacCormac, the sooner she could forget all about him.

Forty-five minutes later she tied the last suture and stepped back. He was still unconscious, for which she was profoundly grateful. If he wasn't awake, she wouldn't have to think about who lay on her table. She could just pretend he was an anonymous stranger who'd had an unfortunate accident near her town.

She wouldn't have to wonder why he was back after so many years and wonder what he wanted. She wouldn't have to look at him and know, with sickening certainty, that things would never be the same again in Pine Butte now that Connor MacCormac had come back.

* * *

The beast sat on his chest, holding him down, smothering him. Its breath smelled of blood and pain. The tentacles spread over his body, enveloping his arms and his legs. With a rush of panic, Connor tried to move and found he was held prisoner.

And it was dark. So dark that he couldn't see a thing except the glimmer of fire. The fire that was pulling him out of the darkness, that was showing him the way out.

But if there was fire, why was he so cold? He could see the flames, but he shivered convulsively. Ice cubes bumped through his veins, chilling him to the core. He had to get closer to the fire to get warm.

Forcing his eyes open took all his will. Now there was light coming from behind the fire. Still the fire hovered over him, just out of reach. He needed it more desperately than anything else. He shivered, his muscles clenching with the cold; his body throbbed with pain. He needed to make the cold go away.

The flame came closer, leaned over him. Forcing his eyes open, he looked into a face. A face surrounded by a nimbus of gleaming red-gold hair.

"Can you hear me, Mr. MacCormac?" It was the voice again, the one that had smoothed away the fear and panic before. The soft sound spread over him like a warm blanket, taking away the chill. It was closer this time, but still seemed to come down a tunnel from a long way off.

He tried to nod, stopping abruptly when a giant hammer came out of nowhere and slammed into his brain, making his head explode with the pain. "Yes," he finally managed to croak.

"Move your left toes for me."

He must have obeyed, because the voice said, "Okay, now your right toes."

After a few moments the woman nodded and turned away. The light seemed to dim as she stepped out of focus. He tried to raise his hand to hold her close to him, but he couldn't lift his arm. Panic returned and he began to struggle against the weight holding him down.

"Please don't move just yet, Mr. MacCormac," her soft, musical voice said. "I need to make sure you don't have a more serious neck or head injury before I untie you."

Neck or head injury?

"What happened? Where am I?" His voice sounded completely foreign to him, slow and indistinct.

The woman with her glowing hair moved closer to him, and again he felt inexplicably soothed by her presence. "You're in Pine Butte, Colorado." Why had her voice changed, become almost frosty? "You had an accident with your motorcycle outside of town and you're in my clinic."

The picture suddenly clicked into focus. He remembered the car careening toward him, the sharp pain before everything went black. Head and neck injuries. "What's wrong with me?" His voice was strained and harsh.

The woman leaned closer, no doubt curious about the change in his voice from confused patient to authoritative questioner. She stepped back, fiddling with his IV line. "I don't think it's life-threatening," she soothed. "We'll know better when the evacuation helicopter gets here."

"I want to know now, damn it. What did you find?"

Even through the pain-induced haze, he saw her eyes turn cool and assessing. "Very well. You have a concussion, possibly with mild subdural hemorrhage. Three or four ribs are cracked. I haven't looked at your X rays yet to determine the severity. There was a three-inch laceration on your left thigh with moderate arterial bleeding. As far as I can tell, there is no bleeding into your abdominal or chest cavities. You're able to move all your extremities, so the possibility of spinal cord injury is slight. Are you satisfied?"

"Yeah." He closed his eyes, letting the pain take him under again. When he woke up next time, it would be less. "Thanks, doc. Sounds like you did a good job."

"You're welcome. And I'm not a doctor," she said tightly.

He lifted his eyelids again, held them open by sheer force of will. "No? You know an awful lot about medicine."

"I'm a nurse practitioner. In Pine Butte, I'm all there is."

"Good thing I landed where I did, then," he breathed, closing his eyes and sliding away into the welcome darkness. The last thing he saw was the red-gold of her hair.

He was back in the hospital. Phones shrilled, people barked instructions in the next room, instruments clattered into trays, and the smell of blood and disinfectant hovered in the air. He had to get up.

Opening his eyes, he swung his legs over the side of the bed and tried to sit up. Pain exploded everywhere, in his legs, his chest, his head. Groaning, he fell back against the hard surface beneath him.

"Mr. MacCormac, you have to lie still." Cool hands slid under his bare legs and lifted them onto the table. "Do you remember I told you about the possibility of head or neck injuries?"

The motorcycle accident. He was in Pine Butte, in a nurse practitioner's office. He remembered concussion, cracked ribs, a lacerated leg.

Eyes closed, he took stock of his injuries, testing his arms and legs, running through his reflexes. "I'm fine," he said finally, opening his eyes again. "Concussion is the worst of it."

"I'm glad you're so certain," she answered, her voice cool again. "I prefer to wait for a doctor to examine you."

"No doctor is going to do more than you did," he answered, gathering his strength. "I'm going to get up now."

Instantly he felt her hands on his arms. "Where do you think you're going to go?"

"To the bathroom." Focusing his eyes, he looked into her blue-green ones. Concern and faint embarrassment were mixed with deep, simmering anger hiding far below the surface. *Is this how everyone in town would look at me?* he thought with bitterness. Was this the legacy of his young life in Pine Butte? Deliberately shoving the thought out of his mind, he forced himself upright, ignoring the pain crashing over him.

"Your ribs haven't been taped," she snapped, holding tightly to his arm as he swayed on the table. "Your leg hasn't been bandaged, either. But if you want to rip out your stitches and poke a hole in your lungs, you be my guest."

"Tape them up now," he ordered. "My bladder can wait that long."

She stood and surveyed him with frustration. Shoving back the red-gold curls that framed her face, she said, "Are you always this much of a pain in the butt, Mr. Mac-Cormac?"

His face relaxed into a tiny smile. "Usually I'm worse. At least to hear the nur—" He broke off abruptly, appalled at what he'd been about to reveal. The knock on the head had made him forget. That was something he'd sworn he'd never do. "You have to do it eventually, anyway," he pointed out, no longer smiling.

She looked as if she wanted to erupt. Instead, she spun around and left the room. Sitting on the table, he acknowledged ruefully that she might well have had the last word. Without support for his ribs, he could neither stand up nor lie down.

A few moments later she reappeared, carrying an armful of bandage material. Setting it down on the table, she straightened and surveyed him. "This is going to hurt you, Mr. MacCormac." She didn't sound as if she was too upset at the idea.

"Just get it done. Once the ribs are taped, I'll be fine."

After watching him for another moment with an inscrutable look in her sea-colored eyes, she abruptly turned away and grabbed a roll of adhesive tape. Moving closer to him, she didn't look at his face again. Instead, keeping her gaze firmly fixed on his chest, she wound the tape around him again and again. When she finally stepped back to admire her handiwork, he felt as if an iron band had been strapped around his chest.

"Perfect," he pronounced, moving experimentally. "Now if you'll get the leg, I'll be ready to go."

"The only place you're ready to go is into the evacuation helicopter and to the hospital in Glenwood Springs," she retorted, slapping antiseptic cream onto the neat line of stitches on his thigh. "As soon as we're done here, I'll call them again and find out when they're coming."

"I don't need to be evacuated to Glenwood," he said, wincing as she pressed the tape over his wound. "I already told you, I'm fine."

"And whose expert opinion is that?"

"Mine. I know my own body."

"I'd rather let a doctor tell me that, thank you."

"What are you going to do, put me on that chopper by force?"

She tore the tape off a little more roughly than necessary. "Obviously I can't force you to do anything. But if you have any sense at all, you'll let a doctor look at you. There could be something seriously wrong with you."

"There isn't." Moving slowly to the edge of the table, he slid onto the floor and waited for the dizziness to pass. Her warm, strong hand gripped his elbow. He felt disapproval radiate off her in waves. "Now if you'll just point me in the direction of the bathroom?"

When he emerged a few minutes later, she stood by the door, worry and anger mixed on her face. "All right, Mr. MacCormac, you win. If you can walk to the bathroom, you can't be too seriously injured. I've canceled the helicopter. But at least stay here in the clinic overnight where I can keep an eye on you. No hospital in the world would let you walk around so soon."

He eyed the hard table doubtfully. "Spending the night sleeping on that thing would probably finish what the accident started."

For the first time a smile softened her lips, and he blinked at the transformation. For just a moment, warmth and caring shone out of her eyes. Something about that smile niggled at his memory.

"I can do a lot better than that." She interrupted his thoughts, and the fleeting memory was gone. When she opened a door at one end of the exam room, he saw a bed in a homey-looking room on the other side. "The clinic is prepared for overnight guests."

He shuffled gratefully toward the inviting vision. By the time he'd reached it, his body was screaming with pain. As she eased him onto the blessedly soft mattress, he looked at her and mumbled, "Who are you? I'm sure I know you."

As soon as the words were out of his mouth, he felt the distance open up like a chasm at his feet. "My name is Sarah Wesley, Mr. MacCormac. Perhaps you remember my sister, Barb?"

Chapter 2

She watched as he dragged himself back from the edge of unconsciousness. It was obvious that Connor MacCormac was as strong-willed as ever.

"Barb." His eyes closed as her sister's name trembled on the air between them. "How is good old Barb?"

His bitterness swirled around her, but before she could respond, he opened his eyes again and stared at her. "You're Barbie's sister?" She heard the surprise in his voice as his eyes scanned her face one more time, then she could see the memory click into place. "I thought you looked familiar."

"I don't look anything like Barb did," she answered coldly, moving away from the bed. If he thought that remark would ensure him a warm welcome, he was about as wrong as he could be.

"No, you don't." His voice was quiet and strangely expressionless as he lay back against the pillows, struggling to stay alert. The pain in his eyes softened as he looked at her. "But I remember you. You had to be, what, thirteen or fourteen?"

"I was fifteen when you left." She felt the familiar anger, and anguish, creep into her voice and clamped her lips together. Whatever else he was, Connor MacCormac was a patient right now. Anything she needed to say to him could wait until he was stronger.

His eyes were closed, but a hint of a smile flickered over his mouth. It was gone so quickly she wondered if she'd imagined it. "You used to be nothing but long legs and red hair. You grew up real nice, Sarah Wesley."

She stared at him, speechless, as a tiny lick of pleasure fluttered through her chest and was quickly subdued. Just what was that remark supposed to mean? She was sure he'd never noticed her when he dated her sister. She opened her mouth to answer him, tell him it was none of his business how she'd grown up, but she realized he'd fallen asleep.

After pausing for a moment by the door to watch the regular rise and fall of his chest, she finally stepped out of the room and closed the door behind her. What on earth was the matter with her? Her heart was racing like a steam engine roaring down the tracks, and she had to wipe her damp palms on her jeans. So what if he remembered her?

He'd been involved with her sister, after all. Under the circumstances, it would've been strange if he didn't remember his lover's family.

And under the circumstances, she reminded herself grimly, it was totally inappropriate to be feeling any kind of connection to him at all. After what he'd done to her family, sympathy for Connor MacCormac was completely out of the question.

Maybe he'd had a rotten deal when he was a kid. It wasn't his fault that his father had died when he was twelve. Nor was it his fault that his mother was incapable of taking care of him and he'd grown up unbroken and unfettered as a wild mustang. But what Connor MacCormac had done to her family had been completely his own choice. There was no one to blame but him.

She moved into the exam room and automatically began to clean up. *Just remember that the next time you get all fluttery inside when he smiles at you,* she told herself grimly, scrubbing the exam table. He was still the same Connor, the same irresponsible and reckless boy he'd been twelve years ago. Having a motorcycle accident in the mountains was proof enough of that. He must have been going too fast or he wouldn't have fallen over the edge.

When the exam room was spotless, she walked to her desk and pulled out a blank patient record, then entered his name on top. She left the address blank. With any luck, he'd be gone before it mattered what his address was.

Her assistant cleared her throat behind her, and she reluctantly turned around. "Yes, Josie?"

"The waiting room is full, Sarah," she offered. "What should I tell them?"

Glancing at her watch, Sarah realized that the afternoon was almost over. Standing up, she fought against the weariness that weighted her arms and legs. "Send home anyone who can wait until tomorrow. I'll take a look at the emergencies right now."

An hour later the last patient walked out the door and Josie quickly locked it behind him. Fiddling with the lock, she stared at Sarah for a long minute, obviously torn. Finally, clearing her throat, she said, "Do you want me to stay here with you?" She nodded in the direction of the room where Connor lay sleeping. "To, you know, help you?"

"Thanks, Josie." Sarah smiled gratefully at the young woman. "I appreciate the offer, but you don't need to do that. He's going to stay right where he is the rest of the night. I'll be fine."

Josie grabbed her purse and unlocked the door. "Okay, if you're sure, I'll see you tomorrow."

"Thanks," Sarah said again to the already closing door. She didn't blame her assistant in the least for being in a hurry to go. With the inside story on a hot gossip item like Connor MacCormac's return to Pine Butte, most people wouldn't even have asked if she wanted them to stay.

Her stomach growled loudly in the silence, reminding her that she'd missed lunch and that dinnertime had already come and gone. Glancing at her watch, she walked to the room where her patient lay sleeping. It was time to check him again before she could think about feeding herself.

Pausing at the door, she watched him for a moment in the dim light. His hands looked both slender and strong resting on the white blanket. Somehow they didn't fit her image of him. She would have expected rough, callused hands, hands used to hard, manual labor, hands that matched the motorcycle and black leather. Instead they looked like a musician's hands, graceful and clever.

Snorting at her fantasy, she walked to the bed. He was sound asleep, and for a moment she hesitated, reluctant to wake him. At least he wasn't in pain while he slept, and when she roused him to check his pupils he would feel the bruises in every bone and muscle in his body. With the head injury, she couldn't even give him a painkiller that would help.

It had to be done. Laying her hand on his shoulder, she bent down and murmured, "Wake up, Mr. MacCormac. I have to look at your eyes again."

He groaned from somewhere deep in sleep, and she laid her other hand on his chest. His respiration was normal, as it had been the last three times she'd checked him. "Wake up, please," she prodded. "Just for a moment."

"Go away," he croaked.

"I will, as soon as you open your eyes."

At that, bright blue eyes stared at her, expressionless. His pupils constricted quickly to black dots as she shined her penlight on his face. When she turned the light off, he closed his eyes again.

"Are you satisfied?"

"Yes, thank you. You can go back to sleep."

He'd already drifted off. She rocked back on her heels and watched him sleep for a moment, amazed. She'd never met anyone with as much control over his body as Connor MacCormac seemed to have. If she hadn't seen him get up and walk to the bathroom earlier, then walk into this room, she wouldn't have believed it. Concussion patients weren't supposed to be able to stand, let alone walk. And the way he'd opened his eyes on command, when she knew every cell in his body had to be screaming to keep them closed, was almost spooky.

Strong-willed didn't even begin to describe him. He had the most iron determination of anyone she'd ever met. She walked to the door, watching the regular rise and fall of his chest. She had no doubts at all that the rest of Pine Butte would find out about that strong will whenever he decided to let them know why he'd come back. Whatever he wanted, she thought with a frisson of apprehension, she had no doubt he would get it.

The sun was just rising over the mountains when Sarah's alarm clock went off for the last time. Stumbling off the couch in her waiting room, she made her way to the clinic bedroom and opened the door. Fear caught in her throat when she saw the bed was empty.

Hurrying to the other side, she was only slightly reassured to see he hadn't fallen out of the bed. Noting the closed bathroom door, her eyes narrowed as she waited for him to emerge.

He walked out wearing nothing but the damned purple briefs and the bandages around his chest and leg. Swallowing once, she forced herself to ignore his wide chest and narrow hips and long, muscled legs. Keeping her eyes on his face, she scowled and said, "What are you doing out of bed?"

He watched her for a moment, his eyes challenging her, then a slow, sexy grin lit his face. "Nature called," he drawled. "As much as I would have enjoyed having you hold a bedpan for me, I figured I could make it on my own."

"Well, you figured wrong," she snapped. She could feel her face flaming but held tightly to her anger, forcing from her mind the images his words had generated. "You shouldn't be out of bed yet."

"But I am," he said easily. "I didn't fall over, rip out my stitches or poke a hole in my lungs. In short, I'm fine."

"You're hardly fine, Mr. MacCormac," she answered tartly, and pulled back the sheets on the bed. "You need to stay in bed for the next twenty-four hours at the least."

"You're the boss." A faint smile crossed his face as he settled on the bed and pulled the blanket up to his chest.

For some reason, that smile fanned the flames of her temper. It even took her mind off his nearly naked body. "You're darn right I'm the boss, and I have no intention of letting you injure yourself more severely while you're staying in my clinic. From now on, if you need anything, you can call me and I'll get it for you."

Raising his eyebrows, he shifted and sat up a little straighter. The sheet slipped down another couple of inches. "Okay, then, how about some breakfast? My stomach is telling me it's missed a few meals."

Why did she feel like she was losing control of this situation? "What would you like?" She hoped her voice sounded cool and authoritative and not as flustered as she felt. It was that damned hairy chest of his that was distracting her.

"Pancakes, waffles, toast, bacon, whatever you've got," he answered, waving his hand in the air. "I'm not picky, just hungry."

"I'll get something from Earlene's across the street and be right back," she muttered.

Closing the door of the room gently, just so he knew she wasn't running away, she leaned against the wall for a moment. She *had* to get rid of him today. If he refused to let the evacuation helicopter come get him, maybe she could drive him to the hospital in Glenwood Springs. He really did need to have a doctor look at him. She was confident in her diagnosis, but she wasn't a doctor and she could have missed something.

Having Connor MacCormac in town was bad enough. Finding herself attracted to him was unspeakably appalling. No matter how often she reminded herself of what had happened twelve years ago, it didn't stop her pulse from speeding up every time she looked at him. And the gleam that lurked in the back of those bright blue eyes didn't help in the least.

She unlocked the front door of her clinic and ran across the street to the town's only restaurant. Earlene Hendricks called out from behind the counter, "Morning, Sarah. Hear you've got an overnight patient in the clinic."

By now, she had no doubt, every single soul in Pine Butte had heard about the accident and who the victim had been. Resigning herself to Earlene's endless questions, she sank onto one of the stools at the counter and answered, "Yeah, I do, and he's hungry this morning. Can you make me up some pancakes and eggs and sausage?"

A moment later Sarah heard the hiss of pancake batter hitting the hot griddle. Then Earlene came around the counter and poured her a cup of coffee, a look of avid curiosity on her face.

"What does he look like?"

"Older." Taking a drink of the hot, strong coffee, Sarah set the cup down and wrapped her hand around it. Her fingers tightening, she added, "But enough the same that I recognized him."

"Did he say anything about, you know, Barb?" Ignoring the two men who'd just walked into the diner, Earlene leaned forward, crossing her arms over her generous bosom.

"He's mostly been unconscious." Sarah's voice was sharper than she intended, and she took another swallow of coffee. "He hasn't had a chance to say much of anything."

Giving her a long look, Earlene reluctantly headed to the kitchen. "You don't know why he's come back here, then?"

"No idea." She'd spent the better part of the night sleepless, wondering the same thing. "And, knowing him, we'll find out when he's good and ready to tell us."

Earlene walked out front, two aluminum containers in her hands and a fierce look on her face. "He gives you any trouble, Sarah, you just tell Sheriff Tom. He'll know what to do with the likes of Connor MacCormac. After all you've been through, and for what you mean to this town, we won't let nobody bother you."

"Thanks, Earlene." Her eyes burned, and she told herself she was just overtired. For all that she dreamed of getting away, Pine Butte was her home and she knew the people here cared about her.

The cook shoved the two boxes at her. "I made one for you, too. You look a little peaked."

"Thanks," she said again, and headed out the door. The two men who'd come in while she was talking to Earlene greeted her, and she saw a dozen questions in their eyes. She just nodded at them and kept going. She was too tired to tolerate endless inquisitions about the man lying in her clinic.

* * *

The click of the door closing reverberated like a gunshot off the four walls surrounding him. Connor eased himself a little higher in bed, ignoring the screams of protest from his bones and muscles, and allowed himself a brief smile as he recalled the fire in her eyes. Little Sarah Wesley was irritated with him. She'd had that same look in her eyes whenever he'd teased her twelve long years ago.

For just a moment he let himself dwell on the clouds of burnished copper hair that seemed to float around her face, on her clear blue-green eyes, on her strong, slender body. Even when she'd been just a kid he'd known instinctively that the shy, gawky adolescent who blushed whenever he looked at her would turn into a beauty.

And now Barb Wesley's baby sister was all grown up. The bitter laughter stuck in his throat. "Don't even think about it," he warned himself harshly. What could be more ironic than being attracted to Barb Wesley's little sister? He was sure someone would see the humor in the situation, but it wouldn't be him.

No, he had to stay as far away from Sarah Wesley as he could during his stay in Pine Butte. His brief stay, he hoped. He'd take care of his business and get out of town as fast as he could. Maybe this time he could forget that Pine Butte, Colorado, even existed.

The knock on the door was quiet, almost as if she hoped he'd fallen asleep again. "Come in," he called, beating down the anticipation. He was just hungry, he told himself.

The door opened and she walked in, carrying a large aluminum container. She wheeled over a bedside tray, set his breakfast on it and fumbled in the pocket of a rumpled-looking sweater for his utensils. Without ever looking directly at him, she opened the container of pancakes, eggs and sausage, then cranked the head of his bed higher. Finally, drawing a deep breath, she looked him in the eye. "Is there anything else you need?"

"A cup of coffee would be nice."

She shook her head. "Sorry. I'm not going to give you caffeine just yet. I don't want anything to raise your blood pressure. How about some herbal tea?"

"I can't drink that slop. Just get me a glass of water. Please."

If she didn't want to raise his blood pressure, she shouldn't walk like that, he thought sourly as she left the room. The graceful sway of her hips and legs in the snug, worn jeans was making his blood pound.

She returned in a moment, setting a glass of ice water on the tray with a snap. "I'm going to be busy today," she said abruptly. "I'll check on you when I can, but I'll be tied up for a while. If you need anything, there's a buzzer over the bed."

Twisting around in the bed, he found the buzzer and pressed it before she was out the door.

As she turned slowly he saw the anger, quickly suppressed, that flashed across her face. "What do you need?"

"Only my clothes."

Her mouth tightened and she stepped into the room. "Sorry, Mr. MacCormac. You're not getting any clothes until tomorrow at the earliest. If you refuse to let a doctor look at you, the least you can do is stay where you are until I'm certain that there's nothing more serious wrong with you."

"Look, I know—" He clamped his mouth shut on the words. What he knew and why he knew it was nobody's business but his own. "I'm fine, Ms. Wesley." His voice was flat. "I appreciate your hospitality, but I need to be on my way. Now get me my clothes, please."

Triumph flashed in her eyes. "Your jeans won't do you much good. I had to cut them off you. I had to cut your shirt off, too. So right now, you don't have any clothes for me to get."

"What about my pack and the stuff on my bike? Where's all that?"

"I don't know." She frowned and jammed her hands into the pockets of her sweater. "I'll ask the sheriff. He probably brought it into town."

"I'll need to talk to him, then."

"I'm sure he'll want to see you. He has to fill out an accident report form." Her voice was cool. "When I see him, I'll ask him to stop by."

She left the room before he could answer, closing the door firmly behind her. For a moment he tensed, ready to crawl out of bed and follow her until she agreed to do what he wanted. Then he smelled the aroma of Earlene's sausage and pancakes and decided that he could wait for a while. He'd almost forgotten how hungry he was.

Twenty minutes later, the aluminum container was empty and he felt much better. He still ached abominably everywhere, but the pounding in his head had lessened to a dull drumbeat. He couldn't take a deep breath without wincing, and his leg still throbbed, but he was damned lucky.

Remembering the way the car had veered toward him, almost deliberately, he knew he was fortunate to be sitting up in this bed in this clinic. He could just as easily have been lying in a drawer in the morgue at the county seat.

Pushing the tray away from the bed, he started to swing his legs onto the floor, but paused as they screamed in pain. Maybe he *should* take it easy for a while longer. According to Sarah, he didn't have any clothes, anyway. A few more hours of rest and he'd be ready to take on the town of Pine Butte. Sliding down beneath the sheets, he closed his eyes and was immediately asleep.

He awakened a few hours later knowing someone stood next to his bed. Opening his eyes, he looked for Sarah's familiar face but found a short, stocky man in a uniform instead.

"How're you feeling, MacCormac?"

"Like I fell off a mountain," he retorted, inching upward against the headboard. He looked at the man standing in front of him, wondering why he looked familiar. "You must be the sheriff."

"Tom Johnson," the other man answered, holding out his hand. The flicker of apprehension in his eyes was so unexpected that for a second Connor wondered if he'd imagined it.

With a barely noticeable start Connor reached out and firmly shook the sheriff's hand. "Connor MacCormac. Pleased to meet you. Are you the one that found me?"

The sheriff nodded, his eyes clearing. "And damn lucky you were that I did, too. If it hadn't been for the sun reflecting off that motorcycle of yours, you'd still be lying up there."

"I owe you, Sheriff."

Tom Johnson waved his hand. "Just doing my job." He jerked his head in the direction of the door. "I left your pack and the stuff in the panniers of your bike with Sarah. Had the bike taken over to the service station. Billy Sullivan over there'll be able to fix it up, I think. He's damn clever with machines."

"Thank you." His voice warmed up as he looked at Pine Butte's lawman. "I appreciate all the trouble you've gone to."

The sheriff shrugged. "It's not a big deal." Apprehension, quickly hidden by a grin, passed over his face. "From what I've heard, your being back in town sounds like it's going to provide a lot of entertainment around here. I'm all for anything that livens up this place."

He couldn't detect an ounce of malice in the sheriff's voice, and Connor relaxed and smiled back. "I suppose you're right. People in small towns don't forget much."

"You remember that, MacCormac, and you'll be fine."

He wasn't likely to forget. "What did you need to know, Sheriff?" The sooner he got this over with, the sooner he could get his clothes and leave.

"Just tell me what happened. I've got to fill out a report for the state, seeing that it was a state highway you fell off of."

"First of all, I didn't fall. I was pushed."

Tom Johnson stood up straighter and pushed his hat back. "What do you mean, you were pushed?"

"Just what I said." In a hard voice, Connor told him about the car that was going too fast, and how it swerved toward him at the last minute, grazing him and pushing him off the road. "That's how I got this," he said, gesturing toward the cut on his leg. "I think the fender caught me."

Tom pulled up a chair and turned it around, resting his arms on the back as he looked at Connor. "That kind of puts a whole different slant on things. Are you saying it was on purpose?"

Connor shrugged. "I have no idea. Nobody knew I was coming here, so it's not like anyone could have been waiting for me. But that car didn't slow down, and it did seem to swerve right at me."

"You see what kind of car it was? Color, make, anything?"

"Sorry. I was thinking more about saving my skin at the time."

After a few moments Tom stood up, looking troubled and somehow anguished. "Let's just keep this between the two of us for now, MacCormac. I want to look into it a little. Are you going to be staying here for a while?"

"For about another fifteen minutes. As soon as I can get my clothes from Ms. Wesley, I'll be out of here. I'll be staying at my mother's for as long as I'm in Pine Butte." He paused, his jaw tightening. "I'm sure any of the good citizens can tell you where her house is."

"I'll get back to you." The sheriff paused at the door, a worried look on his face. "You be careful. There seem to be a lot of strong feelings about you here in Pine Butte."

Connor's mouth twisted. "Don't worry, Sheriff. I'm used to that in this town." He looked at the other man for a moment, that odd feeling of knowing him returning more strongly. "How long have you been sheriff here?"

Ton Johnson looked uncomfortable with the question, and Connor sat up a little straighter, watching him.

"Nine years, give or take a few months."

"You from somewhere around here?" Connor asked casually.

"Meeker." The sheriff licked his lips. "I was on the police force and applied for the job here. The rest, as they say, is history."

Connor nodded slowly, deciding that his concussion had scrambled his brain. He couldn't have seen Tom Johnson before today. He'd never spent any time in Meeker as a kid. "I'm sure as hell glad you moved here, Sheriff."

The other man gave him an odd look, then finally smiled. "I guess you should be, MacCormac."

Connor stared at the floor for a while after the sheriff had left, his mouth twisted. Tom Johnson had no doubt heard all the stories about him as a kid. He was probably wondering if he was going to have trouble with him now, Connor thought with an echo of childhood pain. Well, he didn't give a damn what anyone in Pine Butte thought of him.

He had other things to worry about, anyway. Such as who had tried to run him off the road. Nobody knew the exact date he would show up, but at least one person could have guessed he'd come back. The contents of that anonymous note practically guaranteed that sooner or later he would have to face Pine Butte again.

Maybe it had been coincidence and pure, blind luck. But whatever it had been, he reluctantly acknowledged, the driver of that car had tried to kill him. He'd accelerated and swerved right at him. There had been nothing accidental about it.

Yeah, he'd be watching his back while he was here in Pine Butte.

Reaching around, he pressed the buzzer impatiently. A few minutes later, a young woman he'd never seen before stuck her head in the door.

"Did you need something, Mr. MacCormac?"

"Yeah, my clothes."

"Okay."

Her head disappeared, then returned almost immediately. "Sorry, Sarah says you can't have them yet." She closed the door quickly at the expression on his face.

Slowly he swung his legs off the bed, then rested for a moment until his head stopped pounding. Holding onto the tray stand for support, he pulled himself out of bed and stood on the floor, swaying.

He cataloged all of his aches and pains and decided they were bearable. He didn't want to stay here and have to torture himself with Sarah Wesley and the past any longer than he had to.

He managed to make it halfway down the hall before she saw him. Hurrying from one exam to the other, she stopped dead when she spotted him shuffling down the hall. Her eyes flickered down his body once, then with a surge of color in her cheeks she stared at his face.

"What are you doing?" she asked in a stage whisper. "Get back in that bed."

"Not until you give me my clothes." His voice was implacable.

"One of my patients is going to come out of that room any minute and see you," she said frantically. "You can't stand around in the hall naked like that."

"That's why I want my clothes."

She really did have a temper to match that glorious hair. He saw her fighting it, saw her struggling to hold her tongue. When he took a step closer to her, it finally broke free.

"Fine. You go right ahead and leave. I hope you fall flat on your face in the middle of Main Street. I hope you rip out every stitch in your leg. I don't care if your head feels like it got hit with a bowling ball. If you want to leave, you go right ahead."

"As soon as you give me my clothes, I will."

She whirled and stomped into the small cubbyhole that must be her office. Picking up two brown paper bags and a leather backpack, she marched past him and dumped them on the bed. "You're all set. Don't let the door hit you in the rear end on your way out."

Without another word she flashed past him and into one of the exam rooms, slamming the door. The noise reverberated around his head, making him close his eyes with the pain. Slowly he turned and made his way to the bedroom.

Fifteen minutes later, he'd spread all his belongings on the hastily made bed and taken a quick inventory. Everything seemed to be there. He looked at the T-shirt and jeans he'd tried to pull on and grimaced. Without help, he'd never get dressed. His ribs were still too sore to raise his hands over his head or bend down to pull on the jeans.

Just as he was struggling to step into the jeans without bending over, the door opened and Sarah came in.

"I'm sorry, Mr. MacCormac," she said steadily. "I shouldn't have lost my temper." Taking a deep breath, she continued, "I guess I'm just used to getting my own way when it comes to medical decisions. I shouldn't have said those things to you."

"You're forgiven if you'll help me get these on."

He saw a flicker of compassion in her eyes before the familiar exasperation filled them.

"Doesn't that prove to you that you shouldn't be leaving? You can't even get yourself dressed yet."

"If I just lay here, it'll take me twice as long to heal. I need to move around."

"Where are you going to stay?" She gave in and knelt down, holding his jeans so he could step into them. "There isn't a hotel in town."

"My mother's house."

Rocking back on her heels, she looked up in astonishment. "Nobody's lived there in ten years! You can't stay there. The dirt alone would probably kill you."

"That would make the citizens of Pine Butte happy, I'll bet."

She stood up slowly. "Nobody wants you dead, Mr. MacCormac." The ghost of a smile flashed in her eyes. "Then we wouldn't have anything to talk about." The smile faded as she looked at him, concern on her face. "Would you please reconsider? You're welcome to stay here for a few days, at least until you can get around on your own."

He found himself studying her eyes. She was sincere, he realized. It may have been only her normal concern for a patient, but she was really distressed about the idea of his leaving the clinic.

Something began to shift inside him. He'd come back to Pine Butte determined to hate everyone and everything about the town. She was the last person he could trust, but he found to his surprise that he couldn't hate Sarah Wesley.

"All right, I'll stay," he heard himself say.

Chapter 3

"At night," Connor added, standing and pulling his jeans up over his hips. "I'm not going to lie in this bed all day and rot. I have things to do."

The denim was tight around the bandage on his thigh and the cut began throbbing again. Ignoring it, he reached for the shirt. Sarah grabbed it off the bed and eased it over his head.

"That's fine with me," she said calmly. "You can do whatever you want."

A real smile curved his lips, and he looked over at where she stood stiffly facing him. "That's not what you said a few minutes ago. As I recall, you were pretty vehement about what I was supposed to be doing."

Delicate red color crept up her neck and cheeks. "I have a bad temper, Mr. MacCormac. I'm sorry I lost it."

"And that's another thing. Call me Connor." He watched her for a moment and felt his blood begin to heat. "Especially if we're going to be sharing living quarters for a while."

"The only thing we'll be sharing is this building." Her voice was even, although her cheeks were still red. "My apartment is upstairs. I'll leave the door open at night so I can hear the buzzer if you need help."

"Help isn't what I usually need at night," he said softly, still watching her. She looked so serious he couldn't resist needling her. Those luminous blue-green eyes darkened, then she blinked and looked away.

"Head injuries are funny things...Connor. You never know when you're going to have a relapse." The door closed quietly behind her.

For just a moment, before she turned away, he could have sworn it was longing and not impatience that flashed into her eyes. His body was taut with desire, and his mouth curved down bitterly.

Caught in his own trap, and it was no less than he deserved. He shouldn't have agreed to stay, not after he'd realized who she was.

Imagine him and Barb Wesley's sister. Had Sarah had a good laugh with Barb and her mother after he'd left? Did Sarah think it would be amusing to pick up where Barb had left off, to string the MacCormac kid along one more time?

If anyone did any stringing along this time it would be him, he thought savagely, moving into the hall and slamming the bedroom door behind him. He ignored the pain in his head. Sure, Sarah Wesley was gorgeous. She'd done things to his blood pressure from the moment he woke up and found her standing next to him. But if she thought he'd be putty in her hands the way he'd been for Barb, she was in for a big shock.

He'd stay in Pine Butte as long as it took him to take care of business and not a moment longer. Once he finished here, he'd kick the dirt of this stinking town off his boots forever. He wouldn't have one regret the next time he walked away. He didn't intend to have any reasons to look backward this time.

Moving slowly into the empty waiting room of the small building, he spotted her down the hall, sitting at a desk. Her head was bent over and it was obvious she was writing. He paused at the sight of her coppery hair curling above her slender neck, his body tightening in response.

She was a beautiful woman and he wanted her. Hell, he'd have to be a lot more than half dead if he didn't. But wanting her and needing her were two different things. Now that he was back in Pine Butte, he'd have a hard time forgetting what could happen when you needed someone.

Hobbling over to the door, he eased it open and stepped into the harsh sunlight. He had business. It was time to get it started.

Sarah heard the tiny click of the front door closing and took a deep breath. She'd been frozen in place, feeling his gaze burn into her back—knowing she should have turned around, warned him to be careful, told him where she hid her spare key. But she couldn't have moved if her life depended on it.

And maybe it had. She hadn't mistaken the look in those bright blue eyes or misunderstood his words. He was attracted to her. She had seen the awareness in his eyes, felt it in the tensing of his muscles. Only his injuries, and a thin veneer of civilization, stopped him from acting on it.

Dropping the pen she'd been clutching like a lifeline, she walked into the waiting room and locked the door. Then, knowing she should go back and finish working on her charts, she moved to the window and looked for Connor.

He hadn't gotten far. He'd managed to cross the street and stood, swaying, on the sidewalk opposite the clinic. Her hand tightened on the curtain and she had to stop herself from running out the door after him. He wouldn't thank her for her help, she knew, and would be less than thrilled to admit his weakness.

If she hadn't been so sure that he was basically fine, she wouldn't have let him walk out the door in the first place, she assured herself. Right now he was sore, but his injuries hadn't turned out to be serious.

She watched until he'd turned the corner and disappeared from view, then went back to the pile of records she had to finish before she could get lunch. With any luck at all, she'd have to endure only a few days of his presence. When his motorcycle was repaired and his body recuperated, he'd ride out of town and she wouldn't see him again.

She managed to put him out of her mind and concentrate on her records, refusing to stop until the entire pile was finished. Finally stretching in her chair, she stood up and grabbed her purse. She'd have time for lunch today, after all.

She'd gotten as far as the front door when the frantic screech of brakes outside told her she'd go hungry again today. Tossing her purse onto one of the chairs, she hastily unlocked the door and rushed outside.

The door of a battered pickup truck flew open and her cousin Richard leapt out. "Thank God you're here, Sarah. We had an accident up at the mine." Without waiting for her to respond, he ran around to the back of the truck and threw open the hatch.

Sarah rushed to join him, peering into the dimness of the truck and seeing the motionless figure of a man lying on a makeshift bed of blankets and coats. His left leg was covered with blood, and his face was paper-white against the dark jacket that was balled up under his head.

"What happened?" she asked tightly, picking up his wrist and feeling for a pulse.

"His leg got smashed between two of the rail cars."

Sarah looked up sharply at the voice. Harley Harrison stood on the other side of the truck, looking, for Harley, remarkably subdued. The truculence she associated with him had vanished, replaced by fear.

"Those little cars that carry the rock out of the mine?" she asked.

"Yeah. One had derailed. Chet here—" he nodded at the injured man "—was tryin' to fix it and another one smashed into him."

"That was pretty careless," she commented, laying the injured man's hand down and looking at the mine foreman.

His face darkened. She wasn't sure if it was anger or fear. "It was an accident."

"I'm sure it was. That doesn't help Chet, though, does it?" she tossed over her shoulder. "I'll be right back."

She ran into the clinic and got the stretcher, then hurried to the truck. Her cousin and Harley stood in back of it, looking helplessly at the injured man.

"Richard, you get into the truck. We're going to have to get him onto this stretcher." She watched as her cousin scooted awkwardly to the front of the truck bed, carefully avoiding the bloody spots on the blankets. Good old Richard. He never changed. He might be truly concerned about his employee, but that wasn't about to make him get blood on his expensive suit.

She shoved the stretcher in behind him. "Okay, ease his head and chest over."

Her cousin gently lifted the semiconscious man onto the narrow width of canvas. Sarah's heart twisted as she heard the injured man groan. Lifting up one of the blankets that lay under his injured leg, she eased the lower half of his body onto the stretcher, then grabbed the wooden handles.

"You take the front end, Richard. Harley, you get the door." Her hands tightened and she slowly slid the heavy stretcher out of the truck.

Two minutes later Chet lay on the table in her largest exam room, the same table Connor was on just yesterday. Sarah felt the same overwhelming anxiety, the same fear that she wouldn't know enough to help her patient. At least with Chet the injuries were probably limited to his leg.

"It was only his leg that got caught?" she asked as she started an IV drip.

"Yeah. At least that's what the guys working with him said." The foreman stared at her until she looked away. She was more used to this surliness from Harley.

Sarah adjusted the flow of the IV solution, then reached for a pair of scissors. Lifting up the blood-soaked material of Chet's jeans, she cut through it and pushed it away from his leg.

Her stomach contracted sharply when she saw the white shards of bone stabbing out of his skin. Trying to touch the wound as little as possible, she looked for any areas that were still heavily bleeding. Finding none, she washed her hands and went to the telephone.

She came back a few minutes later to find her patient restless, turning his head from side to side. Taking his hand, she bent down next to his ear.

"Chet, try not to move. Your leg is broken and moving will only make it hurt more. I'm going to give you something for the pain. The evacuation helicopter is on its way, and before you know it you'll be in Glenwood Springs. Shall I call your wife so she can go with you?"

Chet nodded and clung to her hand. "Is my leg going to be okay, Sarah?"

"I don't know, Chet. I'm not a doctor." She tried to keep the bitterness out of her voice. "The doctors in Glenwood are very good. They'll take care of you."

She straightened, looking at the awful wounds on his lower leg. She hoped to God that they could save his leg, and that the delay wasn't going to make it worse. The helicopter was available and would leave immediately. It should be here in a half hour or so.

She squeezed his hand gently, then laid it down and went to get some morphine. Pulling the keys to her safe from her pocket, she turned to her cousin. "Richard, have you called Chet's wife yet?"

Her cousin looked uncomfortable. "Ah, no. We were in too much of a hurry to get him here."

"Do it now, will you?" Her voice was sharper than it should have been, and she turned to get the narcotic out of her safe. "You should have thought of that."

"I'll do it." The foreman moved away from the table and looked around. "Where's the telephone?"

"In the office, Harley." She didn't even look at him as she drew up an injection of morphine. Pushing it slowly into Chet's IV line, she watched with relief as he relaxed, his hands releasing the clenched blanket. Even if all she could do was give him relief from his pain, it was better than nothing.

The door of the clinic opened and she turned, expecting to see Chet's wife. Instead Connor came limping slowly into sight. Seeing the scene in front of him, he stopped dead in his tracks.

Her cousin was the first to speak. "MacCormac. I'd heard you were back."

"You heard right, Wesley." His eyes measured, challenged the other man. "I guess I'm just like a bad penny."

Connor stared at her cousin, his eyes unreadable. Both Richard and Harley stood, looking oddly defensive, and stared back. The atmosphere in the tiny exam room was suddenly crackling with tension, as if an electrical storm on the horizon had every particle of air standing on edge.

Connor's eyes flickered to the man lying on the table and his expression altered. Ignoring Richard and Harley, he walked into the room and looked down at Chet. "What happened to him?"

"His leg was smashed between two ore cars up at the mine." Sarah stepped between her patient and Connor. "Please don't come any closer. He has a serious fracture and needs to have as few people around as possible. The more people that hover over him, breathing on him, the more likely he'll get an infection in his bone."

"You're right." Taking one last look, Connor stepped abruptly backward and out of the room. Pausing to look at Harley and Richard, he said, "The fewer people in the room with him, the better off he'll be."

Flushing, she turned to the other men. "Please go wait in the other room. Nobody should be in here."

Sarah watched the three men retreat to the waiting room. In spite of his injuries, Connor looked lethal, standing staring at her cousin and Harley. Neither of them spoke a word. They just stood, watching.

The door opened again and Chet's wife came running in. When she reached the exam room, she stopped and looked at her husband, color draining from her face.

"Oh, my God, he's dead, isn't he?"

"No, Jilly, he's not dead," Sarah said soothingly. "I gave him a painkiller and he's just sleeping."

Moving over to where the woman stood rooted to the ground, staring in horror at the bloody leg, Sarah gently but firmly led her to the head of the table. "You can stay in here with him, but you can't go near his leg. Just hold his hand

and talk to him. The helicopter should be here any minute."

As she finished speaking she heard the faint sound of the helicopter's rotor in the distance. Saying a prayer of thanksgiving that they were able to be so prompt, she went to her cabinet and pulled out a variety of sterile bandage materials. The evacuation crew would want to protect the wound before they transferred Chet to the helicopter, and she wanted to have everything they could ask for ready. Chet needed to be in a hospital as soon as possible.

Twenty minutes later she stood on the street and watched as the helicopter rose into the sky. As close to the ski resorts as they were, some of the best orthopedic surgeons in the country practiced within one hundred miles of Pine Butte. Chet would be in fine hands.

Just as she turned to go into her clinic, a large black car glided to a stop behind Harley's truck. Her uncle stepped out, walking quickly toward the knot of people in the street.

"How is he, Sarah?"

"He's on his way to Glenwood Springs," she replied. "If anyone can save his leg, the doctors there can." She looked from her cousin to her uncle. "How did you know about it, anyway, Uncle Ralph?"

He nodded in his son's direction. "Richard called me, of course. How else would I have known?"

"I thought you were in such a hurry to get him here that you didn't have time to make any phone calls, Richard?"

Her cousin flushed. "I thought my father should know. It is his mine, after all."

"And it was Jilly's husband." She looked at her cousin with disgust. "You did a good job getting him here right away, Richard, but you never change, do you? The bottom line is always the bottom line."

Ralph Wesley's cane thumped twice on the hard-packed dirt of the street. "That's quite enough. I didn't come here to listen to you two squabble like kindergarten children. I simply want to know what happened and how my employee got hurt."

Richard recited the whole story again while the burly foreman shifted from one foot to the other. Connor stood at the door to the clinic, watching them with hooded eyes. When Richard had finished, Sarah's uncle turned to Harley.

"What's your explanation?"

"He didn't let anyone know the car got derailed," Harley muttered. "That's why the next one was sent along. I guess he thought he could push it right back and nothing would happen."

"I see." Ralph Wesley stared from one face to the other. "It was an accident, then."

It wasn't a question but a statement, and Sarah knew the final word had been spoken. Without another word Ralph turned to get in his car. When he saw Connor leaning against the door of the clinic, he stopped.

"So they were right. You've come back."

"I have." Connor stared at the older man, his relaxed attitude betrayed by the fire in his eyes.

"There's nothing in this town for you, MacCormac. When you've recovered from your injuries, you'll be on your way."

Again, it wasn't a question but a statement. Connor slowly straightened, never taking his eyes off the older man. "I'll be on my way when I've finished my business in Pine Butte, Wesley. And not a minute before."

Sarah knew how injured Connor was. He couldn't possibly make good on the threat in his eyes. Still, she shivered and took a step toward him, intent on restraining him.

Ralph Wesley's cold gaze swept Connor from his head to the toes of his dusty boots. "You never did know how to take advice, MacCormac. I thought maybe you'd gotten a little smarter since you left. I can see I was wrong."

Sarah held her breath, feeling the anger coming off Connor in waves. Finally he smiled, and she shivered again. Cold, ruthless and utterly without humor, it was the smile of a predator who's just spotted his prey.

"I think you'll find you were wrong about a number of things, Wesley." Connor's eyes flickered over the older man, then looked away, dismissing him. Only Sarah saw her uncle's hand whiten on the handle of his cane. When Connor leaned back against the door of the clinic, she and the three men stood frozen for a moment, staring at him.

"Why is he here, Sarah?" her uncle asked, looking at her as if Connor didn't exist.

"Because he's injured and needs to be watched." Her voice was even and she turned and looked steadily at her uncle. "That's what I do, remember?"

"Send him to the hospital in Glenwood, then."

Sarah felt her temper rise at the peremptory order. Glancing at Connor, she saw a muscle in his jaw tighten. "He's not injured badly enough to justify that. Besides, he doesn't want to go. He's an adult. He can make his own decisions."

"So you're living with him. Can you imagine how he's laughing at you, after what he did to your sister?"

"I am not living with him, Uncle Ralph," she answered, clenching her teeth but feeling her face redden as she avoided Connor's eyes. "He is staying in the clinic until he's recovered enough to leave."

Her uncle turned to go, his gaze flicking over Connor dismissively. "Get rid of him, Sarah." He stepped into the long black car and it sped away, leaving a plume of dust behind. She watched it for a moment before turning to her cousin and the mine foreman.

"The hospital in Glenwood will call me as soon as they know anything. I'll get in touch with you, Richard." She paused, looking at the two men. "Thank you for bringing him into the clinic."

The foreman scowled at her and didn't bother to answer as he got into his truck. Richard said, "It was the least we could do, Sarah. I hope he's going to be all right."

She stood on the sidewalk as the battered truck disappeared in the direction of the mine, then turned and looked at Connor again.

He stood in the same place, watching her with unreadable eyes. Her gaze caught his and held for a moment, something dark and dangerous crackling between them like a flash of lightning. As she walked past him into the clinic, her heart began to pound. He followed her in, and the door clicked softly shut behind him.

"I'm sorry," she said quietly after a moment, trying to diffuse the anger she'd felt in him. "They had no right to talk to you that way." She could feel his gaze burning into her back, but she refused to turn and look at him. And why on earth was she apologizing, anyway? Hadn't her uncle and cousin only said what she'd been thinking since he'd landed in her clinic the day before?

"Why are you apologizing for your family? They're big boys."

She flushed and turned around. "That doesn't forgive rudeness."

He shrugged, a tight, bitter smile thinning his lips. "It's no less than I expected. They're just picking up where they left off twelve years ago, after all."

"What do you mean?" It was because of the way Connor had left town that the people of Pine Butte came to despise him.

His mouth twisted and he turned away from her. "Don't tell me you've forgotten, Sarah. Every town needs a bad boy, and I was nominated real early. I always figured it was because I was different—I had a different name, my father was an immigrant. Then my old man died, and it got real easy to live up to their expectations. Hell, I just did what everyone in town was waiting for me to do."

She winced at the bitterness and anger in his voice.

He turned and looked at her, apparently surprised at the shocked look on her face. "Don't tell me that the citizens of Pine Butte are ready to welcome me back with open arms. I'm sure they've filled your ears with a catalog of my sins, past and present."

"Yes, but that's because . . ." She hesitated, then said in a rush, "I had no idea they treated you badly when you lived here."

"You were an innocent, weren't you?" His voice was savage. "I figured everyone in town knew about the Mac-Cormac boy."

"Not everyone."

"It doesn't matter anymore. Hell, I should personally thank every one of them. If it wasn't for the way I was treated here in Pine Butte, I wouldn't be what I am today."

"And what is that, Connor?" she asked softly.

He looked at her for a long time without speaking. His eyes assessed and gradually softened as he watched her. For just a moment, she saw a yearning deep in his soul. Then his eyes hardened and he stood up straight.

"A man who gets what he wants. Remember that, Sarah. When your uncle and your cousin ask you what I'm doing here in Pine Butte, you tell them that I'm here to get justice. And tell them that I always get what I want."

"Is that what my sister Barb got? Justice?" she cried. The question was torn from her, but she couldn't hold it in. He wasn't the only one who had suffered.

"No, she didn't." His face tightened, and he said bitterly, "But there are some things that can't be undone."

"That's certainly true," she muttered. "But if you haven't come back for Barb, why are you here?"

"Like I told you, I'm here for justice."

"Justice or revenge? You sound too angry for justice."

He slowly sank into one of the chairs in the waiting room, and she suddenly remembered his injuries. He stretched his legs out in front of him, and she saw the slight trembling in the injured left one.

"I couldn't have come back, even to av—take care of business, without the anger." Closing his eyes, he leaned his head against the wall. "All I ever wanted to do was forget about Pine Butte."

Stretched out in the chair, propped against the wall, he looked achingly lonely. In spite of the pain and anger she'd carried around for the past twelve years, something inside her wanted to go over and comfort him. The impulse shocked her.

"Don't you know hatred only destroys itself? Go back to your life, Connor. Don't do this to yourself." *Don't do this to me,* she wanted to add.

"Or to Pine Butte?" he asked sarcastically, opening his eyes. "I'm sure your uncle would be happy to hear you say that. He'd be thrilled if I started walking now and never turned around."

"My uncle has nothing to do with it," she cried. "I have no idea why you've come back or what you hope to accomplish." Her voice steadied. "I just don't want to see you hurt yourself or anyone else." Why did she care, for God's sake? After what he did to her sister, she should be more than happy to see him self-destruct.

"That's mighty thoughtful of you, Sarah. I'd be more touched if I didn't think you had an ulterior motive."

"What possible motive could I have? I have no idea what went on here before you left twelve years ago."

"You're a Wesley. That's motive enough."

Her eyes flashed and she stood up. "Who's using names now to lump someone into a category?"

"There's a difference between being the poor Irish immigrant's son and the niece of the most powerful man in town. I wouldn't say it's the same thing at all."

"You're in no physical shape to get into a fight with my family, Connor. Have you forgotten that?"

"I have no intention of fighting with anyone. But you shouldn't worry. If anyone has a different idea, I heal fast."

Levering his bruised body off the chair, he slowly stood up. Instinctively she started over to help him, then stopped. If she had been telling herself it was foolish to let herself feel attracted to him before, it was insanity now. Apparently he'd come back to Pine Butte carrying a grudge against the Wesley family, and he'd lumped her in with the rest of them. If the thought hadn't been so ironic, it would have hurt too much to bear.

"Be careful," she said, trying to sound flippant. "I'd hate for all my good work to be wasted."

"Don't worry, I'm not doing anything more stressful than looking at my mother's old house today." He paused, watching her. "And then maybe I'll go visit Barb, for old time's sake."

The pain came sharp and fast, reminding her again why she despised him. "You won't have to go far," she said bitterly. "The cemetery is just outside of town."

He paled. It was the first time she'd seen him rattled. "Barb's dead?"

She looked at him. "She died eleven and a half years ago."

"What happened?"

"She went into labor in January. There was something wrong and I tried to drive her to the hospital in Glenwood Springs. Eagle Ridge Road was icy and we slipped off the road. She bled to death in the car."

"My God!" His eyes softened and he reached out for her hand. "I'm so sorry, Sarah. But why did you have to drive her to the hospital? Where was the father of her child?"

"You tell me." Pulling her hand away from his, she felt the familiar pain and anger gripping her. "She died giving birth to your baby, Connor MacCormac."

Chapter 4

"Like hell she did." Connor stopped dead in his tracks. Rage filled his face, wiping away the pain that had filled his eyes.

"Is that what you all think of me? That I would walk out on a pregnant eighteen-year-old girl? That I would abandon not only her but our child, as well?" His eyes burned with a fury that made her back up a step.

"Isn't that what you did? As soon as you found out she was pregnant, you took off. Having a child wasn't in your plans," she said savagely. "Isn't that what you told Barb?"

Blue fire flashed from his eyes. "What I told Barb," he began fiercely, then paused. The anger faded, replaced by a weary futility that made Sarah fist her hands in her pockets.

"What I told Barb doesn't matter anymore." All his rage had disappeared. "I'm sorry she's dead, Sarah. It must have been horrible for you."

"Horrible. Yes, I guess that's one way to describe it." She would never forget that cold January night on Eagle Ridge Road. The car's wheels stuck off the side of the road, spinning more deeply every time she revved the engine. Looking at her sister, holding her hand when the contractions came and she sobbed with fear and pain. Watching the trickle of blood between her legs become a steady stream of red, dark and ugly. Remembering her own panic and helpless desperation, and how hard she'd tried to reassure her terrified sister. Remembering her frantic tears as her sister slipped into unconsciousness, praying for a miracle that never happened.

"I'm sorry," he said again quietly, interrupting the memory she'd tried so hard to forget. "I had no idea."

"Of course you didn't. You weren't anywhere near Pine Butte when she needed you."

Connor heard the agony in her voice and saw the effort at control in her rigid back and was halfway across the room before he realized it. Stopping abruptly, he jammed his hands in the pockets of his jeans. She wouldn't welcome comfort from him. She thought he was the man who'd seduced then abandoned her sister, sentencing her to a painful and senseless death.

He couldn't tell her the truth, not right now. She didn't know anything about him and the man he'd become. She would never believe him, and right now he didn't want to face the scorn in her eyes. Looking at her vulnerable back, at the way her bright hair curled softly against her neck, he felt his body tighten. She was becoming too damn important.

"I have some things to do," he said abruptly. "I'll be back later." He had to leave. There was no place in his life for this kind of weakness. Moving stiffly, he turned and walked slowly out the door.

Four hours later, standing on the sidewalk in front of Earlene's restaurant, Connor hesitated with his hand on the door. He didn't want to eat alone. His gaze wandered to the clinic across the street. Maybe Sarah would be finished with her patients and he could persuade her to join him. He needed some way to repay her for taking care of him, he told himself. Then again, after what she'd told him about her sister, maybe all she wanted was to see him gone.

Head throbbing and ribs and leg aching, he limped painfully to the clinic door. Maybe he should have listened to

Sarah, not tried to do so much the day after his accident. His lips thinned as he pushed the clinic door open. He didn't have a choice. Now that everyone knew he was back, he needed to get to the truth as quickly as possible.

"Sarah?" he called, shutting the door behind him. "Are you here?"

"I'm upstairs." Her voice drifted down to him. "I'll be right there."

He headed for the open door that looked as if it might hide a staircase. Before he got all the way there, Sarah came clattering down the wooden stairs.

"I'm glad you're back," she said, her voice neutral. "I was beginning to worry."

The surge of pleasure her words produced took him by surprise. It had been a long time since anyone had worried about him. Even the coolness in her blue-green eyes couldn't diminish the warmth that engulfed him.

"I'm okay." His voice sounded gruff, and he cleared his throat. "I was just wondering if you wanted to go over to Earlene's and have dinner with me."

Her eyes scrutinized him, sweeping him from head to toes. Their clear color was shadowed with old pain, and a faint puffiness told him she'd been crying. Finally she said, "Why don't you eat here tonight? I've got some spaghetti sauce on the stove and salad in the refrigerator. You'll probably be more comfortable if you can relax on the couch."

Her words were carefully objective, spoken only out of medical concern. There was nothing personal about her invitation. She probably invited all her patients upstairs for dinner.

That thought made him scowl. "Thanks, if it's not too much trouble."

She shook her head before she turned to lead the way upstairs, pausing to lock the front door of the clinic first. "I have to eat anyway," she pointed out. "No one makes just one serving of spaghetti sauce."

He couldn't walk into her house with the afternoon's accusations between them. "Sarah," he began in a low voice.

She stopped on the lowest stair and turned.

"About this afternoon. What you said about Barb?" He hesitated, groping for the right words. "I wasn't the father of her child."

It seemed like a long time before she answered. "That's not what she told me." She turned and vanished up the stairs.

"Wait." He followed her up the stairs as fast as he could. When he got to the room upstairs, she stood waiting for him, her whole body tense. The cheery room full of floral prints and bright colors should have seemed comfortable and welcoming. Instead it mocked him, the outsider forever locked away from the warmth. He was the intruder, coming back to where he wasn't wanted, opening old wounds in her life.

"You're telling me my sister's a liar." Her voice was flat and brittle. She watched him with unreadable eyes.

"I'm sure Barb had a good reason for saying what she did." He tried to keep the anger out of his voice. "It just wasn't true. I never slept with her."

"Well, it's your word against Barb's. Guess who I'm going to believe?"

"I know you have no reason to believe me now. I'm not even sure why I want to bother to try to change your mind."

She pushed her hair away from her face with one impatient hand, and his body tightened. He knew why. He just had no intention of telling her right now.

"Connor, as long as you're my patient I'll treat you like I would any other patient. But don't expect me to welcome you back to Pine Butte. That's not part of my job." She turned and walked into the kitchen.

He followed her to the kitchen and hovered near the stove until she turned to him, scowling.

"Will you please just sit down before you fall down? You're standing there swaying on your feet."

Thankfully he lowered himself into one of the wooden chairs that stood around the butcher-block table. "I'm okay," he said again. "Just a little tired."

She stood facing him, skewering the air with a long, thin knife she was using to cut tomatoes. Almost as if it was against her will, her eyes softened. "A little tired, my left foot. You're ready to keel over. You've got the world's worst headache and it feels like ten horses kicked you in the ribs," she said, amazingly accurate.

"Yeah, but other than that I'm fine."

Her lips quivered for a moment, then a tiny smile flashed and was quickly suppressed. A sliver of the ice in her eyes melted. "I guess I shouldn't be so surprised you weren't hurt any worse. With a head as hard as yours nothing could cause much damage."

With a tiny groan he settled back against the chair cushion. "That doesn't mean I'll object to a little tender loving care."

"Spaghetti and salad are about as tender as it gets around here, MacCormac." The smile faded as she turned around and finished slicing the ripe tomato.

They talked intermittently through dinner. By unspoken agreement they tried to keep the conversation light, both avoiding any talk about Pine Butte. She asked, delicately, what he did now, but he deflected the question easily and talked about something else. He enjoyed her company, he might want to do more than just talk with her, but he still didn't trust her. Anything he told her about himself could be used later as ammunition. He wasn't about to give anyone in Pine Butte a single round to use against him.

When they finished dinner he struggled to his feet to help her clear the table. "Connor," she sighed, placing her hands on her hips and giving him an exasperated look. "Will you cut it out? Go on into the living room and sit down."

"Yes, ma'am," he replied meekly, suppressing a smile. She had no idea how endearing she looked, standing there with a spatula dripping water onto the floor.

Her couch felt as if it was made in heaven. Sinking into its comfort, he turned and watched her wash the dishes and stack them to dry. Even doing the mundane chore she moved gracefully, her slim hips tantalizing in the worn jeans. She was warmth and fire, and he longed for just a taste of her.

After she finished she brought him a mug of coffee and a piece of pie. Raising his eyebrows, he said, "You've decided that my blood pressure doesn't need protecting anymore?"

"No, you're fine. If you can spend the day walking around Pine Butte, then a cup of coffee isn't going to hurt you," she said dryly.

They ate the pie in silence. When he finished, he set his plate on the coffee table and looked at her. In spite of the way he felt about this town, in spite of the way he felt about her family, he was too damn attracted to her to let things lie between them.

"About our conversation earlier," he began, but she cut him off.

"Forget about it. I have already."

"You can't tell me you've forgotten about your sister and why she died."

"I'll never forget that." She stared at him for a moment, her eyes hard. "But she's dead, and you're a patient, at least for the time being. I can manage to put our... differences aside and be professional."

"Are you ever anything other than professional?"

She looked at him for a long time, then looked away. "No."

He could believe that. Her apartment, although welcoming, was definitely feminine. It didn't look as though many men spent time in her hideaway.

"Thank you for insisting that I stay here in the clinic." He didn't think he'd tell her what had made him agree.

"I could hardly let you wander around town with a concussion and broken ribs. Someone needed to look after you."

"And I couldn't have picked a better person myself," he murmured, watching her from suddenly heavy-lidded eyes.

She jumped up from the couch abruptly and went to the window. Dusk was just beginning to fall, and he could see the start of a magnificent sunset splashed against the mountains that ringed Pine Butte.

"Why are you here, Connor?" she asked quietly. "What do you want from Pine Butte?"

"Just what I told your uncle today. Justice."

"It's too late to punish the people of Pine Butte for what they did to you when you were a child. You have to forget about it and get on with your life."

"I never said I was here to extract retribution for my miserable childhood. No one can give me that. But there are other things this town took from me besides my innocence. Things that the people responsible are going to pay for."

She couldn't turn around. If she saw his face, saw the anguish in his eyes that accompanied his words, she would be lost. Gripping the windowsill, she thought she might be anyway. Still staring out at the vivid sunset, she murmured, "Even if you hadn't told me so, I'd know that you always got what you wanted." She paused and a note of sadness crept into her voice. "You know the old saying about being careful what you ask for? Be very certain this is what you want, Connor."

For an injured man he managed to move awfully quickly. When his hand touched her shoulder, she jolted and turned around too fast. Her hand brushed his chest, and she looked up into eyes that glittered with something that wasn't pain.

"There's only one thing I'm certain I want right now," he muttered, and bent his head to hers.

It was not a gentle kiss. There were no preliminary caresses, no soft brushing of his lips against hers. His mouth, hot and hungry, took possession of hers. His hands slid into her hair, holding her head for his plundering kiss.

After the first moment of surprise and resistance, her eyes fluttered closed and she felt herself melt into him. Her brain screamed a warning, begged her to stop and think, but she was beyond thinking. The moment his mouth touched hers she was lost.

Feeling her surrender, he deepened the kiss. His hands combed through her hair, barely touching her scalp. Shivering, she leaned against him and tentatively wrapped her arms around his back. She felt his body tighten and tense, then he pulled her closer. His palms slid over her shoulders and down her back, cupping her hips in his big hands. When he pressed her against him, she felt the extent of his arousal and shivered again.

With one hand he held her close, and with the other he wandered up her back. His lips left her mouth, leaving her aching, wanting more. They glided over her cheek, down to her neck and finally settled in the hollow above her collarbone.

"Sweet Sarah," he whispered into her ear. "I've wanted you since the minute I woke up and saw you standing over me." His mouth returned to hers. This time, his tongue teased her lips and she gladly opened to him. The taste of coffee and forbidden passion filled her head.

Desire curled inside her, heated to a throbbing, almost unbearable rhythm. Her arms tightened around him, trying to bring him closer, and it took a moment for his sudden stillness to penetrate the haze of passion.

Realization hit her like a fist in the stomach. Unwrapping her arms from around him, she stepped back. "Your ribs," she whispered, horrified. "I forgot."

"I did, too." Sighing, he pushed her hair away from her face and let his fingers slide down her cheek. "It seems like I forget a lot of things when I'm around you."

But she was remembering. She took another step back and stood trembling, staring at him. They might have been locked together for a minute or an hour. She had no idea. Wrapping her shaking arms around herself, she felt a little sick. How could she have forgotten who he was, what he'd done to her sister? How could she have responded to him so quickly, so completely?

"Sarah," he began, but she cut him off.

"I think you'd better go, Connor. I'll keep the door open in case you need help during the night."

She turned away, but he didn't move. She felt him behind her, pulsating with energy and frustrated desire.

"It doesn't matter, you know. No matter how much I want you, it won't stop me from getting what I came for."

She whirled to face him, but he'd already started out of the room. My God, did he think she was deliberately seducing him? A bitter laugh caught in her throat. The last thing she needed or wanted was any kind of relationship with Connor MacCormac.

Sinking down on the couch, she looked at the place where he'd disappeared just moments before. She had to be honest, at least with herself. Wanting had nothing to do with it. She'd wanted him from the moment she saw him. But having. Now that was a different story.

He was the last man she could allow herself to care about. Even if the past hadn't stood between them, the ugly accusations and suspicions poisoning the air, the present would. He wasn't a settle-down, stay-in-one-little-town kind of man. He especially wasn't interested in staying in Pine Butte, Colorado. He'd made that more than clear. And unless, by some miracle, they could attract a doctor to their tiny community, Sarah was doomed to stay here forever.

Moving stiffly, she undressed and got ready for bed. At least she wouldn't have to worry about one thing, she thought with lingering pain. If he needed her during the night, it would take her only a minute to respond. She wasn't planning on much sleep tonight.

When Connor opened his eyes to the pearl-gray dawn light, he looked around for a moment, disoriented. Where was this room?

Memory came back quickly as he swung his legs over the side of the bed. His side still ached as if he'd been stomped by a horse, but the pain in his head had subsided to a vague throb. When he flexed his left leg, there was only a momentary twinge of pain. As he'd told Sarah, he healed quickly.

Listening intently for a while, he finally stood up and fumbled in his pack for clean clothes. There wasn't a sound from the clinic or Sarah's apartment upstairs. Maybe he could sneak out before she was up. That way he wouldn't have to think about the uneasy guilt he felt whenever he saw the concern in those sea-colored eyes of hers.

Sarah Wesley was concerned only about her precious town, he tried to tell himself. He smiled grimly as he pulled a T-shirt over his head. It sure would be a hell of a lot simpler if he could convince himself of that. But their kiss last night had blown that theory right out of the water.

She hadn't kissed him like a woman who was trying only to protect her town and her family. She'd kissed him like a lover, like she'd meant it. And God help him, he was afraid he'd kissed her the same way.

It wasn't too late to stop, he told himself. One kiss didn't mean a thing. Sure he was attracted to her, but so what? He'd been attracted to a million other women. He'd enjoyed more than a few of them, then they'd said mutual goodbyes without an ounce of regret.

But Sarah Wesley was different. He'd known it from the minute he'd opened his eyes and saw her standing over him in the clinic, soothing away his pain and surrounding him with her warmth. Something in Sarah cut away all the pain and anger, cut right to his core where he had no defenses. And she scared the hell out of him.

He hadn't come back to Pine Butte to get involved with a woman. Especially not Barb Wesley's sister. Of all the betrayals large and small that were his memories of this town, hers had been the worst. The last thing he wanted or needed was to care about her sister.

His stomach still curled with disgust and shame when he remembered the innocent, lovesick child he'd been. He'd been the same age as Barb Wesley, but for all his toughness and bravado on the outside, his heart had been tender and untried.

And he'd fallen in love with her. Maybe it had been the way she'd held him at arm's length, teasing him, letting him take her out but not allowing more than a chaste kiss, that had made him so determined to marry her. Maybe it had been just the starry-eyed idealism of a boy in love for the first time. Whatever it had been, he would never forget the day, just after they'd graduated from high school, when he'd asked her to marry him.

She hadn't actually laughed out loud at him, but he'd known she was laughing inside. When she'd told him she was pregnant, he'd just looked at her, unable to comprehend what she'd said. When her words finally sunk in, when he realized she'd been using him all along, he'd left her without another word. The next day he'd packed his meager belongings and left Pine Butte.

No, the last thing he needed in his life was another dose of a Wesley woman. His heart told him Sarah was nothing like Barb, but he refused to listen. He would leave now, before she was awake, and try not to return until late. By tomorrow he would be able to clean up his mother's house and live there. Once he was away from her, it would be easy to forget her.

As he tiptoed toward the front door he heard a faint rustling behind him.

"You're up awfully early," Sarah's calm voice said.

He spun around and found her leaning against the wall that led to her cubbyhole of an office. She smelled like flowery soap and her hair was still slightly damp from a shower, but no amount of bathing could have erased the huge purple shadows under her eyes.

If she wanted to play it casual, so could he. He ignored the little flare of disappointment. "So are you."

Waving her hand toward her desk, she said, "I have a lot of records to catch up on. What's your excuse?"

"Business." He moved to the door, determined to get out of the clinic and away from Sarah. At the door he paused and looked back at her. "Have you had breakfast?" he found himself asking.

"I'll get something later," she replied, pushing herself away from the wall. "Be careful today."

It looked as if she was as determined as he was to forget about the previous night. Some devil made him ask, "It doesn't look like Earlene has many customers yet. Sure you wouldn't care to join me?"

She was on the verge of saying no. He saw it in her eyes, saw the word form on her lips. Then, slowly, she nodded. "That would be nice." Grabbing the clinic key off the desk, she followed him out the door without another word.

Earlene gave them a sharp look when they slid into a window booth. The faded orange vinyl seats looked the same as they had when he was a kid, and the menu was about as old. Carrying a pot of coffee, the owner of the town's only restaurant rumbled over to their table and stood there for a moment, a hard look on her face.

"Morning, Sarah." The look she gave him was frankly curious. "Hello, Connor. We heard you were back in town."

Earlene and her cohorts had probably been talking about nothing else for the past forty-eight hours. "You heard right." He lifted the cup of coffee she'd just poured and took a gulp of the scalding liquid, closing his eyes in satisfaction. "Nobody on God's earth ever could make coffee like you, Earlene. Are you sure you don't want to run away and marry me?"

She snorted, her lips curling up in a reluctant grin. "You always could charm the rattles off a snake, Connor Mac-Cormac."

Earlene walked away smiling and Sarah raised her eyebrows. "I didn't realize your affections were spoken for."

He grinned. "Honey, you make coffee like Earlene and I'd probably ask you the same thing. At least in the morning."

Without bothering to ask, their hostess brought two platters piled high with pancakes and bacon and hash brown potatoes. They ate in a comfortable silence, and finally he pushed away his empty plate and leaned back against the stiff vinyl.

"Are they going to gossip about you?" he asked.

She didn't pretend to not understand. Flushing, she said, "This isn't the first time a patient has stayed overnight at the clinic. Everyone knows that."

"But it's the first time *I've* stayed there." He couldn't help the bitterness that crept into his voice. "I'll leave today."

"No, you won't." She leaned over the table, her face hot with temper. "I don't care what anyone says. You're not leaving a minute before you should. I'd like you to stay at least another couple of nights."

"I'll stay tonight. After that, I don't know." He wasn't sure he could handle even one more night alone in the quiet building with her.

Sliding stiffly out of the booth, he pulled out his wallet and tossed some bills on the table. "Thanks for joining me for breakfast. With you here, at least Earlene was willing to serve me."

"Something tells me she would have been more than willing, anyway you showed up," she answered dryly.

He grinned suddenly. "Yeah. Now she's going to be queen of the gossips, at least for a day. She actually spoke to me."

Sarah stood next to him, a faint trace of sadness on her face. "Not everyone in Pine Butte is like my family, Connor. Give them a chance."

"Oh, I'll give them a chance, all right. I just won't turn my back on them."

They stood on the sidewalk, Connor oddly reluctant to leave her and get on with his business. It seemed as if Sarah wasn't in any hurry to get back to her clinic, either.

Finally she started across the street. "I'll see you later. What are you going to do today?"

"I'm going to see if the kid at the gas station is finished with my motorcycle, then I have some checking to do. I may not be back until late."

"All right," she said softly.

He felt her eyes on his back all the way down the street. When he finally turned the corner, it felt as if he'd left something important behind.

An hour later, Connor eased the clutch out on the tiny car he'd rented from the gas station and urged it up the hill. His motorcycle wouldn't be finished for a few days, but he was satisfied the kid knew what he was doing. There were parts that had to be ordered, and young Billy Sullivan had been eager to chat about tail pipes and spark plugs. All Connor wanted was to have it fixed and running again, but he'd spent a few minutes with the mechanic. At least there was one person in the town who didn't care about his past.

The car chugged up the hill like an anemic sewing machine, sputtering more the higher they got. "Just another couple of miles," he muttered to the dashboard. He drove past the gate that led to the offices of Wesley Mining Inc. He planned on visiting the mine today, but he didn't think he'd be welcomed in an official capacity. The back entrance would do just fine.

After a slow fifteen minutes, he parked the car off the road behind a clump of trees. It wasn't hidden from sight, just out of the way. Scrambling between trees and around boulders, he finally emerged just above the main entrance to Wesley's mine shaft. Settling himself in the bushes, he watched the activity below.

Ore cars shot out of the hole in the mountain at regular intervals. A swarm of workmen unloaded them and started them down the other track back into the mine. Watching the frantic activity below, Connor saw how easy it had been for Chet to injure his leg.

Ralph Wesley was determined to get as much work as possible out of his employees. The cars came just a hair too fast. If Chet had been trying to replace a derailed car without having the next one stopped, as the foreman had claimed, it would be all too easy to get trapped between the two cars.

Chet was going to be fine. Connor had been in Sarah's apartment the night before when she'd gotten the phone call. He'd had surgery, and although his recovery would be long and painful, he wasn't going to lose the leg.

Watching the activity below him, Connor was amazed that accidents like Chet's didn't happen more frequently. He watched for a while longer, then stood up and retraced his steps. The scene was enlightening, but it wasn't what he'd come for. Unloading ore cars wasn't what had killed his father.

By the time he reached the car, sweat poured off him. Ignoring the ache in his side, he got into the car and pointed it up the road. Eventually, straining and groaning, the car got him to the place he wanted to stop.

He was far from the mine, and not a whisper of sound from the activity below reached this far. All he heard was the twittering of birds in the underbrush and, close by, the gurgle of a little stream.

He needed to sit and think for a while, to try to plan his next move. He'd come back to Pine Butte to find the truth. His father had died when he was twelve, of a heart attack. At least that's what the doctor had said, and he and his mother had had no reason to believe otherwise.

Until he'd gotten the note. After all these years, he'd almost managed to forget this town. Almost. And then one day in the mail he'd received an anonymous note, telling him his father's death hadn't been any accident. That he'd been killed.

Pushing through the bushes, he found the little stream he'd been looking for. This was the place he'd always come as a kid, riding his first small motorbike up the mountain in search of solitude. Easing himself down into the soft moss, he leaned against a tree and idly watched the water ripple over the rocks.

Who had sent the note? And why? If he could figure that out, he'd be halfway to solving the mystery. Why would anyone want to dredge up an eighteen-year-old death?

As he stared at the stream, thinking, it slowly dawned on him that something was different about this place. Frowning, he leaned forward, looking at the water and the trees around it. On the surface, nothing looked changed.

As he studied the stream, his eyes narrowed. Where were the fish? This stream had been his favorite fishing spot, and the trout used to practically jump out of the water into his net. Swarms of minnows used to hide next to the rocks, and all kinds of insects used to skitter across the surface of the water or the sand underneath it.

Now the stream was silent, and empty except for the rocks that lined the floor. Connor stood and walked upstream for a while, sure he'd just found the one barren spot. But no matter where he looked, there was no sign of any fish. There was no sign of any life whatsoever.

As he stared into the water, frowning, he almost didn't hear the crack of twigs behind him. When he did turn around, he was too late. The blow caught him on the side of the head and the world exploded in pain.

Chapter 5

Sarah stood in the waiting room of her clinic, watching her last patient of the day walk out the door. She glanced at the clock on the wall and frowned. Connor had been gone all day, and there was no sign of him yet.

More than one of her patients had reported that he'd rented a car from the service station and headed off into the mountains in the direction of the Wesley mine. That had been hours ago. Twirling one strand of hair around her finger, she looked at the phone, torn with indecision.

She had no idea where Connor had gone or why. But the fact that he'd headed off in the direction of the mine made a knot of fear settle in her stomach. She wouldn't soon forget the hatred that had seemed to flow between Connor and her cousin and uncle. Should she call her cousin Richard, see if Connor had been there?

As her hand reached for the phone, she told herself that anything could have happened to him. He might have passed out in the car, run off the road. He'd suffered a concussion only two days ago, after all. It was no more than her duty as the only medical person in Pine Butte to check on him.

She'd dialed half the numbers for her cousin's office at the mine when she slowly replaced the receiver. If Connor hadn't gone to the mine, he might not appreciate her phoning Richard. Until she had a better idea of why he was here, she didn't want to remind her cousin or her uncle about his presence.

Grabbing the keys to her truck, she hurried out the door. The smartest thing to do was look for him herself. That way, when she found him perfectly safe, she was the only one who'd know what a fool she'd been.

The inside of her truck felt like the desert at high noon. Heat shimmered off the seat, and the steering wheel was almost too hot to touch. She rolled down the windows, then headed for the road that led to the mine.

When she got to the entrance, she stopped the truck but didn't drive in. One glance told her that the tiny economy car Connor had rented wasn't there. Letting in the clutch, she hurried past the gate and drove on, scanning the sides of the road for any sign of his car.

She was about to turn around and head back to town when she saw the flash of metal behind a stand of trees. Jumping out of the truck, she ran over to the car. It was the rental car from the service station, but there was no sign of Connor.

The ground rose in a steep slope just past where the car was parked. Scanning it quickly, she decided that she'd climb it if she had to. Right now, she'd check the other side of the road first.

She heard the stream almost as soon as she'd crossed the road, and stopped abruptly. Maybe he'd come up here to do some fishing. Just because he'd said he had business to take care of today didn't have to mean anything sinister. Maybe his business had been nothing more serious than catching a few trout.

She'd come this far, she told herself reluctantly, and she might as well finish it. If she felt like a fool because she came running to rescue a man who was fishing, then so be it. She'd think of some excuse to give Connor.

When she got to the stream, there was no sign of him.

"He probably wandered downstream," she muttered, trying to ignore the frisson of uneasiness that skittered down her spine. She took two steps toward the car when the eerie quiet made her stop.

If he was fishing she should at least hear the regular plop of the fly hitting the water, or the splashing of his boots as he moved through the stream. The only sound was the quiet gurgling of the water moving over the rocks.

The back of her neck prickling, she pushed through the undergrowth and walked a little farther. "Connor?" she called quietly. "Are you here?"

She walked a little farther, calling again. When there was no answer she leaned over the stream, trying to look ahead. The only thing she saw was a bluish log in the water upstream.

She stared at it for a moment, puzzled by its color. Suddenly she realized that it wasn't a log at all but a person's jean-covered leg. Her stomach clenched in fear as she rushed through the bushes toward the prone figure, ignoring the branches whipping at her face.

Connor lay sprawled on the ground, his legs in the water. An ugly purple bruise discolored the skin next to his right eye.

"Connor!" she screamed. Dropping to her knees next to him, she frantically reached for a pulse.

When she found it, steady and strong, she drew in a shaking breath. At least he was alive. Reaching over his still body, she tugged at his legs until they were out of the water. Her hands flew over him, searching for any other injuries.

When she was satisfied that the bruise on his head was the only problem, she rolled him over on his back. In spite of the searing heat he felt cold and clammy. "Connor," she said urgently. "Can you hear me?"

He groaned and moved his head just a fraction of an inch. The fingers of his right hand clenched and relaxed.

"Connor, you have to wake up! I can't carry you out of here."

He groaned again and his eyelids fluttered open. "Sarah? What're—"

"I came looking for you," she interrupted. "You'd been gone for too long. What happened? Did you feel dizzy, fall and hit your head on a rock?"

His eyes closed, and she was afraid he'd passed out again. "No." His voice sounded groggy. "Gotta get out of here."

"That's right," she soothed. "Do you think you can walk?"

"Try."

He struggled to sit up, and she grabbed his shoulders and pulled him forward. The slight remaining color in his face drained away, and she knew pain had to be stabbing through his head. Squatting next to him, she fitted her shoulder under his arm.

"Hold onto me and try to stand up."

He wrapped both his arms around her and she felt his muscles tense. Slowly, feeling his weight sagging against her, she staggered to her feet. He stood swaying in the sun, his eyes closed against the pain and weakness, using her to support him.

It couldn't be more than fifty yards back to the truck, she thought desperately, turning in the direction of the road. She could get him that far. As long as he didn't fall down, they'd make it.

Her left arm tightened around his waist until a sharp intake of his breath, quickly muffled, reminded her about his ribs. She slipped her fingers inside the waistband of his jeans, catching her breath at the feel of his hot skin against her knuckles. Disgusted with herself, she tightened her grip on his jeans. If she needed any proof that she had to get a life, this was it.

"We're going to go real slow, Connor. One step at a time. Once we get to the road, I'll get the truck and you can pass out again."

She wasn't sure if she was reassuring Connor or herself. She kept up a soothing, running monologue all the way through the woods. The hand hooked into the waistband of his jeans cramped, but she ignored the pain. Whenever she didn't have to use her right hand to hold branches away from his face, she tucked it into his armpit and took some of the weight off her left hand.

By the time she spotted the road through a break in the trees she was practically dragging him behind her. She wasn't sure if he'd passed out again and she couldn't stop to find out. If she lost her forward momentum, she'd never get started again.

When they reached the strip of gravel, she guided him to a tree and eased him to the ground. Her legs buckled under her and she slid down next to him. As she sat there, willing strength back into her arms and legs, she looked at the man next to her.

His face was pasty white, and beads of sweat that had formed at his hairline ran down the side of his face. His eyes were closed. She couldn't tell if he was awake or unconscious again.

"Connor?" she said, suddenly scared. "Can you hear me?"

"I can hear you." His voice sounded harsh and raspy. "How much farther to the truck?"

"It's down the road a little. I'll get it in a minute. You won't have to walk any farther."

Willing her muscles to obey her, she stood up. Her legs trembled and her arms shook, but she ignored it. "I'll be back in less than five minutes."

"Hurry."

"Connor." She dropped to her knees in front of him, her heart thundering. "Is there something more wrong with you than your head? Are you injured somewhere else?"

His eyes fluttered open. The softening in their bleak depths, quickly suppressed, had her reaching for his hand. His surprisingly warm fingers closed around hers and held on.

"No, it's just my head. But I don't want to be sitting on this road alone in this condition."

"I'll run to the truck," she promised. "It's not more than a few yards down the road."

She eased her hand out of his, hating to break the contact. She got to her feet, then turned back on impulse. Dropping to her knees again, she pressed a kiss to his lips.

"I'll be right back."

His eyes snapped open as she jumped to her feet and turned in the direction of the truck. She felt his gaze but she didn't look back. As she ran down the road, fear for Connor churned in her gut, mixing with a queasy apprehen-

sion. He'd had two accidents in as many days. Her heart
thundered as her feet crunched on the gravel. That was quite
a coincidence for a sleepy little town like Pine Butte. Or was
it more than a coincidence?

She tried to banish the ugly thought but it lingered at the
edge of her mind, making her feet move even faster.

The truck was closer than she'd thought and she pulled up
next to him less than three minutes later. She turned the
truck, jumped out and opened the passenger door. When he
heard her coming, he'd tried to stand up. He was propped
against the tree, his knees bent, trying hard not to slide back
to the ground.

"Just a few steps," she crooned, draping his arm over her
shoulders again and holding onto his jeans. Together they
staggered to the truck, and she practically shoved him into
the cab. As he leaned against the seat, she lifted his legs into
the cab then shut the door.

Supporting herself against the hot fender, she closed her
eyes and took a deep, shuddering breath, finally allowing
herself to confront the fear. If she hadn't come looking for
him, he might have died, lying there in the icy water. It
might be summer, but the mountain streams were still cold
and the nights up here could be frigid.

After a moment she forced herself to get into the truck.
Connor needed to lie down somewhere, preferably on an
evacuation helicopter to Glenwood Springs. Ignoring the
pang of loss at the thought of his leaving Pine Butte, she
concentrated on a way to convince him he would be better
off in a hospital with a real doctor.

She started down the mountain, wincing every time the
truck hit a bump in the road. After a few minutes, she
glanced at Connor. His eyes were closed, but she saw him
tense every time the truck bounced.

"Sorry about the ride," she said. "I'm trying to avoid the
biggest holes."

"Don't worry about it." His eyes opened and a ghost of
a smile passed over his face. "Any kind of a ride is a hell of
a lot better than lying facedown in the woods."

Thank God he was at least conscious. "What happened?" she asked softly. Maybe she could take his mind off the uncomfortable ride.

She could almost feel him tense beside her. "Someone sneaked up behind me and knocked me out." His voice was flat and without expression. "I have no idea how long I was lying there."

"What?" she whispered, staring at him. Apprehension blossomed into sickening fear. "Someone knocked you out? I thought you'd slipped and hit your head on a rock."

"I'm sure that was how it was supposed to look," he answered grimly. "But whoever did it screwed up and didn't hit me hard enough." His face softened as he looked at her. "And they didn't count on you coming to look for me. Why did you?"

The truck nearly swerved off the road as she stared at him. Finally, feeling the faint flush in her cheeks, she turned to watch the road. "I was worried," she answered, trying to sound nonchalant. "I knew you weren't as strong as you thought you were. I was afraid you'd had an accident or something." Remembering her concern about a possible confrontation with her cousin, she felt a thrum of dread deep inside her chest. What was happening in her town?

"Yeah, I guess accident would cover it." He leaned back against the seat and closed his eyes again.

"Connor?"

"Later, okay?"

She saw his hand grip the armrest on the door. Every time the truck bounced, his knuckles turned white. He was right. She had to concentrate on getting him to town as quickly as possible. After she'd made sure his injury wasn't serious he could answer her questions.

Sarah pulled the truck around the back to avoid any curious eyes on Main Street. Unlocking the back door to the clinic, she propped it open and hurried to the truck to help him out. When she opened the door, he slid off the seat and stood, swaying slightly, on the hot pavement. "Hold on to me," she directed, and was rewarded with another of his infrequent, blinding smiles.

"With pleasure."

Wrapping his arms around her shoulders, he moved slowly toward the open door. Instead of stopping at an exam room, she went directly to the bedroom and eased him down on the bed.

He sighed and relaxed into the quilt and she wanted nothing more than to soothe away his pain. The realization slammed into her and she slowly took a step backward. What was happening to her? Wasn't this what she'd been dreaming of for the past twelve years, Connor MacCormac helpless and dependent on her? What had happened to her fantasies of revenge? The emotions he roused in her now were neither comfortable nor reassuring.

She should be feeling nothing but dislike and a cool professionalism for this man. His smiles shouldn't make her heart beat faster. She shouldn't be thinking about him so much that she felt compelled to go looking for him when he didn't show up for several hours. She should look at him and realize that he'd finally gotten what he deserved after so many years.

But all she could do was burn with the need for revenge against the person who'd injured him. She couldn't even pretend it was just concern for her patient, because right now it would give her great pleasure to pick up a rock and smash it into whoever had done this. No, there was nothing detached about her feelings for Connor MacCormac.

"Could I have some water?" he croaked.

"Of course," she said briskly, rousing herself. "I'll be right back."

She walked into the room a few minutes later with a glass of water and several instruments. "I want to examine you before I let you have a drink."

"Be my guest, but there's nothing wrong with me other than a knock on the head. I'll be on my feet again tomorrow."

"I was going to suggest a trip to Glenwood Springs. I still think you should see a doctor, now more than ever."

"Trust me, Sarah, I'm fine. Go ahead and do your exam if it will make you feel better, but you're not going to find anything."

Ten minutes later she was forced to agree with him. Other than an ugly purple bruise on the side of his head, there weren't any signs of serious injury. Rocking back on her heels, she looked at him and asked, "How did you know that you were okay? How do you know so much about medicine?"

He shrugged and looked at his hands. "I just know my own body. I can tell if there's anything seriously wrong." Shifting once more on the bed, he looked at her. "What happened to your face?"

"My face?" She reached up to touch her cheek and felt criss-crossing welts. "I don't know."

"You look like you've been in a cat fight."

Suddenly remembering her headlong rush through the bushes after she'd spotted him in the stream, she flushed faintly and shrugged, praying he couldn't see the color in her face in the dim light. "I guess the bushes up on the mountain scratched me."

He watched her steadily, a strange light in his eyes. "Sarah," he began, but she interrupted.

"It's not important. What is important..." She hesitated, choosing her words carefully. "I don't think you should move back to your mother's house just yet. It's kind of...isolated, and you're probably not going to be real quick for the next few days. Think about staying here for a while."

She watched him fight the weariness weighing his body down and saw the exact moment when he couldn't fight any longer. "I'll do that," he grunted. "Later." His eyes drifted shut and he slowly relaxed.

She pulled the quilt over him and stood watching for a minute. For the time being he was safe. She'd have to be satisfied with that, and save her questions for later.

Sarah curled deeper into the waiting-room couch, trying to concentrate on the book in her hands. Darkness had settled long ago on the town of Pine Butte. Only a sliver of pale light from the street lamp crept into the room from a crack in the curtain.

Connor had been asleep for three hours and she was beginning to worry. Should she have trusted her judgment and just let him sleep, or should she have called the evacuation helicopter? She'd been so sure that his injury wasn't serious.

Shrugging off the afghan that covered her, she got up and walked to the bedroom. She saw with relief that at least he wasn't still in the same position, motionless as a dead man. He'd moved around a little, and as she watched him he flung his arm off the bed and muttered in his sleep.

Hurrying to his side, she squatted next to him and watched anxiously. As if he sensed her presence, he rolled over and slowly opened his eyes.

"Sarah," he murmured, and she felt an absurd rush of pleasure at the sound of her name on his lips.

"How do you feel?" She was amazed her voice sounded so ordinary.

"Hungry as hell, but otherwise okay." He pushed the covers back and sat up, closing his eyes briefly.

"Don't tell me your head doesn't hurt."

"Okay, I won't. But I'll survive. I think." He opened his eyes. "As long as I get something to eat."

The relief she felt was staggering. He was still pale, but his eyes were clear. "No problem. What's your pleasure?"

His eyes darkened as he stared at her, and for a moment even the air around them seemed to be holding its breath. Her heart began to pound again, only this time it wasn't with fear.

He reached out a hand and touched her face, his fingers sliding down her cheek to her throat. His touch was as gentle as the whisper of a spring breeze. Then he jerked his hand away and she jumped to her feet.

"I'll see what I have upstairs," she muttered.

She knew darn well what she had upstairs, she thought as she hurried toward her apartment. Leftover spaghetti and refuge from his touch, sanctuary from the look in his eyes. She had to regain her composure before she went downstairs. She couldn't let him see how he affected her.

By the time the spaghetti had been heated in the microwave and the salad had been tossed, her breathing had returned to normal and she'd repeated the twenty-five zillion reasons that she couldn't be attracted to Connor Mac-

Cormac. Satisfied that she and her libido understood each other, she started down the stairs with a tray clutched in her hands.

He sat on the edge of the bed in the shadows, looking dark and dangerous. When he saw her standing in the doorway, holding the tray, he switched on the light next to the bed.

She almost wished he'd left it off. The warm yellow light bathed the room in an intimate glow, softening the harshness of his features and spreading a pool of sunshine over the bed. Quickly she set the tray on the table next to the bed and stepped back.

"It's just leftover spaghetti," she said in a light voice, "but it's hot. Ring the buzzer when you're finished and I'll come get the tray."

"Sarah," he said as she turned to go.

Slowly she turned. "Was there something else you needed?"

"Yeah, you." He flashed her a grin and motioned her into the room. "To talk to," he said. "I wanted to ask you some questions."

"Okay." She perched on the edge of the chair and watched him eat the spaghetti. "Shoot."

"What time did you find me?" he asked abruptly.

She relaxed a fraction at the question. At least it wasn't something personal. "I'd already seen my last patient when I realized you weren't back yet. By the time I got my truck and got up the mountain, it must have been six-thirty or so." She wasn't sure she should mention her debate about calling her cousin. Maybe she'd been reading too much into that exchange in the clinic yesterday.

"Did you call anyone, tell anyone that I was missing and you were looking for me?" His tone of voice didn't change, but she saw the sudden tension in his body and the way his eyes narrowed just a fraction.

"I didn't see a soul before I left, so there wasn't anyone to tell." She flushed a little. "I knew where you'd gone because a couple of my patients had mentioned seeing you heading toward the mine road."

He pushed the empty plate away. "Yeah, I'll just bet I'm a hot topic of conversation around here." His voice sounded bitter.

"This is a small town, Connor. Nothing much ever happens here. *Anything* new or different is a topic of conversation," she said gently. "You're a novelty right now, but it'll wear off."

"I'll be long gone before that happens," he promised, standing up abruptly. "As soon as my business here is finished I'm leaving."

"What is your business, Connor?" He stood over her, watching her intently. He sank back down onto the bed again, his eyes shuttered.

She couldn't read a thing in his face. "You didn't come back just for old time's sake."

"I sure as hell didn't." He watched her for a long time. She forced herself to meet his gaze. Finally he relaxed just a fraction. "I trust you," he said abruptly, "but I don't know why I should. You're a Wesley, but I don't think you'd betray me." He leaned forward just a little. "Would you, Sarah?"

"I would never betray a confidence." She tried to keep her voice even and impersonal. "No matter who it was from."

"But in the final analysis, you're on their side. Is that what you're trying to tell me?"

"In the final analysis I judge for myself. Just because someone shares the same last name as I do doesn't mean I automatically side with them." If only he knew about the battles she'd had with her uncle and cousin, she thought wearily. Some vestige of family loyalty prevented her from blurting them out. It really wasn't any of Connor's business.

He sank back onto the bed, obviously exhausted. "I have to tell someone," he muttered. "I can't trust anyone in this town except you."

"Tell me what, Connor?" Her chest tightened with dread. Somehow she knew she wasn't going to like what she was about to hear.

"I got an anonymous note," he said abruptly. "About a month ago. It said that my father's death wasn't a simple heart attack, that he'd been killed. It didn't say how or who had done it."

She drew in her breath sharply. "What? Who—"

"That's what I'd like to know. Only one person in this town knew where I was, and he's sworn it wasn't him." His lips twisted. "So when I have a convenient motorcycle accident on my way here, and when I'm bashed over the head with a rock two days later, I tend to believe that maybe there was some truth to that note."

Horror grew and spread deep inside her. "Are you saying that what happened on your motorcycle wasn't an accident?"

"A car ran me off the road. The fender caught me in the leg."

"I wondered why that cut was so clean." She realized with a shock she had no doubt he was telling the truth. "They didn't stop to help you?"

"I have no idea whether they stopped or not."

She heard the cold steel in his voice and shivered. The driver of that car better hope Connor never caught up with him. "What can I do to help?" The words were out almost before she'd stopped to think about them.

"Think carefully, Sarah, before you offer to help me. My father worked for your uncle at the mine. He died on the job. If it wasn't a heart attack, then your family probably had something to do with it. Are you sure you want to help me?"

"You can't know that for sure." Her objection was instinctive. Her uncle might be a hard-nosed businessman, but he wouldn't murder anyone.

"No, I can't." He watched her steadily. "But can you think of a better place to start?"

"There must have been people he didn't get along with, someone with a grudge against him."

"The whole town had a grudge against him. He was a foreigner, and the good citizens of Pine Butte don't like foreigners."

"We're not like that anymore."

The look he gave her said, *Yeah, right.* "It doesn't matter how liberal Pine Butte has become. Eighteen years ago, if your name was MacCormac and you spoke with a brogue, you were different and therefore no good." When he saw her about to object, he slashed his hand through the air. "Believe me, Sarah, I know what I'm talking about."

She stared at her hands in her lap. She could feel his eyes on her face, willing her to look up at him. Finally she lifted her head. "I want to help you. What can I do?"

He closed his eyes for a moment and she felt him relax just a fraction. "I don't know." Opening his eyes, he looked at her. The flame began to burn again in his eyes as he watched her. "Right now it's enough to know you believe me."

"I believe you." God help her, when she looked into his clear, steady eyes, she *did* believe what he'd said about his father. And what was worse, she wanted to help him. *I'm sorry, Barbie,* she whispered to herself. Barb had died twelve years ago, and she couldn't ever forget who had been responsible. But now there might be a murderer in her town. Regardless of how she felt about Connor, she would help him find the truth.

Chapter 6

I believe you.

They were only words, Connor told himself, but their impact staggered him.

He stood up to reach for Sarah and the pain stabbed at his head again. The world spun slowly around him, and he closed his eyes. As long as he didn't try to move, he could control the pain. He could ignore it, force his body to do what he demanded. Once he tried to move, though, the demons descended again.

He stood still for a moment, feeling his body sway slightly. In a flash Sarah stood next to him, her hands on his arm.

"Sit down!" The look she gave him was one of complete exasperation. "Honestly, you're as bad as a ten-year-old child."

He turned to her, trying to ignore the sweet torture of her hands on him. "I can't lie around doing nothing, Sarah. I can't let a little bump on the head make me into an invalid." He took her hands and gripped them, willing her to understand his urgency. "My only weapon was surprise. Now that's gone, but I still have no idea what happened to my father. I don't have the time to be hurt."

Her hands shifted in his and she looked at him, her eyes huge and luminous in the dim light. "If you don't give yourself at least a little time to heal, you're not going to be doing anything but lying in a hospital bed." The compassion in her eyes took the censure out of her words.

"I'll be fine. I told you I know my own body."

"And I admit you were right. I've never heard of a concussion patient walking around the next day like you did. But you're not going to do anything more tonight. Sit back down, go back to sleep. Tomorrow is soon enough to fight the rest of the town single-handedly."

A smile transformed her face, and he tightened his hold on her. He wanted to draw her closer, to feel the warmth and fire in her. He wanted all that heat for his own.

"I need some fresh air," he muttered. A dose of cold water was more like it, he thought sourly. What was the matter with him, anyway? How could he even consider getting involved with a Wesley, and Barb Wesley's sister to boot?

"Why don't we go sit on the swing in the backyard?" she said, all solicitous concern. She sniffed delicately at the air. "Last time I checked, hospital disinfectant wasn't exactly a tonic for a headache."

"Sounds good." Anything was better than staying in this room, sitting on the bed with her.

She helped him to his feet and tucked one arm around his waist to help him walk. It was a completely impersonal gesture, but his muscles tightened in response. He glanced at her to see if she'd noticed, but she was looking down and her hair had fallen forward to cover her face. *She's a nurse,* he told himself, closing his eyes. *She does this every day.* He rested his hand on her shoulder, trying to make himself believe it was only because he needed the support, trying to ignore the feel of her warm, pliant skin beneath his hand. She was probably used to men making fools of themselves over her, too.

She opened the back door and a rush of sweet, cool air flowed over him. He took a deep breath, smelling the faint pine smell of the mountains on the slight breeze. Her arm tightened a fraction and he realized she was trying to direct him to a swing that sat in the corner of the yard.

The grass was dry and brown, seared by the summer heat. But the flowers and vegetables that surrounded it were all lush and verdant, showing someone's loving care. The swing blended into its surroundings, a sturdy glider made of weathered cedar.

As soon as they reached it, she slid her arm away from him and waited for him to sit down. In spite of himself, he allowed his fingers to trail down her arm before he let her go. After he'd settled himself, she squeezed herself into the farthest corner of the swing away from him.

For a while the only sound was the slight creak of the swing, moving slowly back and forth. Gradually he relaxed and heard the crickets chirping in the garden and the soft, muted sounds of creatures flying overhead in the darkness.

"It's peaceful out here." He heard the surprise and wonder in his voice.

"You must be used to living in a city."

It wasn't a question or even a request for information. She leaned back against the swing and stared at the moon and stars. She'd said it as if she knew.

"Why do you say that?" He couldn't keep the suspicion out of his voice, and she looked over at him, surprised.

"Only people who are used to noise and traffic notice the quiet in the country. Don't get so defensive. It was just an observation."

After a long time he answered. "Yeah, I've been living in a city. I'd forgotten how many stars there are in the sky out here." His voice was low, the words almost grudging. He was reluctant to part with even that small piece of information.

Her hand relaxed its grip on the arm of the swing and she leaned farther back, a dreamy smile on her face. "I love to come out here and look at the sky at night. I like knowing everyone else in the world is looking at the same sky, seeing the same stars. No matter where you go, you can always look at the sky and see something familiar."

"Where do you go, Sarah, to look up at the night sky?" he asked softly. He laid his arm on the back of the swing and allowed his fingers to touch the silk of her hair. In the moonlight its fiery color was as dark as a pool of water, drawing him under.

She stared at the sky for a long time before she answered. "Nowhere but Pine Butte." She didn't move, but her tension disturbed the night. She finally turned to look at him and he felt her hair flowing over his hand. "But I can imagine."

Was it his imagination or were those words whispered with a soul-wrenching longing? He needed to know. "Sarah? What do you mean?"

Her withdrawal was almost a tangible thing. She wrapped herself in her own thoughts and seemed to move away from him. Shrugging a little too casually, she said, "It was just an idle remark. You are going to stay here tonight, aren't you?" The abrupt change of subject was a pointed reminder that she, too, had places she didn't want probed.

"I guess I am, as long as you'll have me."

"I told you to stay as long as you want." She watched him for a moment, and he felt the tension ease just a bit. "In fact, it might be smart for you to stay here indefinitely. If someone is trying to...hurt you, it might be better if you weren't alone."

"That's exactly the reason I wouldn't stay here. I don't want you getting in the way of someone with a grudge against me."

"Nobody in this town would hurt me." She sat up straighter. "Nobody is that stupid. I'm the only medical person around here."

"Get real, Sarah. That wouldn't stop someone who thinks he's going to be charged with murder."

She turned to him again, sliding closer. "Maybe your father wasn't murdered. Have you thought about that? Maybe he really did have a simple heart attack at work. This could just be someone's idea of a sick joke." The urgency in her voice made him realize how scared she was.

"That's possible. But I can't just let it be. I have to know." His voice softened and in spite of himself he took her hand. "Can't you understand that?"

She let her hand lie in his for a moment, then gently withdrew it. "Yes, I suppose I do."

From the tone of her voice and the shuttered look on her face he realized she was thinking about her sister. "There are some things that you just can't leave alone, Sarah. If you do, they fester in your soul like a cancer, eating away at you. I couldn't live with myself if I didn't try to find the truth about my father."

"Are you trying to tell me I have to do the same with Barb?" she demanded. "Are you saying that my sister would have died in pain, still not telling the truth about her baby?"

"I'm not calling Barb a liar," he said gently. "Like I said yesterday, I'm sure she had a good reason for saying what she did. But the truth is, I *wasn't* the father of her baby." His lips compressed as he remembered exactly how much he had wished it could have been true, that summer twelve years ago.

She jumped up from the swing and stared at the distant mountain for a moment. Swinging around to face him, she drew herself up straight. "Why would she have lied?" she whispered. He heard the anguish in her voice, the doubts she wanted to deny with every fiber of her being.

"I don't know." His voice was almost a whisper, too, in the quiet of the night. "Obviously I didn't know Barb as well as I thought I did." He felt his mouth twist in a bitter grimace. Sarah wasn't the only one who'd lost her innocence with Barb's pregnancy.

"She was my only sister, and I loved her. I can't believe she would lie to me with her dying breath." She stared at him, pain and grief filling her eyes.

He stood up, too, and stared down at her. In the moonlight she looked as fragile and ethereal as a beam of starlight. The pale silver light couldn't show the steel that ran through her or the strength that was such an essential part of her.

"I know, Sarah. Believe me, I don't want that to be your last memory of your sister. But I can't change what happened twelve years ago, either. Whatever you think, though, remember this. I loved your sister. I would never have done anything to hurt her."

She looked at him, her eyes enormous and glistening. "I want to believe that, Connor. But I just can't."

He reached out and let his fingers slide down the satin of her cheek. "I guess that's going to have to be good enough for now." He leaned toward her, and the sledgehammer of pain hit his head again.

She saw him wince, and the mood was shattered. "Connor, I'm sorry," she cried. "I don't know what's wrong with me. I shouldn't have kept you standing out here."

She slid her arm around his waist again, the objective, impersonal nurse firmly back in control. He wanted to protest, tell her that he was fine, but suddenly it took all his strength to get into the house.

When she finally eased him down on the bed he lay there, his eyes closed. His body was telling him just what it thought of all his exertions today. In just a few moments he would get undressed and get into bed, he promised himself.

"Are you all right?"

She sounded worried, and he forced his eyes open. Her face hovered just above him. "Yeah, I'm okay. Just tired."

"Do you need help getting undressed?" It was too dark in the room to see her face, but he felt the heat from her blush. For a moment, he was tempted to say yes. Just the thought of her helping him slide the jeans down his legs had him tensing, though, and he scowled. "I can manage, thanks."

She straightened, looking down at him. "All right, then, I'll see you in the morning. Good night, Connor."

With a soft click she shut the door and he was alone. He unbuttoned his jeans, pulled them off and let them slide onto the floor. He had enough energy left to pull back the quilt on the bed before he fell into a deep sleep.

Sarah pulled a brush through her tangled curls and stared at her face in the bathroom mirror. The angry scratches were fading, but deep purple circles shadowed her eyes, the legacy of three sleepless nights. The other reminders of the past three days with Connor were invisible but no less real.

Connor was a man who would tolerate nothing less than the truth, and for the first time in twelve years she doubted her sister's version of that truth. She closed her eyes, trying to hold on to her faith in Barb, but Connor's face kept intruding. His anger when she'd accused him of leaving town to avoid his responsibilities, his pain when she'd told him about Barb's death, even the sorrow when he'd said he loved her sister looked back at her.

He couldn't be telling the truth, she told herself desperately. He needed an ally against the rest of her family, and he'd figured out that she was the one to choose. Somehow he had smelled the conflict between her and her uncle and had decided to exploit it.

Even as she was trying to convince herself that was all it was, another part of her resisted. Whatever he had been at the age of eighteen, she sensed he was an honorable man now. She'd seen it in his eyes, in his refusal to endanger her. He couldn't be trying to use her.

She walked slowly down the stairs to the clinic, wondering if he was awake yet. It was early, and the sun was still hidden behind the mountains. The pearly light filled the clinic waiting room as she turned to go to her desk, and she hesitated.

With everything that had been happening for the past few days, patient records were piling up on her desk at an alarming rate. She really needed to spend some time this morning and get the mess straightened out, but the room where Connor slept drew her like a magnet.

The records could wait for a few minutes, she told herself. Connor had been exhausted last night, and she needed to make sure he was all right.

Knocking softly on his door, she waited for an answer. When none came, she opened it silently and looked into the room.

He was sprawled over the bed, clad only in a T-shirt and briefs. Orange ones. Swallowing hard, she told herself to pull up the sheet. Rooted to the floor, she watched for a moment as he murmured something in his sleep and flung his arms in the air. Sweat beaded his forehead and she saw him wince with pain when he shook his head.

The next second she was on her knees next to the bed, holding on firmly to his hands. "Connor, wake up," she murmured.

He moved his head again, muttering unintelligible words. Letting go of his hands, she cupped his face gently between her hands. "You're having a bad dream. Wake up."

His hands covered hers and held on tight. Sinking back on her heels, she watched him struggle out of the depths of the dream. A fierce protectiveness swept over her and she twisted her hands to hold onto his. Someone had tried to kill him, not once but twice, and she wasn't going to let that happen again.

His eyes blinked open and softened as he focused on her. The ghost of a smile curving his mouth, he murmured, "Sarah."

Freeing one of her hands, she brushed a few strands of hair off his forehead. "You were having a nightmare. Are you okay now?"

"You're here, aren't you?"

She looked at him sharply, but he slid to a sitting position on the bed and tugged on her hand until she sat down next to him.

"I want you to tell me something. Why did you come looking for me yesterday?"

Trying to pull her hand away, she shrugged and said, "I was afraid something had happened to you. Since you're my patient, I felt some responsibility for you."

"The last thing you want is having me back here in Pine Butte. Don't bother to deny it," he said matter-of-factly when she opened her mouth to protest. "You've told me you think I'm responsible for Barb's death, and I have a serious difference of opinion with your family."

He paused and watched her carefully. "It would have been so much easier for you to forget about me, to just assume that I'd decided to leave town. No one could have blamed you in the least if I'd died up there in the mountains. I'm not your responsibility." His voice softened to a low murmur. "So why did you come after me?"

"Like I said, you're a patient—"

"Forget the patient garbage," he interrupted. "How many of your other patients have you chased up into the mountains?"

Heat swept into her face and she looked at her hands, still lying in his. "None of them. But all my other patients have families here in town to take care of them." She looked at him, meeting his gaze, knowing her cheeks were still red.

"I'm glad you're going beyond the call of duty for me, Sarah. It makes me think there's still some hope."

His voice was low and raspy and incredibly sexy. The gold of the hoop dangling from his left ear gleamed in the pale morning light. His blue eyes darkened to the color of midnight, and he reached out one hand to cup her face.

"Is there, Sarah?" He drew her head closer to his. "Any hope for me?"

"Connor," she murmured, mesmerized by the naked longing in his blue eyes. The heat from his body warmed her and she was powerless to resist. God help her, nothing had ever felt this right before.

His hand tightened in her hair as his mouth touched hers. But instead of the rough possession of his other kiss, this time his lips glided across hers with a gentleness she didn't expect.

She had steeled herself against the surging desire. She had no protection against the sweetness.

His lips brushed against hers with the faint touch of a butterfly's wings. Nibbling, stroking, caressing, he swept past all the barriers she had thrown up against him.

With an inarticulate murmur, she slid closer to him and twined her arms around his neck. The hard wall of his chest tensed and his arms tightened around her. The thin cotton sheet was no barrier at all between them, and she felt the heat of his arousal burn into her thigh.

For the first time since he'd arrived in Pine Butte she realized he could be vulnerable, too. Something inside him had opened, even if just a crack, and he needed her. It might have been only physical, it might have been just an easing of his body's needs, but somehow she suspected that he would have resisted even that if he could.

He'd had a nightmare, she told herself. He'd awoken with the barriers down and she'd been there to give him comfort. It didn't matter. None of it did. For right now, he needed her and that was all that was important.

Because she needed him, too. When he sought her mouth with hot, drugging kisses, she opened to him eagerly. All rational thought had disappeared at the first touch of his hands. The sensations that exploded in her abdomen and bubbled through her veins had nothing to do with thinking. She felt as if she had been waiting forever for Connor to make her whole.

His restless hands tugged the tail of her blouse out of her jeans and smoothed over her back. When she arched into his touch, he groaned and her mouth greedily swallowed the sound.

Suddenly she couldn't wait another moment to touch him. Slipping her hands under his T-shirt, she combed through the soft hair on his chest, exploring the shape of his muscles with her fingertips. Heated by passion, his skin burned. His muscles quivered and tensed, and he roughly jerked her hands away from him and held them together in one trembling hand.

His mouth plundered hers, his tongue sweeping in and tasting every secret corner. He made no effort to hide the extent of his desire, rocking his hips against her as he held her close with iron-muscled arms.

She barely recognized herself. Sarah Wesley didn't act like a wanton around any man. Her legs fell apart as she tried to press closer to him. Twining around him, she lifted her hands to his hair, feeling the thick, springy silk slide through her fingers. As she kissed him with a desperation she'd never felt before, her fingers traced the contours of his face as though she could memorize him with her hands.

His arms tightened suddenly around her and held her still. After a moment, she heard the sounds in the clinic and stiffened in horror.

"It's Josie, my assistant," she gasped. "Let me go."

"In a minute. Look at me, Sarah," he whispered.

She raised her eyes to him and stared at his face. His features were sharpened by passion and frustration. Then his arms tightened around her and he brushed a few tendrils of hair away from her face, his finger gently tracing the ugly scratches.

"I can't let you go yet." He pressed a soft kiss to her mouth, lingering at the corner of her lips. "This is the last thing I wanted, you know," he muttered. "I was determined to hate every Wesley in Pine Butte."

She could only suspect how much the admission had cost him. It wouldn't be easy for Connor to admit he needed anybody or anything. Passion burned white-hot inside her, but she pulled away slowly.

"I wasn't exactly looking to get involved with Barb's old boyfriend, myself." She said the words more for herself than him, and she couldn't keep the pain out of her voice.

His hands slid down her arms slowly, reluctantly, caressing every inch of skin along the way. "I'm sorry, Sarah. I just couldn't resist. When I woke up from the nightmare, you were there. You were all I could see or think of." His eyes still flamed with desire as his thumbs brushed the skin on her wrists. "I'll try to make sure it doesn't happen again."

Disappointment stabbed like an icicle in her chest, but she nodded. "That would probably be best."

Finally letting her go, he shifted in the bed and rearranged the sheet covering his lap. "I won't be here long, Sarah. I don't want to give you any false hopes or expectations. Pine Butte isn't my home anymore. It never could be again."

"I understand, Connor." She tried to smile, painfully. "Thank you for being so honest."

She began to back off the bed, but he grabbed her hands and held them in an almost painful grip. "Sarah, I'm sorry. If I thought you were the kind of woman who indulged in a quick toss in the sheets..." He sighed, running his fingers through his hair and leaving it standing straight up. "I know you're not that kind of woman. Hell, that's why this can't happen again. But that doesn't stop me from wanting you."

"You don't have to explain, Connor." She tried to get away again, but his grip was like iron.

"There is no explanation except that I'm a damn fool." The bitterness in his voice would have had her going to him if he hadn't held her so tightly away from him. Suddenly he dropped her hand as if it burned. "You'd better get out of here before your assistant gets curious," he said gruffly.

Slowly she stood and walked to the door. Turning, she watched him for a moment. He looked everywhere but at her.

"Shall I get you something from Earlene's for breakfast?"

Finally he met her eyes. "No, thanks. I think I'll walk over there." His mouth tightened to a grim line. "It'll be interesting to see who's surprised to see me alive."

Her hand tightened on the doorknob. "Do you want me to go with you?" He was getting ready to take on the whole town and he could barely walk yet.

His face softened and he watched her for a moment. "Not this morning," he said softly. "This morning I need some honest responses from the good citizens here in Pine Butte."

"Connor," she cried, "don't do anything stupid. Give yourself a day or two to recover."

He actually laughed. "Then it's all right to do something stupid? Sarah, I'm just having breakfast. That's it, nothing more than that. Okay?"

He might be smiling at her, but the determination in his eyes was unshakable. "All right," she answered unhappily. "Promise me you'll come back after you eat and rest for a while."

"I can't. I told you last night that I have to have some answers. I'm not going to get them lying here on this bed."

"This is Saturday," she said, thinking quickly. "The clinic closes at noon. If you can wait that long, I'll come with you to do whatever you want."

"As my guardian angel?"

"To help you," she answered steadily. "I told you last night that I would, and I meant it."

"All right." He'd given up too easily, and she looked at him with suspicion. "I'll wait for you."

"Connor..." She looked at him once more, then sighed. "I'll see you later."

A half hour later, Connor walked slowly out of the clinic. Sarah's waiting room was already half full, and he beat down a tinge of guilt about leaving. What he was, how he could help her, was no part of the equation. Anything the people of Pine Butte found out about him could be used against him sometime in the future.

When he walked in the door at Earlene's he saw that the restaurant was crowded. There was a momentary lull in the noise level when people spotted him, then they began talking again just a little too loud. It was almost enough to make him think they were ashamed of their curiosity, he thought with scorn.

Sliding into a vacant booth, he turned over the coffee cup and waited for the Saturday morning waitress to fill it. She gave him a tentative smile and said, "What can I get for you?"

"Pancakes, eggs and bacon."

"Coming right up." She gave him another smile and moved off, pouring a cup of coffee for the people in the next booth before going to the counter and giving Earlene the order.

Connor leaned against the rigid back of the booth and watched her for a moment. She'd treated him like just another customer, he realized. She hadn't even looked back at him after she'd given his order to Earlene, as she would have if she'd mentioned him to the restaurant owner.

Slowly he looked around the small restaurant. No one else looked as if they were paying any attention to him at all. Maybe Sarah was right, he thought slowly. Maybe his arrival was just a two-day wonder. It would have been unusual, he acknowledged reluctantly, for the people here not to be curious about him. After all, he had left town twelve years ago and none of them had heard from him since.

No one was staring at him with the animosity he'd expected since he woke up in Sarah's clinic. He wondered if that had anything to do with Sarah. Was it because everyone knew he was staying at the clinic so they'd decided he was okay? Had Sarah somehow given him the stamp of approval by letting him stay there?

Not everyone in the restaurant was oblivious to his presence. His shoulders itched with an unmistakable warning, and he turned around suddenly. Harley Harrison, the foreman at the Wesley mine, was staring at him from a table in the back. When he saw Connor turn around he looked away, but not before Connor saw the fear, quickly masked, in his eyes.

He stared at Harley for a moment, but the older man refused to look at him again. Talking to a woman Connor assumed was his wife, he concentrated on his breakfast and his conversation.

Slowly Connor turned around in the booth and raised his coffee cup to take a drink. He'd have to make a point of talking to Harley. The foreman of the Wesley mine should have no reason to be afraid of him. Scorn and arrogance would have been what he'd expected, and would have been more in keeping with what he remembered of the man.

By the time Connor's breakfast arrived, Harley and his wife had paid their bill and left the restaurant. No one said anything to him, but he didn't feel any more stares drilling into his back, either. A half hour later, when he walked out the door into the sunshine, he looked around Pine Butte with thoughtful eyes.

Chapter 7

It was a slow Saturday morning at the clinic, and Sarah ducked into her small office for a cup of coffee between patients. Leaning back in her chair, she closed her eyes for a minute and thought about all that had happened in the past twenty-four hours.

Connor thought his father had been murdered. The fact that someone had tried to kill Connor not once but twice made that unpalatable idea a distinct possibility. Acid in her stomach churned with the coffee to make her feel slightly nauseated, and she abruptly slammed the chipped mug onto her desk. She was at work, for heaven's sake. She couldn't afford to get sidetracked now.

Once she started thinking about Connor, she knew just where her mind would wander. Keeping her gaze firmly fixed on the office door, she refused to glance toward the clinic bedroom. What happened between her and Connor that morning was the last thing she could afford to worry about right now. She still had several patients scheduled and needed to have her mind clear.

"Sarah!" Josie burst through the doorway and stood in front of her, her face lit by an almost unbearable excitement. "You'll never guess who's in the waiting room!"

Pushing her chair away from the desk, Sarah stood up wearily. "If it's not a doctor who wants to take over the practice, I don't want to hear about it."

"But it is," Josie answered.

Sarah stopped dead in her tracks and stared at her assistant, feeling the blood drain from her face. "That's not a joke I consider funny, Josie."

"I'm not joking," she insisted. "He said he saw your ad in one of the medical journals and wants to apply for the job."

Sarah sat down abruptly and stared at the excited face of her assistant. "A doctor?" she said carefully. "In our waiting room? To apply for a job here?"

"Yep," Josie answered happily. "And he's a real hunk, too."

"Okay," Sarah said faintly. "Tell him I'll be with him in a minute."

As Josie left the tiny office, Sarah looked around frantically. If she'd had some warning, she could have cleaned the office up. Patient folders and magazines were scattered everywhere, covering all the surfaces. Scooping them up ruthlessly, she dumped three armloads into the closet and slammed the door shut.

She hastily rearranged everything on the top of her desk to give an ordered, neat appearance. She didn't want a potential employee to think the clinic was a chaotic mess.

"A doctor," she said under her breath, pausing for a moment to savor the words. Her ticket out of Pine Butte, her release, her salvation.

"Stop it," she commanded, wiping sweaty palms down the sides of her jeans. She hadn't even met the man, for heaven's sake, and she was already planning the itinerary of her first trip. Closing her eyes, she said a prayer of thanks for whatever had brought him to their town, then took a deep breath and walked into the waiting room.

In spite of her excitement, she noticed Connor first. He sat in a chair in the corner of the room, not even pretending to have a reason for being there, watching her with an enigmatic look in his eyes. Tearing her gaze away from him, Sarah looked over at the immaculately groomed man who sat a few seats down from Connor, reading a well-thumbed *People* magazine. His blond, perfectly cut hair was carefully styled. The suit he wore was obviously a designer model, and fit him like a glove.

She couldn't help but glance over at Connor again. Even in his faded jeans and old T-shirt, his masculine appeal shouted to her over the stranger's superficial slickness. She forced herself to look at the blond man rather than Connor.

"Hello," she said. "I'm Sarah Wesley."

The stranger jumped up to extend his hand and the magazine slid to the floor. "I'm Perry Cummings. I hope you don't mind my coming without an appointment. When I saw your ad, I was so excited that I just jumped in the car and took off."

"Not at all, Dr. Cummings." Her voice warmed at his obvious enthusiasm and she forced all her attention onto him. "I'm delighted that you're interested in practicing in a small town."

"It's been a dream of mine for years," he assured her. When he stepped closer, the overpowering sweet scent of his after-shave swirled around her and she instinctively backed up a step. "I've just been waiting for the perfect opportunity. Your ad sounded like exactly what I was looking for." He took out a white handkerchief and blew his nose. "Pardon me, I have a little cold."

"Why don't you come into the office where we can talk?" She led the way down the hall, turning to look over her shoulder and catching another glimpse of Connor watching her somberly. "You'll have to pardon the mess," she said, jerking her gaze in Dr. Cummings's direction. We've had a busy few days." She took a deep breath. "Just the reason we need a doctor in Pine Butte."

Forty-five minutes later, she escorted Dr. Cummings out to the waiting room. Connor still sat in the same chair in the corner, but she tried to ignore him. "I'll have to talk with some other people before I can make a decision, but I don't think there'll be a problem," she told the man. "Why don't you leave your address and phone number with Josie?"

He pulled out his handkerchief again and blew his nose, then nodded and smiled at the receptionist. "I already gave her my card. I'm practicing now in Denver, but I don't own the practice so it shouldn't take me too long to tie up loose ends."

"Great. You might want to look around the town for a bit before you leave. In fact, if you're going to be here for a while, why don't I take you to dinner tonight? I can answer any other questions you might have after you've seen Pine Butte."

"Thanks, but I don't think I can stay that long. I have to get back to Denver tonight." He looked again at Josie, then smiled at her. "I hope to hear from you soon."

"I'm sure you will, Perry," Sarah replied.

She watched thoughtfully as the door closed behind him. He'd been nothing but charming and polite during their interview, enthused about the practice here and about medicine in general. So what was bothering her?

He was too smooth, for one thing. She never had trusted anyone who was too slick, too polished, too perfect. Shrugging, she turned to go to her office. As long as his references checked out and he was willing to work in Pine Butte, it didn't matter what she thought of him personally. She'd met more than one doctor like him. Most of their patients loved them.

"Who was that?"

She turned around slowly. As excited as she'd been about the prospect of a doctor working at the clinic, she'd been too aware of Connor sitting in the corner, watching her. The realization unsettled her, made her edgy.

"I'm sure you heard." Her voice was cool.

He slowly straightened and stood up. He looked more sexy in his worn jeans and slightly untidy, just-too-long black hair than perfectly groomed Perry Cummings could ever hope to be.

"I wasn't spying on you, Sarah. You said you'd be free at noon, and I was just waiting for you. So who was Perry?"

"He's a doctor interviewing for a job here in the clinic."

"I didn't know you were looking for help."

She sighed and leaned back against the counter, willing herself to relax. Just because she couldn't control her raging hormones didn't mean she had to take it out on Connor.

"We've been looking for help since the day I graduated from nursing school and came back here. I never intended to be the only medical person in Pine Butte for so long. We just haven't been able to find a doctor willing to come to work here. We can't afford to pay a fortune like some of the small towns who lure doctors away from the city. We don't have any nightlife, and the only recreation is fishing or hunting in the mountains. Not a lot to offer someone used to a lot of money and a lot of places to spend it."

"It looked like he was a live one. Why didn't you tell me you were interviewing this morning? I could have taken care of my errand by myself."

"I don't *want* you to do it yourself. And besides, I didn't know he was coming. He just showed up."

His eyebrows rose. "He came from Denver and just showed up this morning? It's at least a four-hour drive."

"He said he was excited about the job," she answered defensively. "Connor, this is the first time in six years that anyone has even shown up here for an interview. Everybody else that's been interested has said no, thanks after talking to us on the phone."

"So don't look a gift horse in the mouth, is that it?"

"Of course not! I intend to scrutinize his references carefully. But if they check out, I'll hire him in a minute."

"Even though you didn't like him?"

"How did you know that?"

He shrugged. "It wasn't too tough." His eyes flickered down to her toes and back again, and a hot gleam suddenly shone in his eyes. "Body language."

She didn't look at him, although she could feel the heat creeping into her face. "It doesn't matter what I think of him personally. I won't have to work with him much. And the people here'll love him. Look at Josie. She's practically drooling over him."

"What do you mean you won't have to work with him? Where will you be?"

"Doing whatever I want to do," she said softly. "I've been here in Pine Butte all my life except for the five years I was in school. Before Barb... Before I went to nursing school, all I ever wanted was to travel, see the world. If there's someone else here to take care of the practice, I can do that."

"So this guy is an answer to your prayers," he said slowly.

"Yes, he is." She sounded defiant, even to herself, and wondered why. She didn't have to answer to Connor MacCormac, especially on the subject of who she hired to work in the clinic. According to his own words, he'd be long gone before Perry Cummings ever showed up to work.

"Be careful what you pray for, Sarah. Isn't that what you said to me?"

She pushed her hair away from her face and shook her head. "I've never been free, Connor," she cried passionately. "Not once in my life have I been able to do what I wanted. This is my opportunity, and I'm not going to pass it up just because I personally don't like the man. As long as his medical credentials are good, I'm going to hire him. And the next day I'm going to pack my bag and buy an airplane ticket to somewhere far away."

His face softened, and she thought she saw regret in his eyes. "Sarah..."

"Let's go, Connor. We're wasting time here. I thought there was a lot you had to get done today."

"There is." He walked to the door, almost all of the stiffness gone. In a day or two she wouldn't be able to tell that anything had happened to him.

Stepping out into the bright noon sunshine, she squinted and looked at him. "Where are we going?"

"My mother's house. I want to look through what's there, see if there's anything about my father's death."

She looked at him, appalled, as her elation dissipated like air flowing out of a balloon. "You don't think your mother had anything to do with it, do you?"

"No. She might have suspected, though. There might be a note, a diary, I don't know, *something* to give me a clue."

"So we're going to look through her papers and things?" The idea of looking through the personal belongings of a woman long dead was faintly disturbing. She didn't want to pry into another woman's secrets.

"That's the idea. I was at her house the other day, but was too weak to do anything." He glanced at her as they walked slowly down the sidewalk. "There wasn't much. It shouldn't take too long."

"It doesn't matter," she said quickly. "I don't care how long it takes."

After a while he said, "She won't care, Sarah. She'd want us to get to the truth." His voice was gentle. "And it doesn't bother me to have you there. Okay?"

"Okay. It just feels like prying."

"It is," he said frankly, "but it's necessary. Murder is a very uncivilized crime."

They turned down the sidewalk of his mother's house and walked up the porch steps. Although the house was old, it had been recently painted and it didn't look like a typical empty house. None of the windows were broken, the stairs were in good repair and she could see where several clapboards had been replaced.

"It doesn't look as if this house has been empty for years."

He glanced over at her, surprised. "Why should it? I've been paying to have it taken care of for the past ten years."

"Oh." Everyone in town had assumed that once Connor had taken off, no one had heard from him again. Obviously someone had.

They walked in the front door, and Connor switched on a light. The furniture in the living room was covered by sheets and resembled a series of misshapen ghosts. Dust hung in the air, but the general air of neglect she'd expected was absent. Someone had indeed been taking care of this house.

"Where should we start?"

"Come sit down for a minute before we start." Connor took her wrist and steered her toward the couch. After pulling off the sheet, he sat and tugged her down next to him.

Turning to look at him, she said, "Okay, what's the plan?"

For the first time since he'd been in Pine Butte, he forgot the plan. The only thing he could think about was how his next words were going to hurt her. He'd give anything if he didn't have to tell her. After what she'd said in the clinic about her dreams and plans, he knew he'd break her heart. But he couldn't stand by and let her hire Perry Cummings. Even if it meant he had to reveal who he was.

"The house can wait for a minute," he said abruptly. "We need to talk about Perry Cummings."

She looked at him sharply. "How did you know his last name? I don't think I ever mentioned it to you."

"No, you didn't. I know him." He took her hands in his. He had to hold onto her while he told her. "You can't hire him, Sarah. He's bad news."

She tried to pull away, but he held on tighter. "What do you mean, he's bad news? Why can't I hire him?"

"He uses drugs," he said bluntly. "The reason he wants to come to work here is that things are getting too hot for him in Denver. He's going to lose his job there soon, and he knows he won't be able to get another one."

"But... that's impossible. He may have been a little too slick for me, but he seemed perfectly normal otherwise. He didn't look like a drug user." She sounded desperate.

"And what do they look like, Sarah?" he asked grimly. "They don't all have needle tracks up their arms and dilated pupils. A lot of them look just like you and me."

"Then how do you know *he* uses drugs?" she challenged.

"Because I've seen him do it," he answered flatly. "And I know he's still doing it because of the way he was blowing his nose. Heavy cocaine users almost always have a runny nose."

She stared at him, horror in her eyes. "How could you have seen him using drugs?"

"It was at a party. He and a couple of the other people there started snorting. Once the drugs came out I didn't stick around, so I don't know how much he did, but he sure acted like he knew what he was doing."

She leaned forward and gripped his hands too tightly. "Who are you, Connor? What have you been doing for the past twelve years? Why do you know about Perry Cummings?''

He stared at her for a long moment, holding her hands tightly. He felt as if he was about to step off a cliff into an abyss, not knowing if there would be a net there to catch him. Could he trust her with this part of himself?

Her blue-green eyes were wide with fear. Fear for him, he realized suddenly. It was like taking a blow to his chest. She was afraid that he had been involved in whatever seamy underside of life had infected Perry Cummings. She wasn't afraid of him, she was afraid *for* him. Something moved in his heart, and feelings he'd thought long dead swept over him.

He ached to tell her the truth. He didn't want to keep secrets from Sarah. But this secret, the one above all others he'd been determined to hide, stuck in his throat like a burr. All his life he'd protected himself by hiding what was important to him, by not letting his feelings show. So he hesitated, the habits of a lifetime hard to overcome.

She turned away, and the moment was lost. "I'm not trying to pry, Connor." Her voice was painfully tight. "I know you don't want to talk about yourself, and I'm trying to respect that. But when you said you were at a party and people were doing drugs, it scared me." She turned to face him again. "I know you could never be involved in anything as ugly as drugs."

"Thank you," he said softly. His throat swelled as he tried to tell her the truth, but the words just wouldn't come. He'd already revealed too much of himself to Sarah, and the fear paralyzed him. Calling himself every kind of coward for not telling her the truth, he avoided looking in her eyes. The hurt that shimmered from her soul was too painful to watch.

"I'm sorry that Cummings showed up at your door this morning," he added quietly, forcing the words out of his constricted throat. "I would have given anything if it could have been someone else, someone you could have hired."

Her eyes darkened and she jumped up abruptly, going over to stand by the window. "I feel like an utter fool," she said bitterly. "I was so eager to be free of Pine Butte that I completely ignored my own instincts about Cummings. Any judgment I possessed went right out the window when he said he wanted to practice in Pine Butte. I practically bought my airline tickets before he was out the door.''

Light from the window glowed like a nimbus around her, darkening her hair and clothes to shadows. He stepped behind her, and the smell of a floral soap drifted up to him. He couldn't touch her, not now. Not with all that remained unspoken between them. Until he told her the truth about himself, he had no right to touch her.

But right had nothing to do with it. As if they had a will of their own, his hands reached out and gripped her shoulders. He felt her stiffen and instinctively try to jerk away from him. When he didn't let go, she slowly relaxed. She didn't move toward him, but she didn't try to pull away, either.

"You're not a fool, Sarah. Not in this, not in anything I've seen. And as far as your judgment is concerned, I should have paid more attention to it." His hands tightened and then he let them drop and shoved them in his pockets. "If I had listened to you, and to what my own body was telling me, I wouldn't have gone up into the mountains yesterday. If I'd waited until I was stronger, I might have been able to catch the person who attacked me."

She looked at him, eyes wide and stricken. "I'd completely forgotten about your head. How is it this morning?"

"I'll live," he answered shortly. When she would have moved away, he grabbed her hands. "And don't beat yourself up about Cummings. I suspect a lot of other people have been fooled by him. He's able to control himself and he puts up a damn good front."

For just a moment, she held onto him as if she didn't ever want to let go, then she dropped her hands and moved to the couch.

"I guess it's a good thing I didn't order those tickets out of Pine Butte. What is it that they say? If something looks too good to be true it usually is?"

"Someone else will come along who wants to practice in Pine Butte."

"Yeah, in another six years." She sounded utterly defeated.

He sat down next to her on the couch. "Why don't you hire a temporary replacement for a while every year so you can get away?"

"We don't have the money to pay anyone. The people in Pine Butte can barely afford to pay me, let alone the kind of money relief doctors charge."

"Couldn't your uncle afford to hire someone?"

"I'm sure he could, but that doesn't mean he will. He could also afford to spend some of his money to hire a permanent doctor and make sure the people in this town have adequate medical care, too, but you won't see him rushing to do that, either."

The weariness in her voice spoke of a battle too often fought and never won. "Why won't he?"

"'There's a perfectly good hospital in Glenwood Springs, and that's just a hundred miles away. There's absolutely no reason to spend good money on a luxury like a doctor for Pine Butte'," she quoted, anger and despair in her voice.

"What about Richard? Can't you make him cough up some money?"

"Uncle Ralph keeps him on a short leash," she said scornfully. "And he's too afraid of losing his inheritance to ever defy him."

"It sounds like Ralph Wesley has this town by the b—scruff of its neck," he said, trying to keep his voice neutral.

She stood up and smoothed her hands down her jeans. "You could say that. Since most of the people in the town depend on him for their paycheck, either directly or indirectly, there aren't too many who'll stand up to him.

"Except you," he guessed, watching her carefully.

"There's not much I can do," she said, swiping at a dust mote dancing in the sunlight. "He has me by the...scruff of the neck, too. Once I threatened to leave unless he got a doctor to help me." She paused and looked at him, her eyes expressionless. "He said he'd sue me to fulfill my contract, and he'd make sure I could never leave Pine Butte."

"What contract? What do you mean?"

She sighed. "Uncle Ralph and a few other people financed my way through nursing school. In return, I signed a contract that said I would provide medical care to Pine Butte as long as they needed me." Her face twisted with scorn. "I was naive enough to think that we'd be able to find a doctor who wanted to move to our town. But without Uncle Ralph helping finance his salary, we don't have a hope in hell."

"That's barbaric." He was appalled. "Indentured servants were outlawed a long time ago. That contract wouldn't have a chance if you took him to court."

"Probably not. But he knows he doesn't really need it. How could I leave, knowing that there wasn't anyone here to help the people I care about? Uncle Ralph doesn't have to threaten to take me to court. I can't go away and abandon the people here. What would have happened to you if I hadn't been here? Or Chet, what about him? Anyone could have called the evacuation helicopter, but his leg might have gotten infected and he would have been in excruciating pain the whole time. No," she said bitterly, "I can't leave until we find a doctor to move here."

"Why didn't you go to medical school yourself?"

"I couldn't afford to." Pain flashed in her eyes and was quickly hidden. "Besides, it would have taken at least ten years for me to go to college, medical school and do a residency. Pine Butte couldn't wait that long."

"I'm sorry, Sarah." The words seemed totally inadequate to express his feelings. No one knew better than he the frustration and helplessness of being trapped in a situation with no way out. When he was eighteen he had just cut and run, but Sarah was too honorable to do that.

"Don't be," she said. Her smile looked forced. "Pine Butte is my home, and the people here mean everything to me. There are worse things than not being able to travel and see the world. At least I feel as if I'm useful. That's a lot more than some people can say."

"Yeah." Ralph and Richard Wesley's faces came to mind, and his fists ached to smash into their mouths. The impulse shocked him. He'd come back to Pine Butte for justice, not retribution. All he was interested in, he reminded himself, was finding out what had happened to his father. That was all.

He wasn't here to be anybody's salvation. Not even Sarah Wesley's.

This was your home once. It could be again. The thought shimmered like a star in front of him, distant and unreachable. He closed his eyes to the sudden pain. He could never live in Pine Butte again, not after what they'd taken from him.

They'd taken his father, then his boyhood and finally his innocence. When he left, he'd been stripped clean. It had taken him twelve years to rebuild himself, and he wasn't about to give this town the benefit of his hard work.

"Connor?"

Her questioning voice jerked him out of his reverie. "Yeah?"

"I hope you're not brooding about the injustice of it all. I don't."

With an effort he pulled himself back to the conversation they'd been having. "You should," he answered bluntly. "Somebody needs to get the better of Ralph Wesley. He's had a free hand in this town for far too long."

"If he wasn't here, Connor, half of the people in Pine Butte would be unemployed." Her voice was so quiet he had to strain to hear her. "Power works two ways."

"I can't believe you're defending him!"

"I'm not defending him, I'm just saying that I'm not fighting him over my contract. I wouldn't leave, even if I took him to court and had the contract declared illegal. Uncle Ralph isn't keeping me here against my will, Connor."

Once again the thought of what he could do for her danced in front of him. He ruthlessly beat it down, turning abruptly and heading for his mother's old desk. It was time to concentrate on business.

"Since we can't solve your problem today, I guess we might as well work on mine." He forced a light tone into his voice.

"You're right. It's going to take a while to go through all your mother's things. We'd better get started." Her tone matched his exactly.

She stood up, breaking eye contact with him, and he felt oddly chilled in the warm house. While she'd talked about her dreams, he'd felt himself heated by the passion that burned inside her. Now it was back to business, the business that had brought him to Pine Butte. What was going to happen to Sarah's world when he found justice for his father?

Chapter 8

Sarah sat cross-legged on the floor, sorting documents into piles. The brittle papers cracked stiffly as she smoothed them flat and laid them in front of her. Connor sprawled against the couch, looking through his mother's old check registers.

"I haven't seen anything yet that could help us." She stretched and shifted on the hard floor. "All that's in this pile are old bills for insurance and from the utility companies."

Connor looked at her, lines of strain in his face. Reading the small, faded numbers in the check register couldn't be helping his aching head. "I don't really think we're going to find anything in her old utility bills. I just don't want to miss something."

"No one could accuse you of not being thorough," she muttered, wiping a drop of sweat off her ear with her shoulder. "Could we maybe open a window or something? It's getting kind of hot in here."

After a moment he stood up reluctantly. "I guess I can open one in the kitchen. There's probably no point in try- ing to keep our visit here secret, anyway."

He strode into the other room, stretching as he went. The movement pulled his T-shirt out of his jeans and exposed his tautly muscled back for just a flash. His smooth skin looked as fluid as his walk and made her fingers itch to glide over it. Flushing, she looked at the stack of papers in her hands and tried to concentrate on what she was doing.

It was useless. Now that she'd let Connor creep into her mind, she could think of nothing but him—the way he'd tasted and felt that morning as he kissed her, the loose-limbed, flowing way he walked, the way he'd looked at her when he told her not to hire Perry Cummings.

He'd looked at her as though he'd known how much it was going to hurt and would have done anything to protect her from it. He'd looked at her almost as if he cared about her.

Connor reappeared suddenly in the door to the kitchen, holding two glasses. "Here's a glass of water. I should have remembered to bring some cold soft drinks, but at least this is wet."

She hadn't realized how thirsty she'd become. "Thanks. Even water sounds good right now."

The water had a tepid, almost rusty taste, as if it had been sitting in the pipes for a long time. She set the glass down carefully, away from the papers they were working on, and said, "Why didn't you do this a long time ago? If you never intended to come back to Pine Butte, why bother to spend the money to take care of your mother's house when you could have sold it and used the money for something else?"

He shrugged. "I guess because I never wanted to come back long enough to go through her papers like this. I wanted no part of Pine Butte. It was easier to just pay the money and not have to think about it."

"Your mother must have missed you," she said softly.

"Yeah, I suppose she did. But she came to see me pretty regularly before she died." He paused, his mouth twisting into a grim line. "She never said a thing about Barb. I guess she was trying to protect me, or maybe it was just easier to pretend the past didn't exist."

"I think she would be proud of you."

"I'd like to think so," he said gruffly. "What happened with me, the way I was raised, wasn't her fault completely, you know. After my father died, she just couldn't cope. Trying to control any twelve-year-old boy would have been tough, and I was really a handful." He shrugged, turning back to the check register. "She did the best she could. I guess, in the end, that's all I could expect."

She wondered how long it had taken him to gain that small measure of peace with his mother's memory. He bent over the small numbers, apparently concentrating only on the job. Her heart ached for him, for the lonely, frightened boy who'd lost his father and whose mother couldn't help him deal with it. No wonder he'd pulled one outrageous stunt after another. He was crying for some attention from someone.

She suspected that he'd finally gotten it somewhere. He knew himself too well, was too self-assured to be still floundering around. She wondered, wistfully, who had finally seen the man beneath the rebellious boy.

She beat down the tiny whisper of envy because he'd been able to escape Pine Butte and live his own life. Connor had certainly paid the price for his dreams coming true.

A wild hope stirred in her chest that he would decide to stay in Pine Butte once he'd found what had happened to his father. She immediately told herself not to be ridiculous. The one thing that Connor had made perfectly clear from the first time he opened his eyes was that he had no intention of staying in Pine Butte any longer than it took to find out what had happened to his father. Another city was his home now, with, she was sure, many friends and colleagues who were important to him. Including one special woman?

She stopped what she was doing, shocked at the path her thoughts had taken and at the unmistakable bite of jealousy that gnawed at her stomach. It was no business of hers, she told herself carefully, if Connor had ten women waiting for him in ten different cities. She and Pine Butte were very temporary distractions for him. As soon as he'd solved the mystery of his father's death, he would be gone.

Resolutely, she put all thought of Connor staying in Pine Butte out of her mind and picked up the next paper in the stack. She stared at it blindly for a moment until she realized it wasn't the usual bill. Then, trying to gather her composure again, she turned to the man next to her.

"You might want to take a look at these, Connor. It looks like we've found your mother's bank statements."

He put the check register aside and leaned over for the stack of papers she handed him. "Her checkbook wasn't telling me squat. Maybe these will."

Sarah picked up the next paper in the stack, glanced through it and put it in the proper pile. She'd checked over several more useless bills when she felt him stiffen beside her.

"What?" she asked, looking at him expectantly.

He looked at her, wonder in his eyes. "I think we've found something." He held the paper out to her. "Look."

She frowned at the columns of numbers. "I'm not even sure what we're looking for."

He scooted closer to her. His thigh touched hers and she froze, held immobile by the fire scorching through her. He didn't seem to notice.

"Look, here's the entry for the pension she received from the mine."

She saw what looked like a pitifully small number, considering that a woman and a growing boy were expected to live on it. "Okay. I see that."

"Now look here." His voice rose with excitement. "Look at this other entry. It's there every month."

The other number was twice as large as the pension. "Maybe it's just her dividends from investments or something."

He gave her a pitying look. "My parents could barely survive on my father's salary from the mine. They didn't have any investments."

"Then maybe it's social security money. She would have gotten some of that, being a widow with a child to raise."

"It's not that, either. Here's the entry for her social security check, on the third or fourth of every month. No, this is another source of money." He shuffled the papers and finally looked up triumphantly. "She got this money every single month until she died. And there's no logical explanation for it."

"What are you thinking?" she whispered.

"Somebody paid my mother to keep her quiet." His voice was flat and very grim. "They knew she needed more money than the pension and social security. My father was already dead and nothing could bring him back. In exchange for keeping her mouth shut and just ignoring whatever she knew, they'd give her enough money to make life bearable."

"Oh, Connor, surely your own mother wouldn't have covered up her husband's death?" She was appalled that he would even think so.

"What if she honestly thought it was an accident? Maybe she decided that whoever paid her was just easing his own conscience. Hell, she probably figured it made it easier for us and easier for the person paying it." His voice gentled. "I can't believe that she would have helped cover up a murder, either, Sarah. She might have been a weak woman, but she wasn't a bad one."

She stared at the papers Connor clutched in his hands. "What do we do now?"

"Now we go to the bank and find out who was giving her this money."

She leaned against the couch and stared at him. The house was almost eerily quiet. Except for the occasional noise from a passing car, the silence was thick and heavy, weighted with years of secrets. Finally she said, "Do you think they'd tell us?" Her voice sounded unnaturally loud.

"They'd have no reason not to. My mother's been dead for ten years, and I'm her legal heir. If I have questions about her estate, who else would I ask?"

"I hope it's that easy." Rising to her knees, she began to pick up the careful piles of papers. "Do you want to look at these?"

He glanced over at them and shook his head. "No, I trust you. If you say there isn't anything in them, I don't have to look for myself."

"I said I didn't see anything," she protested. "You may recognize something that I wouldn't notice."

He was obviously eager to get away and go to the bank. "All right, pile them up over there on the desk. I'll take a look at them later."

Looking around the room, she noticed the glasses of water on the floor and picked them up. She walked into the kitchen, set them on the counter near the sink, then reached up and pulled the window closed. After making sure it was locked firmly in place, she walked to where Connor stood impatiently by the front door.

As they stepped, squinting, into the bright sunlight, he turned to her suddenly. "I didn't even think. Is the bank open on Saturday afternoons?"

She nodded, glancing at her watch. "For another half hour. We have plenty of time."

He folded the bank statements carefully and shoved them into his back pocket. Then he draped his arm casually over her shoulder, and they began to walk toward the center of town.

It didn't mean anything, she told herself, too conscious of his body next to hers. Her hip bumped against his as they walked, and she tried to move further away. Grinning, he tightened his hold on her.

"Everyone'll just think I need some support," he said, reading her mind as his fingers glided over her shoulder in an unmistakable caress. "Don't forget how weak I am."

"You're weak in the head if you think I'm going to buy that line," she retorted. But she didn't move away. She couldn't. More than just his hand held her next to him. Invisible cords bound them together, and now they were slowly pulling tighter.

She was the only one who knew why he was really in Pine Butte, the only one he'd trusted with that information. She was the only one who knew anything about him. And, she thought slowly, she'd told him things about herself that she'd never told anyone else in Pine Butte.

Glancing at him, she saw the planes of his face set in hard lines. There was no softness in his eyes as he looked around his home town, no happy memories to recall. Even though the mercury hovered near ninety degrees, she felt a chill ripple up her skin. There would be no happy endings for

Connor MacCormac and Pine Butte. And no matter what he stirred in her, no matter how connected to him she already felt, there would be no happily ever after for them, either.

His arm tightened around her almost painfully and he pulled her closer. Looking at him in surprise, she saw him staring ahead of them, his jaw clenched tight. When she turned to look in that direction, she saw her cousin Richard striding toward them.

Her stomach churned. Tension flowed out of Connor and made the arm around her shoulders as hard as an iron bar. His steps never slowed, and she felt him gathering himself.

"Connor, no," she whispered urgently. "Leave him alone."

His fingers curled around her shoulder in a quick, hard embrace. "Worried about me, sweetheart?" The look he gave her was fierce with possession.

"Of course I'm worried about you," she answered. "You've got a concussion. You don't need to get into a fight with Richard."

"That wienie isn't going to hurt me." Scorn dripped from his voice. "About the worst thing he's going to do is go tell his daddy that I'm picking on him."

"Please, Connor."

As Richard approached, she could feel Connor's whole body tightening next to her. He stared at her cousin but didn't slow down. She held her breath, praying that Richard would just keep walking.

Her cousin slowed and stopped in front of them, and she and Connor were forced to stop, too.

"Hello, Sarah," her cousin said, never taking his eyes off Connor. "I didn't realize you had such poor taste."

She twined her arm around Connor's waist and moved closer to him. "I guess there are a lot of things you don't know, aren't there?"

Richard flushed and looked at her. For just a second, what looked like hatred glittered in his eyes, then he blinked and it was gone. "I know trash when I see it. And smell it."

"You wouldn't know your own feet if you fell over them," she spit at him. She would have moved toward her cousin but Connor's arm held her immobile. "Unless your father told you about them, of course."

Connor bent his head and nuzzled her ear, saying softly, "It's all right, Sarah. Richard can't hurt me."

"Is lover boy asking you to protect him?" Richard sneered. "What's the matter? Can't he fight his own battles?"

Connor straightened and looked at the other man.

Richard took a step backward and a flash of fear passed over his face.

"I can take care of myself, Wesley. But don't worry, I only pick on people my own size." His gaze raked her cousin and settled scornfully on his face. "I wouldn't waste my time on you."

Sarah wrapped her arm around Connor's waist as if to hold him next to her. He squeezed her shoulder again and then urged her forward. As they passed her cousin, standing rigid with fury in the middle of the sidewalk, Connor didn't even spare him a glance.

As they got farther away from Richard, she felt his muscles gradually relax. Telling herself she should let go of him and put some distance between them, she tightened her grip on his waist. For a few minutes they walked without talking.

"I'm sorry, Connor," she finally said in a small voice.

"What for?"

"For the things my cousin said. He's not speaking for the rest of Pine Butte, believe me."

Ignoring the last part of her statement, he said, "Why do you feel you have to apologize for him? He's an adult. He's responsible for himself."

She tried to pretend she couldn't feel the weight of his arm on her shoulders, his hand curling into her arm. It was impossible. Every cell in her body was aware of him. "I'm not apologizing for him," she finally said. "I'm sorry that he hurt you."

"He can't hurt me, Sarah. I don't give a flying... hoot what he thinks of me. The Richard Wesleys of the world lost their ability to hurt me a long time ago. That was one of the first lessons I learned."

Tightening her arm around him, she murmured, "Then I'm sorry you had to learn that."

He slowed and stopped, turning to face her. "Why does it matter to you, Sarah?" His voice was oddly strained and urgent. "Why should you care about me? I thought, given the circumstances, you'd be glad of any hard knocks that life had dealt me."

She looked at him, seeing the defiant, lonely boy instead of the man. "According to Barb, I should," she agreed, her voice soft. All her doubts about Barb's story flooded back, accompanied by a profound sense of guilt. "But I can't hate you, Connor. Whatever you did twelve years ago, you're an honorable man now. I'm trying very hard to judge you only by what I see now and not by what happened in the past."

Connor could only look at her. The buildings faded away, the dusty street and withered grass of the lawns disappeared. The only thing he saw was the woman in front of him, watching him with her enormous blue-green eyes. Eyes that were a little defiant and a little worried, unsure of his reaction. Eyes that were filled with a wrenching guilt.

Sliding his arms around her, he backed her up into a huge old poplar that stood next to the sidewalk. He ached for her, had wanted her since the moment he woke up in her clinic and saw her bending over him. Hell, he'd probably wanted her since he'd heard her voice while he was unconscious.

"Sarah," he murmured, before he brought his mouth down on hers.

She hesitated for only a moment. Then she was kissing him back with a desire that burned as fiercely as his own. Her mouth opened and her tongue twined with his, frantic to taste him. His body tightened and he pressed into her, trying to absorb her into him. Their clothes were an intolerable barrier, and he clenched his fists to prevent his hands from tearing them away.

He kept one hand wrapped around her, and with the other he pushed against the tree and eased himself back. After a moment, he stepped away from her and closed his eyes. He burned for her. He wanted her with an intensity that frightened him. Never before had one woman so obsessed him, haunting his dreams at night and all his thoughts by day. He had to back off before he found himself in serious trouble.

"I'm sorry, Sarah. I didn't mean for that to happen."

She pushed away from the tree and brushed off her jeans, not meeting his eyes. "You don't have to apologize. It's not like I was objecting a whole lot."

"I'm not sorry I kissed you." He couldn't help looking at her, and for just a moment the desire that throbbed in him was mirrored in her eyes. Jamming his hands in his pockets to keep himself from reaching for her again, he looked at her steadily. "I *am* sorry that I made you a target for every gossip in town."

She sighed. "Don't worry about it. Chances are nobody saw us anyway. Besides, I'm not ashamed to be seen with you."

At her words, the fire burned hotter and he simply stood and watched as she turned and started walking down the street. Finally he caught up and fell into step beside her. This time, he was careful not to touch her or brush against her. He'd been in control of himself for the past twelve years, and it frightened the hell out of him to lose that control now.

"We should just make it to the bank on time." Her voice was slightly breathless, as if she, too, was having trouble with control. His loins tightened painfully again and he closed his eyes, trying to beat down his reaction to her.

"Do you want me to come in with you?" she asked diffidently. "I can meet you back at the clinic if you like."

"I want you with me." He didn't want to examine that statement. He couldn't think about how much he wanted her with him, and for how long.

They paused at the door to the bank and he reached behind him to touch the folded bank statements in his back pocket. They were the first real evidence he had, and he needed to remind himself why he was here in Pine Butte. Using the skills he'd learned over the past years, he blocked out all distractions and tried to focus only on what he would ask Charles Goodman, the banker who'd been handling his mother's affairs.

They stepped into the lobby of the bank and stood for a moment, looking around. There were a few other customers standing at the tables in the middle of the room, filling out withdrawal or deposit slips. Another couple of people stood at the teller windows, conducting business. Light from the tall, thin windows dappled the floor with the golden glow of late afternoon. Nobody seemed to notice them walking across the room.

As they approached the row of teller windows, Connor felt someone staring at him. Glancing sharply around, he saw one of the tellers, a small, mousy woman, sliding her gaze away from him. Narrowing his eyes, he watched her for a second, then looked away. It was probably just another curious resident of Pine Butte.

As they waited in the line for a teller Connor turned to Sarah and said softly, "Do you know the last teller on the right? The one wearing the brown dress?"

He waited for her to casually glance in that direction, unprepared for her start of surprise. "That's Thelma Harrison, Harley's wife. He's the foreman out at the mine. Why did you ask?"

His lip curled. "She was staring at me. I was just curious."

Sarah placed her hand on his arm. Something stirred in his gut, something he didn't want to name. "Don't pay any attention to her, Connor. She's just being rude."

He jammed his hands into his pockets to keep himself from pulling her into his arms right there in the bank. Somehow Sarah Wesley managed to get around all his defenses. He had to concentrate on why he'd come back to Pine Butte, he told himself almost desperately. He couldn't afford to get sidetracked by a woman, no matter how much he wanted her.

It was their turn at a teller window, and he was a little disappointed that it wasn't Thelma Harrison's window. He'd have liked to see how she'd handle dealing with him face-to-face, he thought cynically.

The young man who greeted them was pleasant and professional. "Can I help you?"

"We'd like to see Charles Goodman. Tell him Connor MacCormac is here."

The young man looked disconcerted, as if he wasn't used to problems he couldn't handle. "His secretary is Debbie James. She's sitting over there." He gestured to his left. "I'm sure she can help you."

Connor placed a hand at the small of Sarah's back and headed toward the woman the teller had indicated. It wasn't just an excuse to touch Sarah, he assured himself. It was nothing more than a polite gesture. They had almost reached the large desk when he found himself fantasizing about how the skin of her back would feel. He snatched his hand away from her back as though he'd been scorched.

"Ms. James?" He stopped in front of the desk and waited for the woman to look up. "I'm here to see Charles Goodman. You can tell him Connor MacCormac would like a word with him."

"I'll check and see if he's busy, Mr. MacCormac," she murmured, pushing away from the desk. Her disapproving glance told him that she didn't think much of people who came in without an appointment.

He rocked on the balls of his feet and waited for her to reappear. He had no intention of taking no for an answer, even if he had to barge into the office uninvited. He had nothing to lose, he thought bitterly. Since everyone here was determined to think the worst of him, he might as well give them something concrete.

"He says to come on in." Debbie James looked puzzled and annoyed, as if the intrusion was a personal affront to her. She stood aside and held the door open, and Connor took Sarah's hand and urged her into the room after him.

"Connor." The portly man behind the desk stood up and extended his hand. "It's good to see you again."

Connor shook the older man's hand briefly, then settled into one of the smooth leather chairs that stood in front of his desk. "Thanks, Charles." He had felt Sarah's start of surprise at the cordial welcome and shot her a reassuring look. He probably should have explained about Charles before they got here.

"What can I do for you, Connor? I assume everything's satisfactory at your mother's house?"

"You've done a good job there," Connor agreed. "Everything's fine. I'm here about something I found in my mother's house that I'd hoped you could explain."

The banker's smile became infinitesimally less welcoming. "I'll do my best." Connor leaned forward and pulled the sheaf of bank statements out of his pocket. "I found these while I was going through my mother's things." He laid them on the cool marble of the desktop and smoothed out the brittle pages. Running his finger down a column of figures, he stopped at the unexplained deposit and looked at the banker. "I wondered where this money came from, and I figured you would know."

Goodman picked up the top statement and studied it. After a minute he picked up the next one, then the one after that. Each sheet he examined made his smile fade just a little more.

"I have no idea where this money came from, Mac-Cormac."

Connor silently noted the switch from cordial, firstname basis to the more businesslike use of his last name. "This was a significant sum of money, Goodman. It was more than twice as much as her pension from the mine. Surely you would have noticed a deposit of this size."

"We have a lot of customers, MacCormac. It would be impossible to remember every single transaction from every one of them. This was ten years ago, after all."

"What about the bank's records? Wouldn't they tell you where she got this money?"

Goodman shook his head quickly. "We only keep records for nine or ten years. Anything we'd have about this matter would have been destroyed by now."

Connor stared at him, certain that the banker knew more than he was willing to tell him. Goodman couldn't quite meet his eyes, and he was fidgeting nervously with a letter opener on his desk. "Is there any way we could...jog your memory?" he said softly.

Goodman pushed away from his desk and stood up, blustering. "Are you threatening me, MacCormac?"

Connor raised his eyebrows. "Of course not. Why on earth would I want to threaten you? I was merely asking if there was anything we could do to refresh your memory."

The banker turned his gaze on the woman sitting quietly next to him. "What are you doing here, Sarah? Surely you, of all people, don't want to associate with him."

"I'll decide for myself who I want to associate with, Mr. Goodman." Connor heard the steel in her voice and wondered why she'd let her uncle push her around for so many years.

"And if I were you," she continued, the smoothness of her voice not concealing the meaning beneath the words, "I would think twice about not cooperating with Connor. If I understand correctly, he's done business with your bank and you personally for a number of years. He might be interested in doing an audit of the accounts for his mother's house."

Connor glanced at her, flabbergasted. She sat with her back very straight staring at Charles Goodman. To his complete astonishment, the banker turned a dull red and looked away.

"I'm sure that Mr. MacCormac would find everything in order," he muttered, sitting down slowly. He looked at Connor with an almost pleading look in his eyes. "I'm sorry, MacCormac. If I could help you I would. I simply cannot."

Connor stood up, taking Sarah's hand and pulling her with him. "I'm sorry to hear that, Goodman. Real sorry. You keep thinking about it. I'm sure something will come to you. And if it does, you know where to find me."

The banker didn't offer his hand this time and Connor didn't offer his. He simply turned and walked out of the office. He strode past the secretary's desk, through the lobby and out into the hot sunlight on the street.

Chapter 9

"That was a hell of a curve you threw old Charles," Connor said as they walked slowly to the clinic. He was more tired than he'd realized, and he silently cursed his weakness.

"All I did was explain some facts to him." Sarah seemed surprised by his remark.

"Why did you just assume he was skimming money from the account for my mother's house?"

She smiled sadly. "Human nature. He didn't think you'd ever show up in Pine Butte again, and he probably saw you as a never-ending source of anonymous money. I'm sure he rationalized it by telling himself that he deserved a cut for his time."

"Well, whatever he thought, it wasn't enough to loosen his tongue about those deposits into my mother's account." His mouth tightened with anger. "And I'm damn sure he remembered what they were about."

"You left him with something to think about." A slight smile curled her lips. "I wouldn't be surprised if you heard from Mr. Goodman again."

"It depends on who that money was from."

When she didn't answer, he glanced at her. "If that money was from someone powerful in this town, Goodman might be afraid to say anything," he said more gently. "You know who that means, don't you?"

"My uncle may be used to getting his own way, but he wouldn't murder anyone. He's not like that." She sounded almost desperate.

"We'll see," he said noncommittally. As they approached the clinic he forced himself to put one foot in front of the other. All he could think about right now was that big bed in the back room. He glanced at Sarah's red head as she bent to unlock the door. And Sarah in it with him.

Closing his eyes, he moved a step away from her. He was too tired to deal with those feelings right now. If he wasn't careful, he'd reach for her and say all kinds of things he'd regret later. Things he had no business even thinking about Sarah Wesley, let alone saying.

"I'm going to lie down," he muttered.

She took his arm immediately. He saw the concern and worry in her face. "Are you all right? I was afraid you were going to overdo it today. Do you need some help?"

"I'm fine, Sarah. I just need some rest." His voice sounded too brusque, but he couldn't help it. He wanted nothing more than to turn to her and put his arms around her. He ached to tumble into that bed with her, to sleep with her body tucked in close to his.

He turned away and headed toward the bedroom. Hell, who was he trying to kid? He wanted to do a whole lot more with Sarah on that bed than just sleep. A whole hell of a lot more. And that couldn't happen.

He knew with a desperate certainty that if they made love, he would never be the same. He wouldn't be able to put her aside easily, as he had all the other women he'd dated over the years. She'd be engraved on his soul, burned into all those cold, lonely places inside him that yearned for her. No, Sarah scared the hell out of him. And if he touched her again he would be lost.

As he eased the bedroom door closed he couldn't stop himself from turning around for one last look at her. As their gazes met and locked, he saw his own yearning reflected in her eyes. For just a moment, awareness blazed between them. He closed his eyes to block out her image, and when he opened them again she'd disappeared.

Her footsteps echoed on the stairs up to her apartment, and he shut the door with a quiet click. Moving carefully, he walked to the bed and lowered himself onto the quilt. His body begged for sleep, but he lay for a long time staring at the ceiling.

"I don't think that's a very good idea."

Connor sounded very final, and Sarah sighed. Dealing with a stubborn man wasn't her idea of fun at nine o'clock on a Sunday morning.

"Why not?" She tried to sound logical. "It's a perfect opportunity to get to know some of the people here."

"I didn't say I wanted to get to know the people. I said I wanted to find out what happened to my father."

"Well, if you talk to enough people, maybe one of them will be able to help you."

He pushed back from the table in her small, sunny kitchen and strode to the window. Shoving his hands into the pockets of his jeans, he stood staring at the distant mountains. The worn fabric pulled tight against his hips, and she had to force herself to look up at the back of his head.

"You still haven't figured out who sent that note, have you?"

"As far as I know, only one person in this town knew my address, and that was Charles Goodman. Getting me back to Pine Butte is obviously the last thing he'd want to do. So, no, I don't have a clue."

"You're not going to have another opportunity to see so many of the people who live here in the same place at the same time. I would think the town picnic is just the place you'd want to be."

Why was she trying so hard to persuade him to go with her? Because she simply wanted to be with him, she admitted reluctantly. She couldn't bear the thought of him sitting in the clinic all afternoon, by himself, while everyone else in the town was out having a good time.

"I'll think about it."

"Fine." She kept her voice light. God forbid if he realized what she was thinking, that she had a more personal reason for urging him to go with her. She had enough trouble with the attraction that seemed to spark between them without fanning the flames. "Would you like more coffee?"

"I'll get it." He turned from the window and reached for the coffeepot. "Is there anywhere in town I can get a decent Sunday paper?"

"If you want to walk a couple of blocks, there's a box in front of the grocery store that usually has the Sunday *Denver Post.*"

He moved restlessly around the kitchen like a caged animal, pausing at the window again to look toward the mountains one more time. "I'm going to go buy one," he said abruptly, and headed for the stairs. "Is there anything you need from town?"

"Nothing you could get today." She grinned at him. "We haven't adopted those heathen, big-city ways here in Pine Butte. All of our stores are closed on Sunday."

"All right. Then I guess I'll be right back."

She watched him until he'd disappeared down the stairs, then picked up her mug of coffee and leaned back. He'd been restless and edgy ever since she'd walked downstairs and invited him up to breakfast. Earlene's was closed on Sundays, too, and she'd figured she didn't have much choice. It was either her apartment or a day-long fast.

He'd looked as reluctant to walk up her stairs as she'd been to invite him. The rapport that had flowed between them the previous afternoon had disappeared completely, replaced by a simmering tension that arced between them whenever they were in the same room.

Everything had changed since their kiss yesterday. She was too aware of him, of his arm laying on the table just inches from hers, of his denim-covered legs stretched out under her table, close enough that she could feel his heat.

She told herself it was just hormones and pheromones, a simple alignment of chemicals in their bodies. It didn't mean anything, and it would disappear as soon as he left town. She couldn't possibly feel anything other than dislike for the man she'd hated for so long. Except that she was beginning to suspect she didn't have any reason to hate him anymore.

Barb, is it possible? she cried silently. *Could you have let the whole town, including me, think Connor was the father of your baby?* Guilt roiled with anger in her stomach, twisting her emotions into knots. Only this time, both the guilt and the anger were directed at her sister.

She had to remember Barb, she thought desperately. Simple loyalty to her sister would forbid her from getting involved with Connor.

But as she stood in the middle of her living room, Barb's face refused to come into focus for her. It swam just out of reach, the details blurry and vague.

She shook her head. She'd never forget what her only sister looked like. Grabbing a photo album, she leafed to a page near the end. Barb stood in front of their Christmas tree, her hands on her gently rounded stomach. Sarah drank in the details, fixing them in her mind. Of course she hadn't forgotten what Barb looked like.

As she eased the photo album onto the bookshelf, her phone rang. Hurrying to answer it, she stumbled over the chair Connor had been sitting in. Pushing it under the table with just a little more force than necessary, she grabbed the receiver.

"Hello."

There was silence on the other end of the phone, broken only by the sound of breathing. Her hand tightened on the receiver and she asked, "Who's there?"

"It's me, Sarah." The words were almost whispered in a high-pitched, childish voice.

Sarah slumped against the refrigerator and relaxed her grip on the phone. If she wasn't careful, she'd be seeing bogeymen everywhere. "Who's me?" she asked softly.

"Danny Franklin. I think there's something wrong with my kitten, Sarah." The words tumbled out. "She won't eat anything and she's very sad. Mommy says the vet won't be open today, and I'm afraid Misty's gonna die."

Danny was five years old. Sarah had seen him recently for his vaccinations for kindergarten, and all the child could talk about was his new kitten, Misty.

"Would you like me to take a look at her, Danny? I'm not a veterinarian, but I might be able to help."

"Yes, please, Sarah. I know you'll make her better."

"I'm not sure of that, but I'll see what I can do. How about if I come over to your house?"

"Okay. Bye." The receiver went dead, and Sarah slowly hung up the phone, a smile fading from her face. Knowing Jenna Franklin and the circumstances of her life, she prayed that they wouldn't have to take the kitten to the vet in Meeker, forty miles away. Maybe there was something she could do to help the animal.

She was rummaging around in the clinic, throwing some pediatric medications into her bag, when she heard the door open. "I'm in here," she called.

A few seconds later Connor walked into the room, a thick Sunday paper under his arm. His eyebrows snapped together in a frown. "I didn't think your clinic was open on Sundays."

"It's not." She grinned. "I have an emergency call to make."

"Are you always so thrilled about emergency calls?"

Still smiling, she looked around for anything else she might need and shook her head. "This one is a pleasant change after the kinds of emergencies we've had lately. My patient is about four months old and covered with fur." She looked at Connor's puzzled face and grinned again. "One of my five-year-old patients called. His kitten is sick and he's afraid it's going to die. I told him I'd come over and take a look."

"Do you mind if I come along?" Connor heard himself ask.

She looked at him and smiled again. "Of course not. I'd enjoy the company."

Now why in hell did I do that? Connor pondered the question a few minutes later as they walked down the street. Even though it was early, the day promised to be beautiful. The scorching heat had eased a little, and a gentle wind blew through his hair. He could be sitting on the swing in Sarah's garden right now, reading the Denver Sunday paper and drinking coffee. Instead he was walking down the quiet streets of Pine Butte, on his way to take a look at a damn kitten.

He glanced at the woman walking next to him and knew exactly why he'd asked to go with her. He'd want to be with her if they were heading out to slop the pigs. The words had flowed out of his mouth on their own, but he realized that even the nirvana of a Sunday paper and a good cup of coffee held no attraction if Sarah wasn't there to share it with him.

Clearing his throat, he said, "What exactly do you think you can do for this kitten?"

"Probably not much," she admitted. "I don't know anything about veterinary medicine. I just don't want Danny to be scared, thinking that his kitten is going to die."

There weren't many people, he thought, who would give up their Sunday morning to reassure a child that his kitten was all right. Everyone he knew would have brushed the child off with a careless word about how the kitten would be fine. He couldn't think of another person who would go to the trouble of actually looking at the animal.

But then, he didn't know anyone else quite like Sarah Wesley. She was a thoughtful, caring, *good* person. He ached to pull her close and let her warmth and caring soak into him. He raised his hand to her shoulder, but let it drop before he touched her.

He couldn't let himself be sidetracked by this woman. He had come here for a reason, and it had nothing to do with feminine diversions. Staring straight ahead while he enumerated the reasons he had to forget about Sarah Wesley, he didn't realize she'd turned into a yard until he felt her hand on his arm.

Her touch was like fire on a cold day. He welcomed the pain even while his soul burned. He hoped to God she wouldn't notice his body's response to her simple touch. He had to get out of this town, and fast.

"We're here," she said, watching him for a moment. "Are you all right? Maybe you should have stayed at the clinic and rested."

"I'm fine."

"You look like your head hurts. Are you sure you don't want to go back to the clinic and lie down?"

Lying down by himself wasn't going to do anything to cure what ailed him. "I'm okay, Sarah. Let's take a look at this kitten."

Giving him a worried look, she rang the door bell. Almost immediately the door was opened by a small child with light brown hair and enormous grey eyes. "Hi, Sarah," the boy said, opening the door.

A woman who looked remarkably like the child hurried to hold the door open. "Thanks for coming, Sarah. I hope you don't mind that Danny called you. He absolutely insisted that you would know what to do."

"I'm not sure about that, but I'm happy to take a look at Misty for him. Jenna, this is Connor MacCormac. He's staying at the clinic for a few days. Connor, this is Jenna Franklin, Danny's mother," Sarah said easily.

He held out his hand and she took it promptly. "Nice to meet you, Mr. MacCormac. It was awfully nice of you to come with Sarah. Come on in."

Connor stared at the woman, dumbfounded. He'd expected an assessing look, at the very least. His name alone should have raised her eyebrows, not to mention the fact that he was staying at the clinic. But then, probably everybody in this small town already knew about that.

He entered the house warily, but Jenna Franklin and her son seemed to have forgotten about him. Danny had taken Sarah by the hand and was leading her into a small but sunny living room. There, on the sofa, a small mop of orange fur was curled into a tight little ball.

"That's how she's been since yesterday, Sarah," the child said, looking at Sarah with enormous, frightened eyes. "She doesn't want to play or anything. She doesn't even want to eat. She takes a bite of her food and it just falls out of her mouth."

"He's right, Sarah. The poor thing hasn't eaten a thing since early yesterday and has barely moved off the couch." Jenna Franklin picked up her son and sat on the couch next to the kitten. In spite of the worry Connor knew she felt for the kitten, she seemed like a woman who was utterly calm and at peace with herself. Looking at her, sitting on the couch with the child in her lap, he knew there was nowhere else on earth she would rather be than sitting in this tiny house in Pine Butte holding her son.

Sarah stroked her hand gently down the kitten's back, and the animal stirred, stretching. "Did she get out of the house, Danny? Could she have gotten hurt somehow?"

The child shook his head vigorously. "Uh-uh. Mommy says it'd be dangerous for her to go outside since she's so small. I'm real careful."

He watched as Sarah picked the animal up and held it in her palm. It looked ridiculously small and helpless, like a tiny newborn baby.

Sarah poked and prodded the animal, even pulling out a stethoscope and listening to the small chest. After looking in its eyes and ears and trying without success to get it to open its mouth, she set it gently on the couch and knelt down next to the boy.

"I'm not sure what's wrong with Misty, Danny. Maybe she has an upset tummy."

"Like I get when I have too many hot dogs?"

She hid a smile. "Yes, kind of like that." She took Danny's hands. "I think maybe you'll have to call the vet tomorrow." She looked at Jenna. "Maybe he can prescribe something over the phone."

Connor saw the look the two women exchanged, and the fear and desperation that passed over Jenna's face. He realized instantly that Jenna couldn't afford to take the animal to the vet. Her house was scrupulously clean, but she didn't have much furniture. Both her clothes and the child's were worn and faded.

Without thinking, he reached for the kitten. "Do you mind if I take a look at her, Danny?"

The boy shook his head, watching Connor with eyes that didn't dare hope. "Sarah's almost a doctor, you know. She could fix Misty if anyone could."

"You're right there, Dan. But I just want to take a look at something," he muttered, concentrating on the tiny bundle in his hands. He hadn't missed the way the kitten had resisted when Sarah tried to open its mouth.

Bracing the kitten in his lap, he ignored its needle-sharp claws as he pried its mouth open. Trying to hold it steady for long enough to get a good look inside, he finally spotted what he'd been looking for.

Placing the kitten gently on the couch, he ran one hand down its back as he turned to the child. "I think I know what's wrong with your kitten, Danny. I think she may have been chewing on an electric cord and she burned her mouth. She probably gave herself a little shock, too, which is why she's been sleeping so much."

The little boy wrinkled his nose. "Why would she do that?"

"For the same reason little babies do things like that. They don't know any better. She's probably getting her teeth and needed to chew on something."

Sarah had picked up the kitten again and was trying to get it to open its mouth. "What did you see in there?"

"There's a deep red groove on her tongue and red marks that look like burns on her lips. I'm sure that's what it is."

"What can we do about it?" Jenna Franklin picked up the kitten and cuddled it next to her.

"I think that your vet would probably tell you to mix her food with water so she can eat more easily, and maybe to give her antibiotics. She'll probably stop sleeping so much in a day or two."

"Thank you, Mr. MacCormac." Jenna's eyes shone with gratitude. "How do you know so much about it? You're not a veterinarian, are you?"

"I've had cats," he said gruffly, somehow not willing to lie to this woman who looked at him so trustingly. "It's a pretty common injury."

As Sarah measured out a bottle of a common, pink pediatric antibiotic, Connor sat on the floor and watched the two women. Sarah handed the bottle to Jenna, gave the kitten one more quick caress and stood up.

"You'd better call the vet tomorrow, just to be certain that we're doing the right thing," Sarah said.

"I will."

A look of perfect understanding passed between the two women, and Sarah bent down to give Danny a kiss. "You take good care of Misty for me, Danny. I'll come by tomorrow and check on her."

The child had a smile on his face as he slid off his mother's lap. "Okay."

Jenna Franklin stood up. "I don't know how to thank you, Mr. MacCormac. Misty is very important to Danny," she said softly.

He shrugged, uncomfortable with the praise. "It's nothing. I hope the kitten's okay."

"I'm sure she will be. Are you coming to the picnic this afternoon?"

There was nothing but friendly invitation in the woman's eyes, and he found himself saying, "I thought I might."

"Wonderful. I'll see you there."

Sarah didn't say anything until they were out the door and almost back to the clinic. Finally she said, carefully, "Jenna's wonderful, isn't she?"

He glanced at her in surprise, then slowly smiled. He wanted to kiss her, right there in the middle of the street. She actually sounded jealous of her friend.

"She's great," he said, feigning enthusiasm. He couldn't resist teasing her. "And gorgeous, too."

Sarah fumbled with the lock on the door to the clinic. Shoving it open, she waited until he followed her in, then shut the door just a little too hard. "I'm glad she was able to convince you to go to the picnic this afternoon. I'm sure you'll have a good time with her and Danny."

She headed toward the stairs to her apartment, and he snaked an arm around her waist and hauled her against him. "I'll have a good time at the picnic this afternoon, but it won't be with Jenna Franklin." He nuzzled the fragrant hair at the back of her neck. "She's very nice, but I'm not interested in her."

She turned around slowly in his arms and looked at him. "What are you interested in, Connor?"

"My father," he muttered, unable to look away from her. "I'm interested in what happened to him."

"Is that all?"

In answer he bent his head and touched his lips to hers. He meant for the kiss to be light and quick, a mere brushing of his mouth against hers, an apology for teasing her.

He wasn't prepared for the explosion of desire that hit him. Fire coursed through his veins, making him instantly hard and throbbing with need for her. His arms tightened around her and he pulled her closer.

She came willingly, fitting into him as if she belonged there. Her mouth clung to his, and when he flicked his tongue over her lips she opened to him immediately. Plunging into her mouth, he tasted the sweet, ripe flavor of her. When she hesitantly touched his tongue with hers, he groaned and pulled her hips closer to his, rocking against her so she could feel the extent of his desire for her.

"Sarah," he groaned into her ear, his voice harsh. "I can't even see any other woman besides you."

"I want you, too," she whispered, her voice so faint that he could hardly hear her.

Her hands kneaded the muscles on his back and her hips moved slightly against his. He doubted she even realized what she was doing, but the evidence of her arousal made him afraid he would lose control. Blood pounded in his head, and his legs felt suddenly wobbly.

He steered her toward the couch in the waiting room and eased her down onto it, covering her body with his. She raised her head, disoriented, but when he kissed her again she wrapped her arms around his neck and melted into him.

He couldn't wait another moment. He had to touch her. Gripping the soft material of the T-shirt she wore, he pulled it slowly out of the waistband of her shorts, then slid his hand underneath. Her skin was hot and slick with perspiration. His hand smoothed her stomach and slid up her ribs, pausing when he noticed her sudden stillness as he got closer to her breasts.

He smoothed one finger slowly over the outer curve of one breast, feeling her fingers tighten on his back. Bending to kiss her neck, he teased her for a few minutes. His finger circled and stroked, getting closer but not touching her nipple. She was rigid beneath him, almost holding her breath.

Both her hands dug into the muscles of his back, gripping him almost painfully.

He fought for control, wanting to prolong the moment for as long as possible. He shifted against her, fitting himself into the V of her legs but holding himself very still. If he moved at all, it would be over too soon.

Finally he touched her nipple, one finger gliding over the silky material of her bra. She sucked in her breath and arched against him, her fingers clenching on his back.

Slipping his hand underneath the barrier of her bra, he cupped her breast in his hand. It was perfect, just like the rest of her. Silky and firm, it filled his hand completely. Rolling her nipple in his fingers, he covered her mouth with his and drank in her small moans.

She was moving against him frantically, her hips rolling and lifting, pressing to get closer to him. Her hands scrabbled at his back, trying to pull his polo shirt out of his jeans. He could feel her fingers trembling as she caressed his tense muscles, her hands kneading and testing, fluttering down his spine and back up again.

He had never wanted a woman this much, not even as a randy teenager when he could think of nothing but sex. Closing his eyes, he shuddered with the effort to control himself. It almost took more strength than he possessed to stop himself from stripping off her clothes and plunging into her right here on the couch in her waiting room.

She deserved better than this. He repeated the words over and over until he felt his trembling slow and some spark of reason catch in his brain. When he made love with Sarah, it would be in a bed and they would have hours to explore each other. It wouldn't be on a couch in a public place, where anyone passing by the window could glance in and see them.

And they *would* make love. Even though every instinct he possessed screamed at him to run as far and as fast as he could, he knew he couldn't run from Sarah just yet. She was an obsession burning into his soul.

He knew she'd felt his withdrawal, because she tried to pull away from him. Sitting up, he pulled her close and held on while she tried to stand up.

"Don't, Sarah. Let me hold you for a moment."

Bending her head, she refused to look at him. Her wavy red hair fell forward and covered her face, and he gently pushed it behind her ear. Her cheeks were bright pink.

Pulling her onto his lap, he wrapped his arms around her and held on tight. Closing his eyes, he tried to ignore the feel of her soft bottom pressing into his groin. This wasn't the time or the place, he repeated to himself almost desperately.

"Sarah, look at me." When she ignored him, he took her chin in his hand and turned her to face him.

"I didn't think you wanted to make love in your waiting room," he said gently. "That's why I stopped."

A fresh wave of red washed her cheeks as she looked at the window and realized anyone could have seen them. "I'm sorry," she whispered. "I don't know what I was thinking of."

"I have a pretty good idea." He bent to kiss the side of her neck and felt himself stirring again. "It's probably the same thing I've been thinking about ever since I opened my eyes in your exam room."

"I'm sorry, Connor," she said at last. "I'm not usually... like this," she finished lamely. "I don't... I mean I haven't..."

"Hush. I know. This was the last thing I was thinking about when I came back here. But I can't think of anything but you."

He saw her fighting tears. Finally she burst out, "I feel so guilty, so disloyal!" She turned to look at him, tears spiking her eyelashes and making them even blacker. "I've hated you for twelve years. Now I feel like I should hate myself for the way I feel."

His arms tightened around her almost involuntarily, then he set her aside and stood up. "I want you, Sarah. I won't try to make you think otherwise. You're the last woman I should want, but that doesn't seem to make any difference. I can't promise forever. I can't even promise next week. You know why I'm here, and as soon as I get my answers I'll be leaving."

He looked at her, for once not trying to disguise the longing and need in his eyes. "But I've never felt this way about any other woman. No one has ever obsessed me the way you do. I want you, and I'm not going to deny it. I stopped just now because I didn't want to do anything to embarrass you. Next time I might not be able to be so strong." He watched her, wanting nothing more than to carry her upstairs and finish what they'd started. "Remember that, Sarah."

She stood and stared at him for what seemed like hours. Then, without a word, she turned and walked up the stairs. He stood for a long time, watching the place where she'd disappeared.

Chapter 10

Sarah stood beside Connor at the edge of the park just outside of town and felt the tension slowly coil tighter and tighter. Most of the town was gathered for their annual summer picnic, and she saw his gaze drift from group to group. The smell of grilling hot dogs and chicken drifted on the breeze, and the shouts of children echoed from the trees over by the playground.

She hadn't said anything more to him about the picnic beyond stopping at his room and asking him again if he wanted to go with her. He'd said yes and they'd walked the five or six blocks to the park in a charged silence.

She'd avoided him since their encounter earlier that morning, hiding in her apartment and making up a whole list of chores that absolutely had to be done that day. She'd known it was cowardly, but she just couldn't bring herself to face him yet.

Disturbed and still guilty about the passion that had burned between them, she'd decided she had to avoid him until she'd had a chance to think about what had happened and figure out a logical reason for it.

The explanation that had crept into her mind while she was scrubbing her kitchen floor had been immediately dismissed. There was no way she could be falling in love with Connor MacCormac. Love was a gradual emotion. You came to love a person slowly, after getting to know him, weighing all his good and bad points, and making a rational decision about your future together.

It wasn't this passion that took control of your life, stealing all your logic and reason and turning you into a quivering mass of jelly. You didn't fall in love with the man you'd blamed for your sister's death for twelve long years.

Guilt washed through her again, and she said silently, *Forgive me, Barb*.

Aloud she said, "There's Jenna and Danny. Let's go and say hello."

As they walked toward the woman and child, Connor said abruptly, "Tell me about her."

She looked at him warily, and he smiled. "I'm not interested in her, Sarah." His voice deepened as he added in a whisper, "I thought I explained that to you earlier."

Blushing, she looked at where her friend stood unpacking a picnic basket. "Jenna's wonderful. She's the kindest, most thoughtful person in Pine Butte and one of my closest friends."

"Why couldn't she take her son's kitten to the vet?"

She glanced over at him, surprised. She had no idea he'd picked up on that. "She doesn't have a lot of money," she said carefully. "She couldn't afford to take the day off to go to the vet or pay the bill."

"What does her husband do?"

"Her husband left her when Danny was a year old. She hasn't heard from him since." She didn't bother to hide the fury she always felt when she thought about Sonny Franklin. "Jenna works in the grocery store. She has enough money to take care of herself and Danny, but it doesn't extend to extras like big vet bills."

She saw him clench his jaw. "How could a man abandon his wife and child like that?"

She turned to him, her gaze locking with his. He was waiting for her to say something about Barb, she realized. She saw it in his eyes, the way he braced himself for her sharp, cutting remark. But the words died on her lips.

Was she really choosing to believe this man over her own sister? No longer willing to look at him, afraid he would be able to read the longing in her eyes, she looked away. She let her gaze drift over the crowd. "Let's go get a hot dog," she said finally. "I'm starving." She didn't want to talk to anyone right now.

Before she could move away, he put his hand on her arm. She froze, feeling a jolt of awareness sizzle through her.

"Wait a minute, Sarah."

She turned slowly, afraid to look at him. His gaze burned into her until she reluctantly met his eyes.

"I didn't abandon Barb and it wasn't my child," he said, his voice low. "There's no way I can prove it to you. You're just going to have to decide whether you believe me."

There was no deceit in his eyes, just a steady flame that never flickered as she stared at him. She believed him, she realized with a sudden flood of guilt and despair. God help her, she did.

Barb's face rose up in front of her, contorted with agony as she lay dying on the back seat of their old car. And now Sarah imagined that her dying sister looked at her with disappointment, as well. How could she betray her sister this way? How could she believe the words of the man her sister had accused of abandoning her over the words of her own sister?

"I don't think this is the time or place for this discussion," she said, pulling away from him. Smoothing her palms down the flowered skirt she wore, she tried to hide the trembling in her hands. She could salvage a little of her pride as long as he didn't realize how he affected her.

"Besides—" she looked at him and forced herself to smile "—this is supposed to be a day for fun. Can you forget about everything else and just enjoy yourself?"

He simply stared at her for a moment. "Let's go get that hot dog," he said abruptly, and took her elbow as they began to walk.

As they threaded their way through clusters of people gathered around picnic tables, she saw heads turn and watch them pass. Chin high, she nodded and smiled to everyone who looked at them. One man called out, "Afternoon, Sarah, MacCormac."

Beside her she felt Connor tense again. He turned and looked at the man who'd spoken, and finally nodded. "Hi, Bill. Good to see you again."

There wasn't a trace of sarcasm in Connor's voice, and Sarah darted a look at Bill Winston, the man who'd spoken. He nodded deliberately to Connor, then turned to his family. She hadn't seen an ounce of malice or dislike in his face. Apparently Connor hadn't, either, because she felt him relax just a bit beside her.

Several other people greeted them as they wound their way past picnic tables and blankets spread out on the grass. Connor responded each time, cool and distant, although he seemed to remember a lot of names. By the time they had reached the bank of grills where members of the town council were busy turning hot dogs and chicken, she'd almost convinced herself they would get through the day without a confrontation.

After buying a piece of chicken and a hot dog for each of them, Connor turned to Sarah. "Do you think Jenna Franklin has had a chance to buy a hot dog for Danny yet?"

"Probably not. They looked like they'd just gotten here."

He handed her their two plates and asked for two more, and as she watched him she felt the last resistance in her heart melt away. He'd noticed the worry that shadowed Jenna's too-serious eyes when they talked about taking Misty to the vet. And after what Sarah had told him about the Franklins, Connor knew darned well that Jenna wouldn't be buying a hot dog for Danny or chicken for herself.

But he wouldn't embarrass her friend by playing the lord bountiful, either, she realized as they walked up to where Jenna and Danny sat on a blanket on the grass. Dropping down next to them, he handed the plates to Jenna and said easily, "We managed to get to the grills when there was a lull in the crowd, so I grabbed stuff for you and Danny, too. I didn't figure you'd want to fight the people and try to hold onto a wriggling kid at the same time."

Jenna stared at the plates and then glanced at the few people standing in line for food. She opened her mouth to object, then looked at her son's face. Danny was gazing at Connor with adoration.

"Thank you, Mr. Cormac," the child said.

"You're welcome, Danny."

"Yes, thank you, Mr. MacCormac. I was just waiting until the line got smaller." She reached behind her for her purse, but Connor raised his hand.

"Forget it, Jenna. It was my pleasure. And my name is Connor."

Jenna paused, her hand still on her purse, then she released her grip and slowly smiled at him. "Thank you, Connor," she whispered. "Danny was looking forward to a hot dog."

A look that spoke volumes passed between the two adults, and Sarah felt her heart expand until she thought it would leap out of her chest.

Leaning back and picking up a piece of chicken, Connor deliberately changed the subject. "How's Misty feeling?" he asked Danny.

"She's still very sad." The child frowned, then his eyes brightened. "But she likes her medicine."

Connor nodded thoughtfully. "It's a very big job, taking care of a sick kitten. But I think you can handle it."

"Oh, I can," Danny reassured him. "I made her a bed in my room and covered her with my favorite blanket."

"Sarah and I will stop by tomorrow and check on her, okay?"

"She'll be all better by then." The boy nodded confidently.

"Maybe not all better," Connor said gently. "But I'll bet she'll be eating a little."

Tenderness washed through Sarah as she watched him talk to Danny. He knew exactly what to say to the child. He'd be a wonderful father someday.

Stop it, she told herself vehemently, banishing the fantasies of a happy family from her mind. Connor had made it more than clear he wasn't staying in Pine Butte a second longer than it took to find out what had happened to his father.

A feeling of utter desolation and loss swept over her, and for a second she thought about leaving Pine Butte with Connor. They could travel together, she thought. All the faraway places she wanted to visit, all the exotic sights she'd been reading about for years tumbled through her head. Freedom danced in front of her, close enough to touch.

Slowly she opened her eyes and looked again at Connor. Munching on a piece of barbecued chicken, he looked out over the crowd and assessed it with thoughtful eyes.

This particular fantasy certainly had no basis in reality. Even if she was willing to abandon the town of Pine Butte, Connor had never even hinted that he wanted her to leave with him.

Danny's giggles interrupted her thoughts, and she looked up, startled, to see Connor waving a hand in front of her face and grinning.

"What planet were you visiting?" he teased.

She smiled bleakly. "One that hasn't been discovered yet."

His smile fading, he settled back and stared at her. Uncomfortable with his scrutiny, she jumped to her feet.

"Let's go walk around. You never know who we may run into."

Unfolding his long legs, he stood up and watched her for a moment. She glanced away, pretending to look around the picnic ground. Those bright blue eyes of his would see right into her heart and dissect all her secrets if she wasn't careful.

"Are we looking for anyone in particular?" he finally asked after they'd said goodbye to the Franklins.

She shrugged, still pretending to scan the crowd. "Not really. I just thought you wanted to mingle and pick up, uh, vibrations."

"I'm picking up vibrations, all right. From you. What's wrong?" he asked bluntly.

"Nothing's wrong," she answered, still not meeting his eyes. *I'm afraid that I'm falling in love with you, and that you're going to break my heart. Other than that, things are just peachy.* "I'm just looking for someone who might be able to help you."

She moved a step away from him, only to stop dead in her tracks when his fingers curled around her arm.

"What's bothering you, Sarah? And don't say nothing," he warned, "because I know better."

Her gaze scanned the crowd frantically. She didn't want to have this discussion at all, let alone in public. "Look, there's Tom and Mary Johnson. You remember him, don't you? The sheriff? He talked to you the morning after you were hurt."

"Yeah, I remember him." Connor looked away from Sarah reluctantly and glanced over to where the Johnsons sat on a blanket with their two children. He hadn't heard a word from Tom Johnson since the morning after his accident when he'd told the sheriff he'd suspected someone had run him off the road deliberately.

"Let's go say hello."

She was already moving away from him. He hadn't missed the relief on her face. She'd have hurried toward anyone right now, even her uncle. Frowning at Sarah's back, he slowly followed her.

She'd dropped down onto the blanket and was talking animatedly to a thin-faced, pale woman who held a toddler on her lap. As he stood looming over both the women, Sarah looked up at him.

For just a moment, she forgot to shield her face. Her eyes softened when they met his, and something unbearably tender lurked in their sea-colored depths. Then she blinked, and the mask was in place again.

But he hadn't mistaken that look. His heart pounded and his chest tightened. Impossible as it might seem, apparently the desire he felt for her was mutual.

He refused to call it anything other than desire. He didn't believe in anything more than that. There was no such thing as love and happily ever after. Two people had a mutual itch, they scratched it and that was that. He refused to make it more complicated.

Except with Sarah, it had been more complicated than that from the very beginning.

"Do you remember Tom Johnson?" Sarah's low voice asked.

"Of course." He extended his hand and gripped the sheriff's firmly. "How're you doing?"

The short, stocky man shrugged. "Pretty well." He glanced around nervously. "You enjoying our town picnic?"

"So far. Whoever's in charge cooks a mean chicken." He nodded at the two small children. "Are your kids having fun?"

Tom licked his lips and nodded. "Mary can barely keep up with them, the way they run around." He glanced over at her. "She has to hold them down to get any rest."

Connor looked at the woman and noticed that she did look exhausted. The little boy in her lap suddenly jumped up and ran off, and he realized why. She was in the advanced stages of pregnancy.

Out of the corner of his eye he saw that Tom had quickly jumped up to chase after his son. The expression of relief that flitted across his face set Connor's antennae quivering, but he was suddenly distracted by the woman in front of him struggling to stand up.

He jumped to his feet and extended a hand to help her up. When her hand curled around his, he felt the swelling in her fingers and wrist. Studying her face, he realized that she was, indeed, too thin for this far along in her pregnancy. Glancing down, he saw what he'd expected. Her feet were swollen almost out of her shoes.

"You must be having a hard time in this heat," he murmured.

She looked startled, as if his words were the last thing she'd expected him to say. Then she nodded slowly. "That, and keeping track of two other kids." A tiny smile crossed her face. "I'll try to plan better next time."

Connor smiled back, but continued to watch her. It was far more than the heat and stress of two kids that was making Mary Johnson's face so pinched. And her hands and feet so swollen. Making a mental note to ask Sarah about her, he turned and followed the direction of her gaze.

Tom had swung their son, who looked to be about three, onto his shoulders. He held their daughter, a thin, delicate-looking child, by the hand as the trio walked slowly back to the blanket.

He knew, with a certainty he couldn't doubt, that Tom was hoping they'd be gone by the time he got back to his wife. Connor stood and watched him as he approached. Tom Johnson's behavior was the first odd thing he'd noticed today, and he had no intention of walking away. The tiny frisson of something wrong washed over him again, the same feeling he'd had the first time he'd met Tom.

Tom swung the child off his shoulders and stood watching as he ran around his mother. According to what the sheriff had said, he hadn't lived in Pine Butte when Connor left. So why did he look so damned familiar?

Refusing to meet Connor's eyes, the sheriff asked, "Have you remembered anything more about that car that hit you?"

"No, I haven't." His lips curved slightly upward. "Other than it was big."

Tom darted a look at him and smiled nervously. "I haven't heard a thing. Nobody's taken their car into Billy at the service station for bodywork, and no one's reported any accidents. I've been checking around, looking at cars and asking some discreet questions. If anybody knows anything, they're not talking."

Connor looked at the sheriff in surprise. Somehow, with the way he'd been acting around him, Connor hadn't expected the sheriff to be pursuing his problem in more than a very superficial way. It sounded as if he'd been spending some time with it, actually making an effort to find out what had happened.

"Thanks," he said slowly. "I appreciate that. But I doubt if you're going to find anything."

"Probably not," Tom agreed. "It's been five days. If it was really an accident, someone would have come forward by now."

He seemed a lot more comfortable talking about Connor's problem than making small talk, and as Connor watched him, some of the suspicion in his chest began to ease. There were a lot of people who were more comfortable talking about their field of expertise than chatting socially.

"Let me know if anything turns up."

"Will do." The sheriff cleared his throat. "You still staying at the clinic?"

He nodded casually. "Sarah insisted. Said something about head injuries," he answered easily. "I figured it wouldn't be smart to alienate the only medical person in town."

A quick flash of relief passed over Tom's face. "Our Sarah can be pretty stubborn," he agreed.

Was he concerned about Sarah, he wondered, staying alone with him? Or did Tom have some other motive for asking where he was staying?

Connor turned away abruptly. Everyone in this town was a suspect, he reminded himself. Even the sheriff, who had been surprisingly ready to help him. Maybe the man was just a good actor.

Sarah turned away from Mary Johnson just then and gave him a questioning look. He nodded slightly even as he wondered about the understanding that flowed between them. Why did he seem to know so easily what she was thinking?

"I'll talk to you soon, Mary," she said. "Remember, I want you to come into the clinic sometime in the next few days. At this stage of your pregnancy, I should be checking you every week."

"All right, Sarah. But you're worrying about nothing."

"Come in and prove it to me."

Connor said goodbye to Tom and Mary and looked at Sarah as they walked away. "What is the nothing that you're worrying about?"

"I just don't like the way she looks," she answered slowly. "This pregnancy has been a hard one for Mary, and worrying about her daughter, Jenny, hasn't helped any."

"What's wrong with her daughter?"

"She needs heart surgery, and Mary's worried sick. About the danger, about the expense, about everything connected with it."

"I didn't think Mary looked very good, either," he said slowly. Looking at Sarah, seeing the worry on her face for her friend, he wanted to gather her close. "You would have made a good doctor." His voice sounded gruff.

She looked at him then, a sad smile on her face. "Thank you. I always thought so, too." She straightened her back and said fiercely, "But I am a damn good nurse practitioner."

"That you are," he murmured. *Tell her,* he told himself fiercely. *Tell her now.* But the same fear that had him in its grip when Perry Cummings came to town grabbed him by the throat and wouldn't let go. He wanted to be free to tell Sarah about himself, to tell her his secrets, but the fear and caution he'd learned over his lifetime sealed his lips. He would tell her later, he assured himself, when they weren't in public and surrounded by an audience. She wouldn't want him to tell her now, anyway.

She interrupted his thoughts by veering abruptly to the left. "Let's go over here."

He automatically looked the way they'd been going and stopped dead in his tracks. Ralph Wesley was holding court near the center of the picnic activities, and Sarah had obviously swerved to avoid him. "Sarah, wait."

"Not here, Connor." Her voice pleaded with him. "Save your confrontation for somewhere a little more private. Don't make the people in Pine Butte choose publicly between you and my uncle."

"I wasn't planning on confronting him. But I don't have any intention of letting him scare me away, either. If he wants an ugly scene, I'm not going to stop him."

"All I'm asking is that we not walk right into him. That's all."

He looked at her. Her eyes pleaded with him to walk away with her, and he was helpless against her. "All right, Sarah. Let's pretend we're fascinated with the horseshoe game over there."

"Thank you," she murmured, looking at the ground as they walked.

He took another look over his shoulder and saw Ralph Wesley and Harley Harrison, his foreman, deep in conversation. Every once in a while the foreman's eyes flickered in his direction.

"I can wait," Connor said softly. "But not for long."

The rest of the day drifted by in a haze of barbecue smoke and memories of long-past Pine Butte town picnics. To his surprise, Connor actually found himself having a good time. More and more people stopped him to say hello, and although most of them were a little tentative, no one was hostile. That seemed to be confined, he thought wryly, to the Wesley family. With one exception. He glanced at Sarah again.

She hadn't budged from his side all day. He couldn't miss the speculative looks directed at her by some of the townspeople, but she'd merely held her head higher and moved a little closer to him.

As dusk swallowed the daylight behind the mountains, they wandered toward the edge of the crowd. Suddenly he wanted, more than anything, to be alone with her. He needed to wrap himself in her courage, lose himself in the depths of her eyes that shone like emeralds in the dim light. He needed some of her strength for himself.

"Let's go home," he whispered, and she turned to look at him. Her eyes flashed with something that made him hold his breath, then she licked her lips and slowly nodded.

"Yes."

He reached for her hand, threading his fingers between hers. As the voices and laughter faded away behind them, she moved closer to him.

They were still in the park when her uncle Ralph suddenly appeared in front of them. For a moment, he seemed just as startled as they were. Then he looked from Sarah to Connor and something dark and ugly flashed in his eyes.

"Stay away from him, Sarah. He's nothing but trouble."

If Connor hadn't reached out with his free hand and grabbed her wrist, she would have stepped in front of him. For a second he looked at her, puzzled; then he realized what she was doing.

Sarah was trying to protect him from Ralph Wesley. Another door in his heart, one he'd thought nailed shut forever, swung open with a rusty creak. The hand that held her wrist gentled and his thumb stroked her arm softly.

"It's all right, sweetheart," he whispered.

Her eyes widened at the endearment and she just stared at him. Stepping in front of her, he looked at Ralph Wesley.

His fists clenched as he stared at Ralph. A man who very likely knew exactly what had happened to his father. Who might have had a role in his death. Closing his eyes, he tightened his hold on Sarah's hand. *Not now,* he warned himself. Not with Sarah standing next to him.

"Sarah's a big girl," he finally answered, his voice carefully neutral. "She can make her own decisions."

Fury gathered in Ralph Wesley's face, and his eyes narrowed to slits. "I wasn't talking to you," he said with venom.

"But I'm talking to you. Tell me, Wesley, exactly what is it that you have against me? You've never really said."

Ralph Wesley's face mottled with rage. "As if you had to ask. Coming back here, after the way you left, after what you did to my niece . . ." His voice trailed off and he stood staring at Connor with hard eyes. Finally he said, "You're no damn good, MacCormac, just like your father before you."

"It always comes back to my father, doesn't it?" Connor answered softly. "But he's been dead for eighteen years."

Still holding Sarah's hand, he stepped around the older man and walked away. He didn't have to turn around to know Wesley was staring after him. The spot between his shoulder blades burned.

As they turned a corner and disappeared from Ralph Wesley's view, Connor heard Sarah draw a shaky breath. Dropping her hand, he draped his arm over her shoulder and pulled her close as they walked.

"I'm sorry. I promised no confrontations today."

"It wasn't your fault." She took another deep breath, and it seemed to Connor that she moved closer to him. "He came looking for us."

"I don't think he did," Connor answered thoughtfully. "I think he was as surprised as we were."

"If that's true, he sure made a quick recovery."

He heard the chagrin in her voice and looked at her in amazement. "You're not responsible for what your uncle says or does. Why are you ashamed?"

It was a while before she answered. Finally she burst out, "He makes me ashamed to be a Wesley, to be related to someone who thinks like that. What he said was...was despicable."

He felt his eyes burn. He couldn't remember the last time anyone had defended him so passionately. "What he said about Barb?" he forced himself to ask.

"No, what he said about you." Her answer was immediate. "And about your father. He sounds like he was an honest, hardworking man."

"He was." His mouth tightened. If Ralph Wesley was responsible for his father's death, it would give Connor great pleasure to make him pay.

"I'm going to the mine tomorrow," he said abruptly. "It's time to have a little talk with both Ralph and Richard."

"I'm coming with you." Her response was immediate.

"You can't, Sarah. It could be dangerous."

"All the more reason for me to go. Not even my cousin Richard is stupid enough to do something in front of a witness."

They'd reached the door of the clinic and she fumbled with the lock. Stepping inside, she reached for the light, but he stopped her. "I don't want anything to happen to you, Sarah. I couldn't leave here with that on my conscience. I have no idea what's going to happen tomorrow at the mine, but I think it's a safe bet that it won't be pretty. You're too...important to me to let you take that kind of chance."

She faced him in the darkness, only her silhouette visible in the faint moonlight. Her eyes gleamed like the sea at midnight. "And you're too important to me to let you go alone. I can't do it, Connor."

"Sarah, no," he groaned. "Don't say things like that."

"Why not?" She lifted her chin a notch. "It's true. It's too bad if you don't want to hear that people care about you. I do." Her voice softened. "You're a good man, Connor MacCormac. It didn't take long for me to see that."

"You blame me for your sister's death." He desperately brought up the one thing guaranteed to push her away from him. He had no defenses against her. She had to be the one who stopped him from making a fool of himself.

"You told me it wasn't you," she said slowly. "And I believe you." Guilt, sorrow and pain flashed over her face. "God help me, I do believe you."

"Sarah," he whispered, closing his eyes and reaching blindly for her. "Sarah, I'm sorry."

He pulled her against his chest and held her there, burying his face in the fragrant mass of her hair. A hot dampness burned through his shirt, and he realized she was crying.

"I'm sorry," he said again, his arms tightening. "I should have let you go on believing it was me."

Raising her tear-drenched face to his, she said fiercely, "No! Why would you want to let me think something so wicked of you?"

"I would do anything to spare you this pain." He smoothed one hand down her hair, letting the silk flow over his fingers. "You shouldn't have to face this kind of betrayal after losing your sister."

"You'd rather I think you were capable of abandoning her and her unborn baby?"

"It would be less painful for you," he muttered, trying to ease away from her. He was supposed to be comforting her. Some comfort he would be if she realized how aroused he was.

"Barb's been dead for almost twelve years." She leaned back in his arms to look up at him. The light in her eyes made him want to pull her close again. "Yes, it hurts terribly to think that she didn't trust me with the truth. It would hurt far more, though, to think you were capable of such a terrible thing."

"I'm trying to do the right thing here, Sarah," he groaned. "You can't get involved with me." He sounded desperate, even to his own ears.

She inched her arms around his neck. "It's too late, Connor. I already am involved with you. I think it was too late the moment I saw you lying on the side of the mountain on Eagle Ridge Road."

He closed his eyes while the need stabbed him. Tensing every muscle in his body, he tried to step away from her. "It's not too late to stop. I don't want to hurt you, Sarah. And if you don't go upstairs to your apartment right now, alone, I'm going to hurt you. Eventually."

"Maybe you will. But I don't want to play it safe anymore. I can't."

She paused, and his hands crept up to frame her face. In the darkness he felt the heat sweep into her cheeks. "I want you, Connor." Her whisper echoed in the darkened room. "Do you want me?"

"More than life itself," he groaned, lowering his mouth to hers. "God help us, Sarah. I think I'll die from wanting you."

Chapter 11

As Sarah stared at Connor she saw pain and desperate need in his eyes. His heart boomed against hers where she pressed against his chest, and his arms were like steel bands around her.

His struggle to step away from her was mirrored in his face. As she tightened her arms around him, she wondered briefly what had happened to the cautious, careful woman who hadn't been involved with a man since she'd come back to live in Pine Butte.

Now all her caution, all her good sense, had flown out the window, along with all her inhibitions. Her face flamed as she thought about what she'd just said. Sarah Wesley most definitely didn't ask men if they wanted her.

"Sarah?" he whispered. "Tell me to stop now. Please. If you don't, I won't be able to stop."

Slowly she shook her head. "I don't want you to stop, Connor."

The rest of her words were swallowed as his mouth descended on hers. She tasted his pounding need, his passion, in a kiss that seemed to draw out her soul. She gave it to him freely.

He pulled her even closer, until every inch of their bodies was touching. Suddenly he lifted her up and moved a few steps until her back pressed against the wall. His mouth fastened to hers, he let her slowly slide down his body. She had no doubts about the degree of his desire for her.

He swept his tongue into her mouth, searching out all the secret places and twining around her tongue in a sinuous dance. He tasted of passion and heat, like every forbidden pleasure she'd ever wanted. Cupping her hips in his gentle, clever hands, he rocked against her, making her cling more tightly to him as wave after wave of sensation washed over her.

His hands fumbled with the buttons of her blouse. She could feel them trembling as he tried to push the tiny buttons through the buttonholes. Feathering her hands over the soft material of his polo shirt, she traced the outline of hard muscles as shudders wracked him.

Her fingers found his hard, flat male nipples through the thin fabric and lingered for a moment, softly exploring. He surged against her, his hands clenching in the soft cotton of her blouse.

"Ah, Sarah, be careful. That couch is too close for comfort." He leaned back and looked at her, his eyes glittering. "And I remember how it feels all too well."

She pressed against him again and reached up to kiss him. "I didn't want to stop then, either."

He groaned. "I want to make love with you all night long, in that big bed of yours upstairs. If you're not careful, we'll never make it that far."

Sliding her hands slowly down his chest, she lingered for a moment at the waistband of his jeans. Dipping one finger inside the fabric, she twined it around the hair that feathered down his flat, hard belly. "I don't think I would mind standing right here with you all night," she whispered.

He shifted suddenly and pulled her toward him. Nuzzling her neck, he took her hand and led her toward the door to her apartment. "Not a chance, Sarah. I have plans for you. And they don't include the floor of your clinic."

"Who said anything about the floor?" she murmured as he started up the stairs. "I was having fun just where we were."

Curling his arm around her, he led her up the dark stairwell. His hand casually brushed her breast and she stiffened. "I know some games, too, love." He dipped his head and kissed her thoroughly. When he raised his head she looked around, disoriented. They were in her bedroom. The moon dappled the white lace of her bedspread with a pearly light, making it glow in the darkness.

Lowering her onto the bed, he stood for a moment and looked at her. She felt suddenly cold and foolish without his arms around her and his body pressing against hers. He'd think she was an idiot, teasing him like that.

"Don't, love," he whispered, pulling his shirt over his head. "Don't think it, not even for a second." Unbuttoning his jeans, he shucked them down his legs then straightened, standing in front of her in low-cut red briefs that did nothing to hide the extent of his arousal from her.

"Don't think what?" she asked, feeling her cheeks heat.

"Don't think you're making a fool of yourself. That's what you're doing, isn't it?"

How could she be so transparent? Slowly she nodded.

"I love every minute of it," he said passionately. "Can't you tell?"

She looked at him again, letting her gaze rest on the bulge straining the front of his briefs. She nodded again and let her gaze roam upward. He was as magnificent as she knew he'd be. His flat belly was dusted with dark hair, and his chest was sleek with muscle. She'd completely forgotten about the bandage wrapped around his ribs, and when she saw it she sat up straight.

"Connor, I forgot all about your ribs." She sprang up from the bed and touched the bandage gently. "Won't it hurt, to, you know..."

He caught her hand in his and brought it to his mouth. "No, it won't hurt. Trust me."

Bringing her other hand to his bandaged chest, she gently caressed the injured ribs. "I don't know. It's only been a few days since your accident. I kind of forgot all about it—" she waved her hand toward the stairs vaguely, "—back downstairs." She felt her face flame but kept doggedly on. "Maybe we shouldn't take a chance that you'll hurt yourself again."

"Sarah, stop. I'm hurting now." There was a smile in his voice but she refused to look at him. "There's another part of my anatomy that's going to be permanently damaged if we stop now. You wouldn't want to be responsible for that, would you?"

Her lips curved in a little smile and she finally looked at him. "Absolutely not. As a medical person, I took an oath to do no harm. You could probably report me to the authorities."

He smiled back at her, one of his dazzling, all-too-infrequent smiles. Catching her breath, she could only stare at him.

He drew her off the bed and pulled her close, resting his chin on the top of her head. His sigh vibrated through her. "I want you more than I've ever wanted anything or anyone in my life." He bent his head, nuzzling her neck. His warm breath stirred the hair behind her ear and made her shiver. "I want you so much I'm scared to death."

"I'm scared, too, Connor. I didn't plan on fa—getting involved with you or anyone else."

He pulled back just enough to see her face. "Then give me your hands and we'll face it together."

Slowly she raised her hands and twined them with his. As they held tightly to each other, their mouths met in a tender, gentle kiss. She told him everything that she couldn't put into words, everything that she wasn't ready to say and he wasn't ready to hear. Still holding hands, they tumbled onto the bed.

The moonlight bathed his strong, lithe body as he lay next to her. Propping himself up on one elbow, he swept his fingers over her hair, down her cheek, and rested them in the hollow of her collarbone. She knew he could feel her pulse pound. He watched her for what seemed like a long time, then he bent and kissed her again.

This time he made no effort to hide his desire. His mouth locked on hers and his tongue swept past her lips. Shifting his legs, he slid on top of her and fitted himself into the V of her legs.

He was on fire. His chest burned her, even through the cotton of her blouse. With one knee he pushed the fabric of her skirt out of the way and twined his bare legs against hers. Heat pooled in her belly and burned its way down to the place between her legs. Her arms and legs were too heavy to lift.

He trailed his lips down her cheek and stopped at her ear. Taking her earlobe between his teeth, he suckled it gently while one hand unbuttoned her blouse. Shivering, she clutched him more tightly and waited, muscles tense, while he swept her blouse off her shoulders.

A quick flick of his fingers and the clasp to her bra came unfastened. Suddenly she felt very vulnerable, lying in the moonlight bared to the waist. He lifted his head from the side of her neck and stared at her.

Finally he looked up. "You're magnificent. All of my dreams pale beside the reality. Sarah, I—" He stopped and kissed her again, pouring himself into her. One hand cupped her breast almost reverently. When he drew his thumb slowly across the hard nipple, she arched, feeling the stab of need all the way down to her core.

He looked at her, a hot look glittering in his eyes. "You like that?"

"You know I do," she gasped. "Please, Connor..."

Bending his head, he nuzzled between her breasts, a finger on each nipple. Kneading, stroking and gently squeezing, he explored thoroughly. She was in a frenzy of need when he finally took one hard bud into his mouth.

She wrapped her legs around him and moved against him. Reaching down with one hand, she tried to pull his tight briefs down his legs. His hand reached for her wrist, gentle but firm.

"Not yet, love. I want this to last for a while. If I was naked against you..." His voice trailed off in a groan and he surged against her. Letting go of her wrist, he fumbled desperately with the waistband of her skirt until he found the button that held it together. Sweeping the skirt down her legs, he hooked his fingers in her panties and pulled them off, too.

She lay naked in front of him, but all her self-consciousness had disappeared a long time ago. This was Connor, and nothing had ever been so right. Running her hands up his back, she gloried in his tense muscles that quivered at her touch. She was awed by the knowledge that she could bring him to this, that she could make him hold onto his control by a single, thin thread.

He slid his hand down her belly to the juncture of her thighs. Cupping her in his hand, he lay still for a moment. She felt his struggle with control even as she squirmed against him. He shuddered once, then began to stroke her.

It was too much. She felt herself hanging on the edge, and she reached down to pull his briefs away again. "I need you, Connor. Now." She barely recognized her voice, trembling with passion.

"I don't want it to be over yet," he answered, the agony of control in his voice. "You deserve more than this."

"I can't wait," she whispered, reaching down and slipping her hand inside his briefs. Closing her hand around him, she felt him grow even harder. His hips jerked and he rolled away from her suddenly.

Stripping off the briefs, he sat up on the edge of the bed and reached for his jeans. Moonlight reflected off the little foil packet he ripped open. The next second he was laying on top of her, spreading her legs and lowering his mouth to her breast again.

When she arched into him this time, he drove into her. She gasped and froze, feeling him fill her. Jerking his head up, he looked at her, stricken. "I hurt you. I'm sorry."

"You didn't," she said fiercely. "It's just...been a while."

"Sarah," he began, but she wrapped her arms around him and pulled him close.

"Love me, Connor. You don't know how much I want you to love me."

He moved a little and she froze again, overwhelmed by the sensations coursing through her. She slid her hands up his back, slick with sweat from his battle to go slow. Arching into him, she twined her legs around him. When she reached down to cup his hips in her hands, the last vestige of his control fled.

Murmuring her name over and over, he moved faster and faster, harder and harder. She wrapped her arms and legs around him as she felt herself falling, and suddenly everything exploded in light and color. Clinging to him, she felt him stiffen and whisper her name again and again as he emptied himself into her.

They lay entwined for a long time, holding each other tightly as their breathing returned to normal. Connor shifted once and tried to slide off her, but she refused to let him go.

"I don't want to hurt you."

"You're not."

"How about this, then?" He spoke as he turned suddenly, and she found herself stretched out on top of him.

"Mm," she said, snuggling closer to him.

"Sarah." Brushing her hair away from her face, he willed her to look at him.

Opening her eyes, she looked at his face. The faint echoes of passion were still reflected in the hard planes of his cheekbones. "What?" she whispered.

His face softened as he watched her. "Nothing, just 'Sarah.'"

"Connor," she mocked softly. "What's wrong? Are you regretting this?"

"Never." He gave her a slow, deep kiss. "I'll treasure this night for the rest of my life. I was just afraid that you were having some regrets."

"How could I?" she asked. "I lo—" She bit her lip and corrected quickly, "I loved every minute. Couldn't you tell?"

He stroked one hand down her back and over her buttocks, and the heat began again. "I thought so, but I wasn't sure."

"Well, I'm a nurse, so that means I'm a scientist. Maybe we should use the scientific method."

"Mm." His hand kneaded one hip and slipped between her legs in a brief, feather-soft touch. "You mean see if the results are reproducible?"

"Something like that," she moaned as his hand found her again.

"I like the way you think." He slid her down his body and she felt him, hard and ready. "There're a lot of different experiments that I have in mind, though."

Closing her hand around him, she murmured, "Well, what are you waiting for? We have only another twelve hours before tomorrow gets here."

"I think I could get to be a real fan of the scientific process."

Daylight streamed across her face and Sarah rolled over, bumping into something hard and warm in her bed. Sitting up and opening her eyes with a start, she saw Connor sprawled on the bed next to her, the sheet barely covering him and leaving nothing to her imagination.

She lay down slowly, feeling an unaccustomed stiffness in her body from the night before. She ached in places she'd almost forgotten she had. Pulling the sheet over herself, she looked at him and smiled softly.

It had been an enchanted evening, full of magic and moonbeams. However, this morning would be quite another story, she was afraid. Knowing what she did of Connor, she was sure that any hint of clinging or possessiveness would be enough to send him flying away from her. The last thing he wanted was to feel bound to her.

Well, she could play it casual with the best of them. She'd give him all the time he needed to realize he couldn't live without her. Slowly laying down, she slid over until she nestled against him. In a few more minutes it would be back to reality. For now, she could pretend she belonged there.

Connor stirred and stretched, noticing with satisfaction that his ribs hardly hurt at all. Suddenly he realized he wasn't alone in the bed, and his eyes snapped open.

Sarah was curled around him, her eyes closed and a dreamy smile on her face. Memories of the night before cascaded over him and he felt his body responding. Before he knew what he was doing, he reached out and pulled her into his arms.

She opened her eyes slowly and smiled at him. "Good morning." Her voice was husky with sleep and pleasure, and deep contentment filled her face.

His arms tightened and he bent to kiss her. If he lived to be a hundred, he didn't think he'd ever get tired of waking up next to her.

Except that there was no way he could get used to it. Slowly, as if he was tearing away a piece of himself, he moved away from her and sat up. "Good morning, Sarah."

She watched him for a moment, a tender smile on her face. Then she sat up, clutching the sheet above her breasts, and shook her hair out of her face. "Do you want to use the shower first, or shall I?"

What he wanted was to pull that sheet away from her and sink back into her sweetness, to spend the rest of today and the next several lifetimes in this bed with her. "You go ahead," he said gruffly, leaning against the headboard. At least he could watch her walk to the shower.

Jumping off the bed, she twisted the sheet around herself and headed for the bathroom down the hall. She paused at the door and turned around, saying softly, "I'll only be a minute."

Then she was gone, and he leaned forward, resting his elbows on his knees and frowning at the place where she'd disappeared. She was being awfully casual about this whole business, as if waking up in bed with a man wasn't that unusual.

But he knew otherwise. Every move she'd made, every surprised little cry and subtle tensing of unused muscles had told him it had been a long time for her. Standing up, he looked around for the clothes he'd discarded so hastily the night before. She was probably just trying to make it easier for him, and he stood in the hallway and stared at the closed bathroom door.

He'd give anything if he could have met Sarah Wesley in a different place and under different circumstances. He hadn't known people like her still existed. She was good to the core, a luminous, shining woman. And she made him burn with a desire that was like a fever.

Who had he been fooling? One night with her would never be enough. It had just whetted his appetite, made him realize what he'd be missing when he went home to Denver.

And going home to Denver was inevitable. There was no place for him in this town. And he didn't care. He didn't want Pine Butte, either.

Hearing the shower stop, he turned and headed for the stairs and his clean clothes and shower in the bedroom in the clinic. Knowing he had to go, he tried to tell himself he could leave Sarah alone, that he wouldn't hurt her any more than he already had. As he stood in the lonely room downstairs, hearing her padding around in the apartment above him, he wondered who he was trying to fool.

Walking slowly up the stairs twenty minutes later, he heard pans clinking on the stove and a radio cheerfully reciting the time and temperature. When he hesitantly entered the kitchen, Sarah turned and gave him a bright smile.

"I thought I'd make pancakes and bacon. I'm starving this morning."

Her face colored slightly at the last words and she turned to the stove. Without thinking, he walked over to her and wrapped his arms around her waist.

"Me, too." He nuzzled her neck. "What do you say we have dessert first?"

For just a moment she melted into him, then pulled herself together and stood up straight. "Everyone knows you don't have dessert with breakfast. You need something substantial to start the day."

"What I have in mind would be very substantial. And it would be a great way to start the day." His hands crept upward until they cupped her breasts. In spite of all his lectures to himself in the shower, he wanted her as much as he had the night before. More. Now he knew what it would be like.

Dropping the spatula into the frying pan with the bacon, she turned around slowly in his arms. "I've never had dessert for breakfast," she whispered. "But I'm always open to new experiences."

Closing his eyes, he bent and kissed her. It was too late to pull away, to play it casually the way he'd planned to do. He was going under fast, and there was no lifeline in sight.

Taking her hand, he led her out of the kitchen and into the bedroom. She'd made the bed and picked up her clothes, leaving the room looking as pristine and untouched as it had been before last night.

Staring at her for a minute, trying desperately to distance himself from her, he gazed into her wide, trusting blue-green eyes. It was like gazing into a pure, crystal-clear stream. He could see all the way into her soul, and there wasn't a shadow of doubt in her.

Finally, releasing the breath he hadn't even realized he'd been holding, he kissed her again and felt her drawing him down onto the bed. As she murmured his name, he closed his eyes to block out the truth. For now, he would see only what he wanted to see. And that was only Sarah.

When they finally ate breakfast, the bacon was burned and the pancakes were dry. Taking a bite, she wrinkled her nose. "Are you sure you don't want to go to Earlene's?"

"Positive," he replied. "We wouldn't have nearly as much privacy at Earlene's." He watched her, feeling his body stirring again as a blush washed over her cheeks. "And there are certain times when a man wants privacy."

Her cheeks still red, she pushed away from the table and began running water to wash the breakfast dishes. "We've had about all the privacy we're going to get, for the morning at least. Josie'll be here soon and my patients won't be far behind her."

"And I need to get going, too."

She spun around, fear on her face. "You're not still planning to go to the mine, are you?"

"I have to, Sarah. Nobody's going to come up to me and say, 'Oh, by the way, MacCormac, you want to hear what happened to your father?' If I want any answers, I have to dig them out myself."

She leaned against the counter, a soapy dark blue coffee mug clutched in her hand. "All right, then, I'm coming with you. I told you I would last night and I meant it. I don't want you going out there alone."

"You have patients coming this morning, Sarah. You can't just take off." He figured that appealing to her sense of duty would be the quickest way to head her off.

"Josie can reschedule them. We won't be gone all day. And besides," she said firmly, her eyes filling with excitement, "I have the perfect reason to go out to the mine."

He could see a plan churning in her mind, and in spite of his determination he felt himself getting caught up in her excitement. "What's that?"

"There are a bunch of papers I have to fill out for workers' compensation about Chet's accident. It would be natural to go out to the mine to get Richard's signature and pretend I had to check up on some facts."

"Why would you have to check on things at the mine for Chet's accident? Wouldn't that be Richard's job?"

"Probably, but he won't realize that right away. By the time he does, we'll be gone and you'll have checked what you need."

"I think you missed your calling," he said ruefully, knowing it was inevitable he would give in to her. "You should have been a detective. I can just see you in a long trench coat, badgering some poor sap into confessing just to get you off his back."

"Is that why you're agreeing with me, just to get me off your back?" She grinned at him and pushed a strand of hair away from her face, leaving a trail of soapsuds across her cheek.

"I didn't say I agreed with you," he grumbled, smiling in spite of himself as she turned back to her chore. "Besides, who said I wanted you off my back?" His voice dropped as he watched the subtle tug of her jeans against her rounded fanny as she moved back and forth at the sink.

"Good, it's settled, then." Throwing an impish smile over her shoulder, she said, "I'll check with Josie and then we can leave."

The sink made a sucking sound as she pulled the plug. She hurried out of the room. After a moment he shook himself and stood up. If he didn't watch himself, he was going to be in way too deep. There was no way anything could work out for him and Sarah. They both knew that once he found out the truth about his father he was leaving Pine Butte, and there was no way he could ask her to go with him. Hell, she couldn't go with him if she wanted to. And he knew her well enough to know she would never abandon her patients here in Pine Butte, not even for him.

Twenty minutes later they were sweating in her old truck, bouncing up the steep grade to the entrance of the Wesley mine. They hadn't said much on the drive, and now she looked at him, worry in her eyes.

"What exactly are you going to do?"

"I'm not really sure," he answered slowly. "I know damn well that Ralph Wesley and your cousin Richard aren't going to tell me anything, and I'm not stupid enough to ask them any direct questions. Two accidents in a week are plenty."

He stared out the window, not noticing the breathtaking scenery all around him. "But there has to be someone who knows something besides them," he said slowly. "A lot of these guys have worked at the mine forever, right?"

She nodded. "There aren't that many other jobs in Pine Butte." Her voice was subdued.

"So I'm just going to keep my eyes open. If anyone looks guilty, or scared, or anything other than curious, I'll talk to them later, when Ralph and Richard aren't around to stifle the conversation."

"Don't you think that if there had been something suspicious about your father's death, and anyone else knew about it, there would have been rumors long ago?"

He heard the agony in her voice and longed to comfort her. But there was nothing he could say. Before he was finished, he had no doubt that her family would be implicated, one way or another.

"Maybe not. He was dead, and my mother and I sure didn't have a lot of friends in this town. Nobody was going to stick up for the foreigner's widow and wild kid, that's for sure."

"Connor, I'm so sorry about that," she said impulsively. "Nobody here is like that anymore, believe me."

A sarcastic answer formed on his lips, but he closed his mouth as he looked at her. "Maybe not," he said finally, astonished to realize that she might be right. Not a soul he'd talked to at the picnic yesterday had been anything but courteous and polite. They were all reserved, but he acknowledged grudgingly that they had good reason to be. Undoubtedly they all thought what even Sarah had believed was true—that he'd gotten Barb Wesley pregnant, then run off and left her to die by herself.

"From everything I've heard, maybe you gave them good reasons to dislike you," she said softly.

"I was just a kid."

"Who didn't act like the other kids," she pointed out. "Maybe they were afraid of your influence on their sons and daughters. These are average, middle-class, conservative people, Connor. You were probably a wonderful person." He heard her voice soften and wanted to reach out for her, right there on the road. "But you never gave them a chance to find out. You were too busy acting out your pain and anger.

"Think of it from their point of view," she urged. "Parents are already scared when their kids hit puberty and the teenage years, and most of them try to clamp down even harder on their own kids. Imagine how you would feel about a wild rebel in your midst if you were a parent. You'd be pretty nervous, too."

He was silent for a long time. Finally he said, "How did you get to be so damn wise at your age? You don't even have any kids of your own." His voice was gruff.

"I just listen to what my patients tell me." She glanced at him, her eyes tender. "How did you know how to talk to Danny Franklin when you don't have any kids of your own?"

He opened his mouth to respond to her when he saw the entrance to the mine ahead of them on the road. Swiveling around in his seat, he snapped to attention as they passed the gates. Sarah waved casually to the man sitting there in a folding chair.

"Here we are," she said, unnecessarily. "Are you ready?"

"I've been ready for eighteen years."

Chapter 12

Sarah drove toward the old two-story building that housed the offices of Wesley Mining, Inc. Dusty and in need of a coat of paint, it squatted on the side of the mountain, looking as if a strong wind would send it down into the parking lot below.

Dreary and cheerless, that office had always seemed to Sarah a perfect symbol of the mine itself. Employees hurried from place to place, heads down and unsmiling. A line of men stood beside the tracks and waited for the ore cars to shoot out of the hole in the ground. As they hurried to unload them, there was no talking or joking. They worked in grim silence, barely emptying one car before another took its place.

"Fun place," Connor muttered as he stepped out of the truck.

"Uncle Ralph doesn't believe in having fun at work," she answered dryly. "All work and no play makes the Wesleys a lot more money."

"And makes accidents like Chet's inevitable. Those ore cars are coming too close together. Even I can see that." He stood, hands jammed into the pockets of his jeans, and watched the men work for a minute. "For your sake, I hope Chet doesn't hire a sharp lawyer."

"Why would it matter to me? If he's entitled to compensation for his accident, I hope he gets it."

He looked at her, a question in his eyes. "Your father owned part of this mine, didn't he?"

She nodded. "He did, but apparently he sold his share to Uncle Ralph before he died. I have nothing to do with Wesley Mining."

"And no income from it." His eyes were shrewd as he watched her. "Good old Ralph is sleazier than even I thought."

"I wouldn't take any money from Uncle Ralph if he got down on his knees and begged me." Her voice rose passionately, and she cleared her throat and jammed her hands under her armpits. As hot as the day was, even thinking about accepting anything from her uncle chilled her. "I'm still paying for the last time he 'helped' me. No, I don't want anything to do with the business."

Connor nodded his head toward the old office building. "Apparently your buddy Richard doesn't feel the same way."

Her cousin hurried toward them. Even from a distance she could see the fury on his face. "He's Uncle Ralph's son. Naturally he feels like the mine is his business, too."

Connor turned to look at her. The expression on his face was almost unbearably tender. "I think you could find an excuse for a serial killer. You're too nice, Sarah. You don't belong in this family."

She raised her head. "I'm proud to be a Wesley. My father was a wonderful man."

He took a step closer to her. "Don't ever make the mistake of thinking that you're like Ralph and Richard. They're not fit to lick the mud from your shoes." He stood barely a foot away from her. She would have stepped into his arms if her cousin Richard hadn't come blustering up at that moment.

"What are you doing here, MacCormac? This is private property. Get out! Get out of here right now!"

"Chill out, Richard. He came with me." Sarah turned to face her cousin. "I have a bunch of papers you need to sign about Chet's accident. Let's go into the office and take care of them."

"*He* doesn't have anything to do with Chet's accident."

"He was a witness to the extent of the injury," she improvised quickly, ignoring the wink Connor sent her. "But he doesn't need to sign any papers. He can wait for us out here."

She grabbed her cousin's arm and steered him toward the ramshackle building. She glanced over her shoulder once when Richard glared behind her. Connor was leaning against the side of her truck, his arms crossed over his chest, looking faintly bored.

"This shouldn't take too long," she soothed as they walked into the depressing building. "You know how the government is, especially when it comes to workers' compensation. They need to have everything spelled out, then written down in triplicate. Since you're in charge out here, you're the one who has to answer most of the questions."

They walked into Richard's office and Sarah positioned herself so she blocked her cousin's view out the window. Perched on the edge of his desk, she pushed a paper toward him and showed him where to sign. Every once in a while she risked a glance over her shoulder, looking for Connor in the yard.

Fifteen minutes later, she couldn't think of another excuse to keep him in the office. Standing up, she gathered the sheaf of papers together and waved him into his chair. "You don't need to see me out," she said breezily. "I can find my way."

Her cousin stared at her for a moment, then stood up. "That's all right, Sarah, I don't mind in the least." His voice was flat and ominous.

She should have remembered that Richard wasn't really stupid. Just because he caved in to his father didn't mean *she* could push him around easily. She hoped to God that Connor had finished whatever it was he intended to do and was waiting by the side of the truck when they walked out.

But when they stepped into the bright sunlight, Connor was nowhere in sight. She felt Richard stiffen beside her, and suddenly he broke into a run.

Hurrying to keep up with him, she clutched the papers under her arm to prevent them from scattering across the parking lot. When Richard got to her truck, he stopped abruptly and looked around.

"Where is he?" He was furious. "What are the two of you trying to pull?"

"Where is who?" At least she could stall for a little more time.

Her cousin grabbed her arm roughly and shook her. "Don't play your little games with me, Sarah. What's going on?"

"Let go of her, Wesley. Now."

Connor's low, deadly voice came from behind Richard, and he dropped her arm and spun around.

"You touch her again and you're a dead man. Understand, Wesley?"

"She's my cousin. And you can't tell me what to do."

Connor's eyes narrowed and his face hardened. "I'm only going to tell you one more time. If you so much as breathe heavily on Sarah, I'm going to kick your worthless tail into the next county. And I'll be waiting for you there when you finally wake up."

Richard took step backward. When he was out of arm's reach, he sneered, "How touching. Too bad you didn't feel as strongly about her sister, MacCormac."

Connor's eyes flashed, but he relaxed against the truck, refusing to be baited. "That's ancient history. And you will be, too, if you bother Sarah again. Am I making myself clear?"

Richard took another step backward. "Where were you?" he demanded, apparently deciding to take the offensive. "This mine is private property."

Connor watched him for a moment, and Sarah saw the rage slowly disappearing from his eyes and his usual scorn for Richard taking its place. Finally he answered, "Just looking around. You've got a real interesting setup here, Wesley."

Richard stared, thrown off-balance by Connor's remark. "Well, it's none of your business," he muttered. "And if you're looking for a job, the answer's no."

Connor laughed with real amusement. "Thanks for the vote of confidence, Wesley. I don't think you have to worry about having another MacCormac working at the Wesley mine."

Sarah saw her cousin stiffen at the mention of Connor's father, but it was so slight that she didn't think Connor had noticed.

"No," he continued as he pushed away from the truck, "I was just admiring your operation here." He waved his hand toward the yawning opening in the side of the mountain. "Very precise and tidy." He faced Richard again. "There isn't even a pile of rocks lying around. But then, you always did have a problem with anything out of order. Still demanding perfection even in the messy world of gold mining, are you?"

Richard's face bleached white and he took another step backward. Then, gathering himself, he moved toward Connor, his eyes glittering. "Get out of here. Now." His furious gaze swept over Sarah, as well. "Both of you. And don't come back here. If there are any more papers that have to be signed about Chet's accident, I'll come in to your office in town to sign them."

Connor didn't move. "Maybe the lady doesn't want you in her office, either. If I were Sarah, I wouldn't be too anxious to be seen publicly with you."

Her cousin's face twisted with rage and he moved blindly toward Connor. Sarah suspected that it was just what Connor had been hoping he'd do. Grabbing Connor's arm, she said to him, "Let's go. Don't let him make you do something you'll regret."

His arm was as hard and tense as an iron bar. Slowly he looked at her, and she saw the rage fade from his eyes. "Something that he'd regret, you mean." His voice was soft and deadly, and his gaze flickered over her cousin.

"He's not worth it, Connor. Not now."

After a long moment she felt his muscles ease just a little. "You're right. Let's go, Sarah. We both have more important things to do."

She didn't let go of his arm until he was in the cab of the truck. Then she hurried around to the other side, jumped in and started the engine. The heat in the cab was stifling and the hot steering wheel burned her hands. Still she gripped it like a lifeline as she carefully drove out of the wide mine yard.

When she was out of sight of the mine entrance and any curious eyes, she pulled the truck over to the side of the road and killed the engine. Leaning back against the cushion, she took a deep, shaky breath.

"I thought you were going to kill him."

"I wanted to." He reached out gently and took the arm that Richard had been holding. Pushing up the sleeve of her T-shirt, he looked at her upper arm.

When she glanced down, she saw the faint imprint of her cousin's fingers. She tried to pull away from Connor, but he held on and stared at the marks on her arm. When he finally looked at her, she sucked in her breath at the expression on his face.

The rage and anger were gone. All that was left was a deadly, determined glitter in his eyes, one that was completely implacable. "Richard Wesley," he said, his voice cold and distant, "is going to regret the day he was born."

"I'm all right, Connor. He didn't hurt me. I just bruise very easily." She was babbling. My God, she'd never seen anyone look like this before. He looked like a deadly, impersonal machine bent on vengeance.

She laid her hand on his arm. "Connor, remember why you're here. This is about your father, not me. I can handle my cousin."

"So can I." His voice was so soft she had to strain to hear him. "And I will."

"Please, Connor. Don't let this distract you. You need to focus on what happened to your father, not the way my cousin treats me. Can't you just forget about it?"

"What do you mean? Has he done this before?"

She should have known he would pick up on her little slip of the tongue. "I can handle Richard," she repeated. "You know how bullies are. They back right down the minute anyone challenges them." She lifted her chin. "He knows he can't push me around."

For a long moment the air in the truck was supercharged with emotion. Finally she felt him relax slightly. Leaning back against the seat cushion, he drawled, "I smell a good story here. What happened?"

Flushing, she shifted in her seat and reached for the ignition key. "It wasn't anything, really. A couple of years ago I saw several of the men from the mine with back problems. After talking to them, I realized that the ergonomics of their work stations was wrong. I told them what they had to do to stop hurting their backs, and told them they couldn't go back to work until it was fixed."

"And Richard didn't like that much." It was a statement rather than a question.

"Not at all," she said ruefully. "When he came into the office to complain about my advice, we got into a little fight."

"And?" he prompted.

She shrugged, smiling a little. "He fixed what was wrong at the mine and nobody has had back problems since. At least not because of that particular job."

"How exactly did you persuade him?"

She grinned, remembering the fierce triumph she'd felt when her cousin had caved in without a word. "I promised him I wouldn't tell anyone else. But he knows better than to threaten me again."

Not enough, though, to get rid of the mistress he had tucked discreetly away in Meeker. As long as his crotch ruled his brain and he stayed married to his very particular wife, she had nothing to fear from her cousin.

She glanced at Connor, sitting so close to her, and saw that he had relaxed. Exhaling slowly, she eased the truck into gear, pulled onto the road and headed toward town.

"You did that very well," he said after a while.

"What?" She looked over at him.

"Don't look so innocent. You defused that situation like a pro. Just don't think I'm going to forget about that sorry excuse for a man that you call your cousin. From now on, I'm going to be on him like ugly on an ape. If he knows what's good for him, he's not going to get any closer to you than he would to a cougar."

"Thank you, Connor," she said after a while. Her eyes prickled with tears and her heart expanded in her chest. "No one has ever stood up for me before. I think I like it."

"Your cousin won't bully you again, at least not as long as I'm in town," he said gruffly.

A cold chill pricked down her skin. *As long as he was in town.* Those were the operative words, weren't they?

Despite what had happened between them the night before, he had no plans to stay in Pine Butte. But he'd never told her otherwise. He'd said from the beginning that he was here only to find out what had happened to his father. Even last night, in the throes of passion, he hadn't made any promises.

"Forget about Richard and worry about your father." Her voice sounded small and forlorn, and she swallowed and sat up straighter. "Did you see anything while Richard and I were in the office?"

"I don't know what I was supposed to be looking for." His voice sounded thoughtful. "But I did seem to provoke quite a reaction from old Dickie boy when I mentioned how neat and tidy the mine looked. I'm not sure if that was significant or if I finally just got to him."

"You've been trying to provoke him." She looked at him in astonishment.

"Give the lady a cigar. Of course I've been trying to provoke him. Your uncle, too. I figure if I make them mad enough, they're bound to let something slip."

"Connor, you don't know for sure that they're responsible for your father's death," she said desperately.

"No, I don't. But if it was something connected with the mine, I'm sure they know about it." His voice softened and he half-turned to face her. "Sarah, all I want is the truth. I can't bring my father back. I can't even make it up to my mother anymore. I just want to know what happened. If it was an accident, so be it." His face hardened. "Except I don't think it was. And I think someone at the mine knows exactly what happened."

She shivered, chilled in spite of the blazing heat. "What are you going to do next?"

He stared out the windshield, and for a minute she didn't think he was going to answer. Finally he said, "I think it's time to pay a visit to my favorite fishing stream again. Someone was real anxious that I not wander around up there. It's made me curious to see why."

Her stomach clenched with fear, but she said, "When are we going up there?"

"*We're* not going anywhere. You're going to provide my cover in Pine Butte while I look around tonight."

"You can't go back there by yourself." She was appalled. "Especially in the dark. I had a hard enough time finding you in the daylight."

His lips curled in a faint smile. "You're not going to have to rescue me this time, Sarah. I'm as good as new now, and believe me, nobody'll sneak up on me again. Besides, you're going to have everybody in Pine Butte convinced that we're spending the evening together at your apartment."

"How am I going to do that?" She didn't try to keep the exasperation out of her voice.

"Well, you're going to get two dinners from Earlene's. A couple of her best steaks. Then you're going to pick up a couple of movies from the video store. Something that wouldn't be your usual taste."

"Like senseless violence."

He gave her a grin, ignoring her sarcasm. "Exactly. And when you rent them, you're going to point out that they're not something you would normally watch, but you have to humor your patient. In other words, no one in Pine Butte is going to have any idea that I'm not sitting in your apartment, eating dinner and watching bad movies."

"In the meantime you're going to be climbing all over the mountain, not sure what you're looking for."

"Got it in one." He brushed the hair away from her face, and his fingers ignited a fire in her belly. "Someone was damned determined to keep me away from that stream. I've waited this long because I realized it was stupid to go up there before I was completely recovered. But I have to go back. You understand that, don't you?"

The problem was, she did. "At least let me go back there with you."

"No, Sarah." His voice was very gentle. "I have a better chance of getting up there and getting back in one piece if everyone thinks we're together in your apartment. You provide my cover and I'll wander around up there by myself."

Drawing in a trembling breath, she whispered, "I'm scared, Connor."

"Don't be. This time I'll be ready. No one's going to hurt me, sweetheart."

The truck dipped as the front wheel hit a hole, and she swung the wheel sharply to the right. "All right," she muttered. "But if you're not back here by midnight, I'm coming to look for you."

"Don't worry, I'll be back." His hand slid around to her neck and tangled in her hair. "Wild horses couldn't keep me away from you tonight."

The afternoon dragged by, the minutes ticking away unbearably slowly. They'd gotten to the clinic just in time for the afternoon hours to begin, and Connor had left her at the back door with a quick, hard kiss. By the time Sarah had opened her eyes, dazed, he'd disappeared.

She moved through the exam rooms like a robot, her mind on the plans for the evening. Every time she had a minute between patients, she rehearsed what she would say in Earlene's and the video store. Feeling like a fool, she told herself that she could pull this off. All she had to do was act normally, for God's sake.

When anyone asked about her live-in patient, she told them the truth. It took a long time to recover from the injuries he had received, and he was still getting his strength back. She didn't tell them that Connor MacCormac had the constitution of an ox and had been perfectly fine, as far as she could tell, for the past three days.

Josie stuck her head into the door of the office. "Only four patients left. Mary Johnson is in the second exam room. She's next."

Sarah slid off the edge of her desk and hurried out the door. She had almost forgotten about Mary, but she was glad she'd kept her promise and come into the clinic. Pushing Connor firmly out of her mind, she opened the door and walked into the room.

"Hi, Mary. I'm glad you came in today. How are you feeling?"

Mary sighed. "The same. The kids are a handful and this heat is sucking all the energy out of me." Smoothing her hand over her rounded abdomen, she continued, "I can't wait for the next month to be over and this baby to be here."

Sarah helped her friend onto the scale and frowned as she noted her large weight gain since her last visit. "Your weight is really shooting up, Mary."

"I don't know how it could. I've been so tired, and the heat is bothering me so much that I just haven't been eating."

At her words a cold fist squeezed Sarah's chest and she helped her friend onto the table. *Please, God, no,* she prayed as she wrapped the blood pressure cuff around her friend's arm.

Taking Mary's hand in hers as she pumped up the cuff, she noticed the woman's swollen hands. Almost afraid to look down, she forced herself to look at Mary's feet. Just as she'd feared, they were so badly swollen they looked as if they were overflowing her shoes.

Holding her breath, she checked Mary's blood pressure. Slowly unfastening the cuff on Mary's arm, she asked quietly, "Did you bring in the urine sample?"

The woman nodded toward the counter where a small bottle stood. Sarah walked over to it and dipped in the test stick, already knowing what she would find.

Staring at the bright green positive color, she took a deep breath and turned to face her friend. Taking Mary's hand, she looked at her for a moment.

"I'm afraid I have some bad news, Mary."

Mary clutched her abdomen. "What's wrong?"

"You have toxemia." At Mary's bewildered look, she elaborated. "Your blood pressure is way too high, and you have protein in your urine."

Mary's face crumbled and she clutched her abdomen more tightly. "What does that mean? Is the baby okay?" she whispered.

"Lie down and let's see."

A few minutes later she helped Mary sit up again and put her arm around her friend. "The baby's fine right now. His heartbeat is strong, and he's already dropped. And if you're real careful, nothing will happen."

"What's toxemia? What's wrong with me?"

"Nobody knows why some pregnant women get toxemia. But it causes high blood pressure and that's dangerous to both you and the baby." She paused, unhappy about worrying Mary any more than she already had. But she had to know. "The problem is when you go into labor. If your blood pressure goes too high, you may have a stroke. Or the baby might."

Mary's face became even whiter. "What can we do, Sarah?" she whispered.

"First of all, you're on complete bed rest, as of now. Get your mother to come and stay with you and take care of Jenny and Tommy." Sarah bit her lip, knowing how her friend was going to react to her next words. "And I want you in the hospital in Glenwood Springs as soon as possible. You need to be in the hospital in case you go into labor early. If we can't get your blood pressure down, you may have to have a Caesarean section."

"Leave Tom and the kids by themselves? This baby isn't due for another month." Her face looked shocked and uncomprehending.

"Your life could be at stake, Mary. Yours and the baby's. Toxemia is dangerous." Sarah took her friend's hand again. "Please, call your mother. Have her get here as soon as possible. I don't want you to take any chances."

Mary slid awkwardly off the exam table and stood up. "Thanks, Sarah. I'll do . . . I don't know what I'll do. I'll think of something."

"Think of it fast, Mary." Her tone softened as she looked at her friend. "This is not something to fool around with. And stay off your feet. I'm coming by tomorrow to check on you."

Sarah slumped against the wall as she watched Mary make her way out the door. *Toxemia.* Fear for her friend clutched at her, propelling her toward the waiting room. She'd tell Mary to get Tom and get in the car now and drive to Glenwood Springs. Mary shouldn't even wait until her mother could get here to watch the kids.

But by the time she reached the door, Mary was gone. Mary was an intelligent woman, Sarah reassured herself. She wouldn't take any chances with herself or the baby. By tomorrow, or the next day at the latest, she'd be in the hospital in Glenwood Springs, her blood pressure constantly monitored and a team of doctors ready to intervene if there was any danger.

She'd call the hospital as soon as she'd seen her last patient. Turning wearily to the exam rooms, she opened the next chart and studied it for a moment before walking into the room.

Connor wanted to see Sarah one more time before he went up the mountain. He told himself it was just to make sure she knew what she was supposed to do and when she was supposed to do it. Needing to hold her, to kiss her again, wasn't the reason at all.

Besides, need had nothing to do with his feelings about Sarah Wesley anyway, he reminded himself. He wanted her, that was all. Wanting he could control. But needing her was different. When you needed someone, they owned you. And no one was going to control him that way, ever again. The last person he'd thought he needed was Barb Wesley. There was no way he was going to let another woman have that kind of power over him.

Pushing open the door to her office, he looked around. Josie sat at the desk behind the counter, writing. She looked up and smiled when she saw him.

"She's in with a patient right now. The last one of the day, so she'll be finished soon."

"Thanks, Josie." He gave her a casual wave and headed for his bedroom. He would *not* hang around the waiting room like a teenager mooning over his first girlfriend.

Stretched out on the bed, he heard the low, indistinguishable sounds of two voices talking. In a few minutes a door opened and as they walked into the waiting room, the voices grew more faint. He wasn't about to jump up and dash out there after her. He'd give her time to get her records in order, then he'd make sure she was all set for tonight.

The front door had barely closed when he stood up and strolled into the clinic. She wasn't in the waiting room, so he headed for the office.

He paused in the doorway. Sarah was slumped at her desk, her head in her hands. His carefully casual air disappeared in a rush of panic.

He was across the room in three strides, crouching next to her and swinging her chair around to face him. "What's wrong?"

At the sound of his voice she started, raising her head to look at him. For just a moment he saw pain and anguish in her eyes before she blinked and smiled at him.

"Hi." She took a deep, shuddering breath. "I didn't hear you come in. What have you been doing?"

"Sarah, don't change the subject. What's the matter?" he asked roughly.

Sighing, she settled back in her chair and watched him for a moment. "It's one of my patients," she said finally. "I'm worried about her."

"Mary Johnson?" he asked, uneasy at how quickly he seemed to know.

She looked startled. "How did you know?"

Shrugging, he looked away. "I know you were worried about her yesterday, and I remember you telling her to come in today. It wasn't that big a leap."

But it was. Never before had he felt this kind of connection to anybody. It was almost as if he could read Sarah's mind, and he didn't want to think about why.

"She's got toxemia." The word fell between them, somehow more frightening for the matter-of-fact way she said it.

"It's high blood pressure associated with pregnancy. I told her she has to go to the hospital in Glenwood Springs and stay there until the baby's born, but I don't know how soon she'll get there." She took a deep breath and said in a rush, "She's not due for a month, but the baby's ready to be born. I'm terrified that something'll happen to her on the way to the hospital."

His hand tightened on the arm of her chair, then he deliberately relaxed it. "Like it did with Barb, you mean."

She nodded, not looking at him. His heart twisted at the agony in her face, and he pulled her out of the chair and into his arms. "She'll be fine," he murmured, nuzzling her bright hair away from her neck and kissing the spot just below her ear. "It's the middle of the summer. There isn't going to be any snow on Eagle Ridge Road, and Tom will get her there in plenty of time." His lips wandered across her cheek and found her mouth. "Nothing is going to happen, Sarah."

Her mouth clung to his, returning his kiss with a deep hunger. He pulled her closer and cupped her hips in his hands, pressing her against his already aroused body. "Don't worry, sweetheart, everything is going to be fine," he whispered.

As he smoothed the hair away from her face, he struggled for control. He had to stop this, right now, if he expected to turn around and walk out of this room tonight. Clearing his throat, he said, "I just came in to see if you needed anything before I left."

Fear shadowed her eyes again. It gave him a fierce pleasure to know that this time it was for him. Jamming his hands in his back pockets, he forced himself to step farther away from her. "Are you going to be all right tonight?"

She nodded. "I'll be fine." Giving him a shaky smile, she added, "I've been practicing all afternoon. I think I've got my lines memorized."

He couldn't resist one more quick, hard kiss. "Don't worry about me. I'll be back before you know it."

He turned and left the room without looking back.

Chapter 13

The orange ball of the sun, hanging low in the sky, glinted off the bare rocks as Connor headed the small rental car up the mountain. Sarah had offered him her truck, but he'd refused. He didn't want anyone thinking Sarah was involved in his business. After he left she would be too vulnerable.

His hands tightened at the thought. Slowly and deliberately, he loosened each finger. Sarah would be fine when he was gone. She belonged in Pine Butte. He never would.

When he reached the place he'd parked last time, he stepped on the accelerator and swerved on the loose stones in the road as he hurried past. There was nothing there except a stream with no fish in it. He'd have to go higher up the mountain to find what he was looking for.

The problem was, he didn't know what he was looking for. Something was going on at the Wesley mine. Richard's behavior earlier had confirmed that for him, and his gut instinct told him to look up the mountain. Whoever had bashed him in the head the other day wasn't just out for a good time. Someone was trying to protect something, and he had no intention of leaving tonight until he knew what it was.

He drove upward until the trees began thinning out. Spotting a decent-size stand of pine, he pulled the little red car behind it, then kicked at the dirt to hide his tire tracks. Then, standing by the side of the road, he took a deep breath and looked around.

The sun hovered near the edge of the mountain, ready to slip behind it and plunge the area into blackness. The few scrubby pine trees cast long, contorted shadows across the rocky ground. Boulders dotted the gentle slope, and as he stood in the twilight the only sound he heard was the moaning of the wind through the trees.

Pulling his black leather motorcycle jacket out of the car, he put it on and zipped it up and shoved his hands into his pockets. It might be late summer in the valley down below, but up at the top of the mountain the nights were damnably cold already. After a moment's thought, he reached into the trunk of the car and lifted out the small black bag he always carried with him. Holding its comforting weight in his hand, he looked around again.

He crossed the road, heading in the direction of the stream. He'd never been this far up the mountain, but the stream had to originate up here somewhere. It would at least be a landmark, something to keep him from getting completely lost in the inky darkness that would descend in a matter of minutes.

The ground was hard-packed dirt and stones, barely covering the solid rock underneath. It was a wonder anything survived up here. Even the few trees that dotted the area were hunched over, clinging tenaciously to the thin soil.

Connor walked slowly, his booted feet kicking loose stones and scuffing over the rocks. Every few feet he stopped and listened. The only sound was his own heart pounding in his ears. Evening on the mountain was silent, almost eerily so. The animals that lived in the sunshine were gone, holed up for the night, and the nocturnal creatures hadn't yet ventured out.

Blackness engulfed the mountain by the time he found the stream. He heard it gurgling before he saw it and stopped, straining to hear in the darkness. The only sound was the splashing of water on rocks, and after a while he moved forward until he stood on the edge of the small stream.

Nothing. There was no sign of life anywhere around him, no smell of acrid sweat, no gathering of tense muscles close by. He was alone in the night next to the stream.

There was also nothing suspicious about the stream, at least where he stood. Stepping back from its edge, he headed upward. Somewhere on this mountain lay the answers he searched for. It was up to him to dig them out.

It seemed as if he walked for hours. The trees became fewer and fewer, until he knew he had passed the tree line. The only vegetation was the occasional scrubby bush that lay almost flat against the rock, and the moss that covered everything.

Suddenly he stopped short. A wall loomed in the distance, rising abruptly out of the stream. This was no beaver dam or fallen log. It looked as if it was made of stone, and it stood at least six feet high. Tightening his grip on the small black bag in his hand, he approached it cautiously.

Sarah checked her watch one last time and wiped her sweaty palms down the thighs of her jeans. It was time to move.

Connor had been gone for twenty minutes, and she had to make sure everybody thought he was waiting for her in the clinic. Peering up the stairs to her apartment one more time, she was reassured by the flood of light that flowed down to her. She started for the door, then paused. Turning around, she strode to the bedroom where Connor was supposed to be staying and flipped on the lights there, too. If anyone looked at her building, she didn't want them to have any doubts that it was occupied.

Her feet felt as if they were weighted with lead as she walked to the small video rental store. It did a brisk business most of the time, and today was no exception. Several people crowded around the shelves, looking for a movie to relieve the boredom of a small town evening. They all greeted her by name and she murmured hello to each of them, telling herself it was good to have witnesses. The whole purpose of this charade was to convince everyone Connor was with her tonight.

"Hey, Sarah," the teenage clerk called. "We've got that movie you've been wanting." He held up a box displaying a romantic comedy she'd been trying to rent for a few weeks.

Rolling her eyes, she shook her head. "Can't tonight, Pete. My patient claims he needs something a little livelier than that." Looking at the shelf of new releases, she picked up a box at random that featured a large gun on the cover. "How about this? Is it any good?"

The clerk looked at it doubtfully. "I don't know if you'd like that, Sarah. It's awfully violent."

She didn't have to fake her shudder. "Then it's just the thing. I have to catch up on some paperwork, anyway. Connor can enjoy it by himself."

"Okay." The clerk typed her number into his computer, and a minute later he handed her a receipt to sign. "I hope he likes it."

"I'm sure it's just what he had in mind," she assured the clerk, clutching the box in her hand. "He'll love it. And if he doesn't, next time he can pick out his own movie," she said, smiling weakly.

The clerk grinned at her and waved as she walked out of the store. Heading down the sidewalk toward Earlene's, she took a deep, shuddering breath and relaxed just a bit. That hadn't been so tough. And, thanks to the clerk, she hadn't had to do a thing to make sure the other people knew she was renting a movie for Connor.

She repeated the process at Earlene's, leaving the videotape in a prominent place on the counter while she waited for her two steak dinners. When Earlene saw the tape, Sarah had to explain again that the movie was for Connor and she was going to do paperwork that evening.

By the time she got to the clinic and locked the door behind her, she was trembling so much the tape slipped out of her hands and clattered on the floor. Drawing in a deep breath, she carefully set the two aluminum containers from Earlene's on the counter and picked it up. Tucking it under her arm, she headed up to her apartment.

The steak tasted like the bottom of her running shoe and the mashed potatoes stuck to the roof of her mouth. Finally she shoved the plate away from her and put the box holding Connor's dinner into the refrigerator. She was supposed to be working on records, so it better at least look as if she was in her office.

She glanced at her watch on the way down the stairs. Connor had been gone for an hour and a half. Flipping on the light in her tiny cubbyhole, she threw herself into the desk chair and leaned back, looking at her watch again. She had no idea when he would return. She didn't have to start worrying yet, she assured herself. It could be hours before he found anything up there in the darkness.

Pulling her chair up to her desk with determination, she told herself she might as well get something done. Grabbing the first record in the pile, she stared at it with unseeing eyes. All she could picture was Connor, alone in the night up on the mountain.

Connor ran his hand over the wall and narrowed his eyes. Someone had gone to a lot of trouble to build this wall. It was made of stones and mortar, and it ran down the middle of the stream until it turned sharply to the left and continued on into the darkness.

He couldn't tell how far upstream it extended, but he'd check that out later. Right now, he wanted to know why someone would build a wall up at the top of the mountain. What did they want to keep in? Or out?

With one hand on the wall he followed it into the night. The small stream soon disappeared from sight and sound, but the wall didn't seem to be getting any lower. Finally he stopped, measuring the distance to the top.

It was just a shade over six feet high, about the same height as him. It would be an easy enough task to hoist himself over the top. Placing his hands on the uneven surface, he tensed his muscles and prepared to jump.

A tiny arc of red flew through the sky, and he pulled his hands away and dropped to the ground. A moment later the sharp, distinctive smell of tobacco smoke drifted past him.

Someone on the other side of that wall had just finished a cigarette and flicked the butt into the air.

He leaned against the wall and drew in slow, deep breaths. Frozen in place, he waited for the sounds that would tell him he'd been spotted. Barely moving his head, he looked for something to use for cover. There were no trees. The only rocks were no bigger than small dogs, certainly not big enough to hide a man.

After a while he heard the faint scrape of boots on rock. The sound got more and more faint, and as it became obvious that the person was moving away from him he allowed himself to relax just a hair.

He *had* to know what was behind that wall. Whatever it was, it was somehow connected to the Wesley mine and what had happened to his father. When he couldn't hear the footsteps any longer, he stood up and quietly began to follow the wall again.

After another hundred feet or so it began to get shorter. Finally he could see over it, and he stooped and approached the wall cautiously.

He listened for a long time before he raised his head. The night was as silent as it had been before, with no sounds from the person he knew lurked on the other side. Standing just high enough to see over the stones, he scanned the area, then dropped to his knees.

There wasn't a soul in sight, and he raised himself up once more. When he heard no shout, no sounds of someone approaching, he let himself look at what the wall was supposed to hide.

There was nothing but a huge pool of water surrounded by piles of rocks. The wall in the stream had obviously been built to divert some of the water to build this pool. But why? And where did these rocks come from? They just as obviously weren't from the top of this mountain. They must have been brought in from somewhere.

He had to get closer, get a better look. The full moon was just rising from behind the mountain peaks. In another twenty minutes the area would be brightly illuminated, and he needed to be gone long before then. He needed the cover of darkness.

Following the wall, he walked until it was no more than a couple of feet high. He stepped over it and paused, waiting for any sign that he'd been seen. The pool in front of him was eerily still, not a ripple disturbing its glasslike surface. There wasn't a sign of the person who'd thrown the cigarette, and he walked quickly to the edge of the pool and knelt down.

The air was heavy with dust and another, unfamiliar smell. The rocks that were piled haphazardly around the water seemed to be tumbling into it. In several places he could see piles of rocks rising out of the water.

Rocking back on his heels, he stared at the water and the rocks and knew they were connected with the Wesley mine. Maybe this was the debris that had been so conspicuously absent from the mine today. But why would anyone haul it up the mountain? That made no sense at all.

Except that Ralph Wesley was no fool. If this was connected to the mine, then there was a damn good reason for it to be here. He'd have to do a little bit of research about gold mining.

He began to back away from the pool when the rising moon glinted off something to his right. Scooting closer, he saw with a faint chill that it was a dead bird. One of the gray jays that were so common in the mountains, it lay on its side next to the water.

Connor stared at it for a long time, then reached for his black bag. Groping inside it, he curled his hand around a couple of specimen bottles. Kneeling next to the pool, he carefully filled both of them with water without getting his hand wet.

He'd capped the first one and replaced it in his bag when he felt something hard poke him in the back. "What do you think you're doing?" asked a low, guttural voice.

Connor tensed, still holding the other bottle of water. He didn't answer, just crouched next to the water and waited for the other man to make the next move.

"Turn around, nice and slow."

Connor spun around and dashed the contents of the specimen bottle in the other man's face. When he instinctively threw up his hands to protect himself, Connor knocked the gun out of his grasp.

The man lunged for the shotgun as Connor got one arm around his neck. Tightening his grip, he waited for his opponent to pass out. When the man slumped unconscious into his arms, Connor eased him to the ground and stripped off his shoes, socks and belt. Tying his hands behind his back, he stuffed his socks in his mouth and pitched his shoes and the gun into the darkness. Pausing only to grab his bag, he vaulted over the wall and headed toward the stream, running as fast as the darkness would allow.

Sarah had long since given up on her records. Leaving the light burning in her office, she headed to her apartment. She refused to look at the clock. It was her enemy, inexorably ticking off the minutes and hours that Connor had been gone. Every time she glanced at it, her anxiety cranked up a notch higher.

There was no way she could even think about sleeping until she knew Connor was safe. Pacing the living room, she spied a romantic suspense book she'd been reading and picked it up. Throwing herself onto the couch, she opened it and began to read. A few minutes later she dropped it on the cushion next to her. Even the complex, riveting plot wasn't able to hold her attention tonight.

Her gaze locked on the clock in her kitchen. Eleven o'clock. He'd been gone almost five hours. How long did it take to drive up the mountain and look around? He should have been back long before this.

She had no choice. Running into her bedroom, she pulled on a heavy sweater and her hiking boots. Nobody would see her leave at this time of night, she told herself. And if anyone did, they'd assume it was because of an emergency somewhere. She wasn't going to leave Connor alone on that mountain for one more second. Remembering what had happened to him the last time he'd gone up there, she clamped her lips together to stop them from trembling and ran out the door.

She was just easing her truck into gear, cursing the noisy muffler, when Connor's little car swung around the corner and rolled to a stop next to her. She stared at him for a moment, unsure whether he was real or just a vision conjured up by her desperate heart.

When he jumped out of the car and wrenched open her door, she closed her eyes with a thankful prayer and slid into his arms. Wrapping herself around him, she held him tightly and whispered his name.

"Where were you going?" he asked, holding just as tightly to her. "Is there an emergency somewhere?"

"I thought there was one up on the mountain," she answered into the cool leather of his jacket. She tightened her grip. "I was worried about you."

She felt him smile into her hair. "You were going to rescue me again." It was a statement rather than a question. His hands moved, slid down her back and under her sweater. "I thought I told you to stay here."

"Anybody who saw me would have assumed just what you did." She tried to push away from him and he pulled her closer. "Damn it, Connor, I was scared to death. Do you know how long you've been gone?"

"Too long," he said softly, and bent his mouth to hers.

Her anger disappeared in the flood of fierce love and desire that washed over her. Her hands clenched his jacket and she opened willingly to him. All the fear and anxiety of the evening faded, replaced by a need for him that consumed her.

Backing her against the truck, he pressed against her so that his rock-hard body burned into her. Tongues twining, hands digging through layers of clothes searching for skin, they stood outside in the cool night air for what seemed like forever.

Finally Connor broke away and pulled her head next to his heart. "Let's go inside." She felt him straining to regain control and heard it in the tremor of his voice. "Aren't you even a little interested in what happened tonight?"

Slowly she raised her head, looking at his profile in the moonlight. The full moon stood directly above them, bathing the angles of his face with a luminous glow. His tiny gold hoop earring stood out starkly against his black hair. He looked beautiful and fierce, and she knew that the fact that he was back, safely, mattered far more to her than whatever he had found.

"Other things seemed more important to me," she said evenly, watching as his face softened momentarily. Then he backed up a step, as if remembering why he was here and chastising himself for allowing her to distract him.

"I want to tell you," he said, taking her hand and leading her into the clinic building.

He made himself a cup of instant coffee and pulled her down on the couch. "How much do you know about gold mining?" he asked abruptly.

She shrugged. "They dig a hole in the ground and take out the gold. What more is there than that?"

"I don't know, but I'm willing to bet a lot that there's more to it than that." He told her what he'd found, and ended by saying, "I took off running and I'm sure nobody followed me. He must have been up there by himself." Taking a long gulp of the scalding hot coffee, he looked at her again. "That guy sure looked a lot like a guard."

"I can't think of any other reason for him to have a gun," she agreed. "Nobody ever goes that high up on the mountain. There's nothing up there."

"There is now." He took another gulp of the coffee and set the mug down on a table. "I'm going into Glenwood Springs tomorrow to have that sample checked at a lab and do some research on gold mining. Are you sure you don't know anything about what your family is doing with the mine?"

She frowned, thinking. Some faint memory niggled at the back of her mind. "I do remember something, a long time ago," she said slowly. "I was just a kid, but I overheard my father and Uncle Ralph arguing. I remember being scared, but I have no idea why." She looked at him. "It was something my father didn't want to do, and Uncle Ralph was pressing him."

He brushed the hair from her face. "Don't worry about it. When I'm in Glenwood tomorrow, I'll find out all I can about gold mining. If that pond is connected with the Wesley mine, I'll find out what it is."

His hand lingered on her cheek, and her heart began to pound. Turning to face him, she reached out to press her fingers against his lips. "I don't want to discuss the mine anymore tonight," she whispered.

Slowly he pulled her to him. "There are a lot more interesting conversations we could be having," he agreed. Sweeping her onto his lap, he flicked his tongue over her earlobe. "Such as what you were going to do on that mountain in the pitch dark."

"I would have found you." Her voice was fierce.

"I think you would have." She heard the wonder in his voice, and then his mouth was on hers. She forgot all about the mine, the pond he'd found and the reason he was in Pine Butte. All that existed was this moment, her body straining into his and his hands molding her to him.

Swinging her into his arms, he stood up. "The couch isn't going to be suitable for what I have in mind." His hand slid up her side to cup her breast, and he bent his lips to hers again as he strode into her bedroom.

Laying her on the bed, he paused long enough to strip off his clothes and hers. Kneeling next to the bed, he watched her in the moonlight. His eyes were dark and unreadable as he slowly smoothed his hand over her face. "I don't want to hurt you, Sarah," he whispered.

"You won't. You didn't last night," she answered, deliberately misunderstanding him. There would be no regrets about this, no matter what happened. Reaching out, she drew him onto the bed. "I want you. Come to me, Connor."

Connor stood in the doorway of Sarah's bedroom, watching her stretch in her sleep. She had to be exhausted. God knows he was. They hadn't slept much in that bed of hers last night.

His body stirred at the memory, and he turned away to get more coffee. He had to leave, this morning, before anybody got a chance to come looking for him. His motorcycle would be ready, and he'd be out of town and on his way to Glenwood Springs by the time one of the Wesleys came to call.

And come they would. The next time they had a little chat, though, he would know what they were doing up on the top of that mountain. He suspected that would turn out to be his ace in the hole.

Grabbing his black bag and a small duffel bag of clothes, he headed for the stairs. He paused at the top, and almost against his will walked slowly back to the bedroom.

She knew he was going to Glenwood Springs today, he told himself. She wouldn't be upset to find him gone. But he couldn't leave without saying goodbye to her.

The springs creaked as he sat down next to her. The sheet had slipped, and she was exposed to the waist. Just one touch, he told himself, staring at her creamy breast. Bending to kiss her mouth, he reached out and skimmed his hand over the smooth curves.

A jolt of desire struck him and he dropped his bags and reached for her. He wanted nothing more than to bury himself in her, to spend the day making love with her. Thoughts of his father, of justice, of the Wesleys faded from his mind. All he wanted was Sarah.

She stirred, and he felt her smile against his lips. "Good morning."

The sound of her husky, sleep-filled voice was almost too much to bear. He forced himself to take his hands off her, finger by finger. "I didn't want to leave without saying goodbye."

Her eyes snapped open, filled with panic. "Where are you going?"

He cursed himself for letting it matter so much. "Just into Glenwood Springs, remember? I'll be back by sometime tomorrow."

The panic faded from her eyes, replaced by wistfulness. "I'll miss you."

"I'll miss you, too," he muttered. Pressing a hard kiss against her lips, he stood up before he could weaken and crawl back into that bed with her. Staring down at her, he told himself the wrenching emptiness he felt in his gut was only worry about her safety. "Be careful. Don't leave the clinic tonight, and don't open the door to anyone after dark."

"I'll be fine, Connor." Her voice was gentle, and she sat up, pulling the sheet with her. "You watch yourself." She studied him, and then to his surprise a faint pink color washed her cheeks. "Could you call me tonight?"

"Absolutely." He reached for her one more time, brushing his fingers against her lips. "I'll see you tomorrow."

He strode out of the room without looking back. One glance, and he would be lost. He wouldn't make it out of Pine Butte this morning. He refused to think about the next time he had to leave.

Two hours later he was sitting on the edge of a desk in the pathology lab at the Glenwood Springs hospital. He knew the head resident there. She'd been a bit dubious about his request, but when he'd explained where he'd gotten the sample, she'd become as intrigued as he was.

She walked into the room, hands shoved into the pockets of her white jacket and her glasses pushed on top of her head. "Consider it done, MacCormac. We should have the results by late this afternoon."

He slid off the desk. "Thanks, Julia. I owe you."

"In a big way," she agreed. "And I expect the first payment to be a complete explanation."

"When I know, you will." He studied her for a moment. She was stunningly attractive, and he'd always intended to ask her out. Now there wasn't even a spark of interest when he looked at her. Not even the most beautiful woman in the world could come close to Sarah.

Sighing, he walked to the door. "I'll call you later, Julia. And thanks again."

His next stop was the public library. He scanned innumerable entries in their electronic card catalog, looked at more reference books than he could count. Apparently there wasn't a lot of public interest in the intricacies of gold mining.

Turning to the *Reader's Guide to Periodical Literature*, he saw several articles listed on gold mining. Scribbling the titles down, he searched until he had a stack of magazines with articles on the subject. Then he sat back and began to read.

When he closed the last magazine, dusk was falling outside the library windows. Staring into the distance, he felt an emptiness in his chest, the pain of loss, long forgotten. He knew how his father had died. And why. He knew just what was in that pool of water up on the mountain. He'd call Julia about what she'd found, but he already knew what she'd say.

He had to get back to Sarah. His head ached, the gash on his leg throbbed, and his ribs had stiffened up. Spending another hour and a half on a motorcycle so soon after being injured wasn't the smartest move in the world. But he had to get back to Sarah. He had to tell her what he'd found and let her kiss away the pain. He had to lose himself in her and let her warmth begin to heal his soul.

Shoving the chair away from the table, he headed toward the lobby and a pay phone. After a brief conversation with Julia, he got on his motorcycle and headed into the night.

Chapter 14

It was close to midnight by the time Connor saw the lights of Pine Butte twinkling below him. He drove cautiously over the dark mountain pass, pulling into town fifteen minutes later to park behind Sarah's clinic.

All the lights were out, and he squashed a wave of disappointment. She had no idea he was coming back tonight. He hadn't even called her the way he'd promised, he thought with a twinge of guilt. Maybe his homecoming would make up for his lapse.

He headed for the back door and the place where she hid an extra key. His hand on the door, he paused as the sound of music drifted through the air.

Shoving the key into his pocket, he walked down the block and found that the one and only bar in Pine Butte was in full swing. A country song blared out of the jukebox, and the singer wailing about the woman who done him wrong competed with the loud babble of voices.

He glanced toward Sarah's building and saw that all the lights were still out. He could stop in here for a few minutes. He needed to know if word had gotten out about his escapade the night before.

When he stepped through the doors, conversation stopped abruptly for just a moment as the men huddled around one corner of the bar turned to stare at him. Then they turned away and all began talking at once. Connor sauntered over to the bartender and asked for a beer, then slid onto a barstool and surveyed the small group of people.

There were seven or eight men slouched on bar stools or against the wall, lifting long-necked bottles of beer to their mouths and waving cigarettes in the air. None of them seemed to be paying any attention to him, and he leaned against the bar and let his glance slide over them.

A couple sat in a booth in the corner, completely absorbed in each other. Another couple was dancing next to the jukebox, but the woman seemed more interested in Connor than in her partner. The glances she cast his way were explicit and unmistakable, and he looked away with distaste. He let his eyes wander toward the men at the bar again.

They were apparently debating an obscure professional football rule. It seemed extremely important to all of them, as they were punctuating their pronouncements with their beer bottles and raising their voices as the discussion progressed. All of them were involved except one man who sat at the bar, his back to Connor, silently and steadily drinking from a bottle of beer.

When the man turned around to ask the bartender for another, Connor saw it was Harley Harrison, the foreman at the Wesley mine. Connor stared at Harley, willing him to meet his eyes. The foreman turned slowly in Connor's direction, and when he saw Connor sitting at the bar, he froze in place.

The look on Harrison's face was pure, sweating fear. There was no doubt about it. Grabbing his beer from the bartender, Harrison slapped a couple of dollar bills on the bar and spun around on his stool. The stiffness in his back told Connor the man was very aware of the eyes watching him.

Connor tilted his bottle and drained it, then signaled the bartender for another. Wrapping his fingers around the neck of the bottle, he slid off his stool and sauntered over to where the foreman sat, rigid.

"How're you doing, Harrison?" He settled in beside the foreman and set his bottle on the bar.

"What do you want, MacCormac?"

Connor considered the question. "What makes you think I want anything? Maybe I'm just being social."

Harley Harrison grabbed his beer bottle and took a long drink. "And maybe I'm Santa Claus. I heard about what you were doing up on the mountain last night."

"And what was that?"

"Messing around where you had no right to be."

Connor's smile didn't extend to his eyes. "I wasn't aware that I was on private property. Last I heard, that land belonged to the government."

Some of the bravado faded from Harley's eyes, replaced by a whisper of fear. "I don't know about that. All I know is you don't belong there."

"I don't think your boss does, either." Connor eased off the stool and jerked his head toward one of the booths against the wall. "Why don't we sit down where it's a little more... quiet?"

Harrison's eyes darted toward the group of men around him. They were all intent on their discussion, and none of them looked as if they were paying much attention to the other two men. Fear blossomed in Harrison's eyes, and he gave a jerky nod as he stumbled off the stool. "Maybe that's a good idea."

"I think so," Connor said pleasantly.

Connor stood and waited for the foreman to go first. Harrison fell into the booth and clutched his beer in both hands as he watched Connor slide in across the table.

"I know you know what's going on up there, Harley," Connor began without preamble. "I do, too. Right now you're an accessory and just as liable as the Wesleys. But you call up the Environmental Protection Agency, tell them what you know, and I figure it'll go a lot easier for you."

"Why should you care what happens to me?"

Connor leaned across the table, fixing his eyes on the frightened man watching him. "I don't give a rat's rear end about you, Harrison. All I want to do is find out what happened to my father. And I think I know. I just need proof, and I think you're the one who can give me that proof."

Harrison licked his lips. "I wasn't there, MacCormac. I didn't see a thing."

"But you know." Connor was relentless. "You know exactly why he died, and what killed him. Don't you?"

The foreman's eyes were riveted on Connor's face. Connor stared back, willing the other man to tell him what he needed.

Suddenly the foreman's eyes widened and he jerked his beer bottle to his mouth, gulping down the rest of the contents. Popping the empty bottle onto the table, he slid out of the booth and stood up. "I gotta go, MacCormac."

Connor turned his head. A woman stood rigid next to the bar, staring over to where he and Harley had been talking. Her thin lips were compressed into a tight line, and she glared first at Harley, then at him. Harley scrambled to where she stood and bent down to whisper something to her. Then, with a final glare, she took Harley's arm and led him from the bar.

Connor swiveled in his seat and stared out the window at them, watching them walk down the street. When they finally disappeared from view, he turned and picked up his beer, smiling faintly as he finished it. Who would have thought tough old Harley Harrison would have a wife even meaner than him?

His smile faded as he thought about their conversation. Obviously Harley knew what was going on at the Wesley mine, and just as obviously he didn't like it. If his wife had shown up just a few minutes later, Connor was sure the foreman would have told him everything.

He didn't need to, Connor assured himself as he pushed away from the booth and walked out the door. Just his reaction had been proof enough. Tomorrow he'd take another trip out to the mine and have a little chat with Ralph and his boot-licking son, Richard.

Taking a deep breath of the crisp evening air, he tried to clear his lungs of the cigarette smoke that had hung in the bar. The full moon illuminated Main Street with a ghostly glow, and the black sky was dusted with millions of stars.

Walking slowly to the clinic, he savored the quiet of the town, the silence of its streets. He thought about his own apartment in Denver, high above one of the busiest streets in the city. Even at four o'clock in the morning, the sounds of traffic kept up a steady rumble outside his windows.

Sarah's clinic was still dark and quiet. She'd gone to bed thinking he'd forgotten to call. Or maybe she thought he just hadn't wanted to bother. That thought pierced him, and he dug the key out of his pocket and shoved it in the lock.

He took the stairs two at a time, then paused in the living room. The house was dark and silent as a tomb. Looking into her bedroom, he could just make out her shadowy form in the bed.

He started toward her room, then stopped. He'd spent almost four hours today on a motorcycle and had just come from a bar. Maybe he should take a shower before he woke her. Turning to go down the stairs, he paused, then spun toward her room. He wouldn't have her thinking he'd forgotten her for another minute. He'd just tell her he was home, then go take his shower.

She'd worn a nightgown to bed, something sleeveless and long and white. His blood heated in anticipation. He'd enjoy taking that off her. The bedsprings dipped and sent her rolling toward him as he sat down on the edge of her bed.

"Sarah," he whispered softly. "Sarah, I'm back."

She murmured in her sleep and her hand moved, but she didn't wake up. Bending, he brushed his lips over her mouth and down her throat. "Wake up, Sarah."

Her eyes still closed, she reached for him, pulling him down onto the bed. The long white nightgown tangled around her legs as she turned to him, trying to draw him closer. As far as he could tell, she was still asleep. She hadn't once opened her eyes or said a single word.

"Are you still asleep?" he murmured.

In answer she just burrowed more deeply into his coat, as if she wanted to get as far inside him as she could. Leaning away from her, he peeled off his coat and kicked off his boots. Then, drawing her closer, he proceeded to wake her up.

Sarah struggled out of the depths of the dream. At first it had been lonely and cold, and she was wandering in the darkness all alone. Then suddenly the sun had come, warming everything with its glow and shining its light into the far corners of her soul. Someone whispered her name, told her to wake up, but she couldn't let go of her dream. She wanted to stay here forever.

The sun took shape and reached out for her, and she saw it was Connor. Smiling, she melted into his arms and raised her face to his. "I'm home, Sarah," the voice whispered, and for just a moment it was as if it was really true.

Then he kissed her, and the feelings swirling through her were more vivid than any dream she'd ever had. Forcing her eyes open, she looked up at Connor, whose deep blue gaze looked black in the dark room.

For a moment all she could do was stare, disoriented by her dream. Finally she reached out to touch his face, murmuring, "Are you really here?"

He kissed her again, a deep, lingering kiss. "What do you think?" he teased. Brushing his lips over her cheek, he added, "I didn't think you were going to wake up."

"I didn't want to. I was having a good dream."

"I hope it was about me," he murmured, nibbling at her neck.

"I'm not going to tell you what it was about. You're already too cocky as it is," she said, sliding to sit up in the bed. He sat up, too, and looked at her. Lines of exhaustion were etched into either side of his mouth, and his eyes looked utterly weary. "What are you doing back here tonight?" she asked, reaching out to smooth the lines from his face.

His eyes darkened. "I'm not going to tell you. You're already too cocky as it is," he mimicked, pulling her toward him. "Let's just say I wanted to sleep in a familiar bed."

She studied him, her hand lingering on his cheek. "I missed you," she said softly. "You didn't call."

"I wanted to surprise you." His answer was gruff, and he wouldn't meet her eyes.

Her lips curved in a smile. He was afraid she was going to be upset with him for not calling. "I'd much rather have you in the flesh than just your voice on the phone."

"Oh, you'll have me in the flesh, all right," he muttered, drawing her back down on the bed. "I couldn't think of anything but you all the way home."

She liked the sound of the word *home.* Even though she knew it was only temporary for him, it sounded so right. Home was wherever Connor was. Cupping his face in her hands, she drew him down to her.

He resisted, trying to pull away. "I should take a shower," he muttered. "I'm a mess."

"You're fine." Her voice was fierce and her hands burrowed under his shirt. "Don't leave me again tonight, Connor."

"I couldn't, love," he whispered, sucking in his breath as her hands trailed over his ribs. Pulling his shirt over his head, he said, "Dynamite couldn't get me out of this bed tonight."

He sat up and pulled off his jeans, briefs and socks, then lay down again, naked. His hands skimmed down her nightgown, lingering on the swell of her hip and dipping between her thighs. "Did you wear this just for me?"

"I wore it because I didn't think you were going to be here." Her voice caught on the words as he brushed his hand over her breasts, and she reached down to pull it off.

"Wait." His fingers folded around her hand and he gently moved it away. "Let me."

He raised the ankle-length nightgown inch by inch, kissing every inch of her skin he exposed. His lips and hands lingered, cherishing her and telling her without words that she was precious to him.

When he reached the juncture of her thighs, he stroked his finger gently over her, following it with his mouth. She arched off the bed in surprise and wonder, gasping, "Connor!"

He looked up at her, smiling tenderly. "Is something wrong?"

Desire pounded a heavy rhythm through her blood and made her ache. "No! I just...I don't..." He touched her again and she felt the spasm shake her body. "I need you, Connor. Now."

"I've just started with you, love." He glided over her again and she shuddered, falling apart in his hands. He waited for the tremors to ease, then raised the nightgown a little higher. He dipped his tongue into her navel, and she felt the tension gathering again.

By the time he reached her breasts, she was panting and writhing underneath him. When he curled his tongue around one nipple, she moaned his name and reached blindly for him. He went completely still as she closed her hand around him. He was hot and smooth and hard.

"I can't wait any longer, Connor."

"Ah..."

She felt his muscles tremble with his effort at control. "I wanted to show you how precious you are to me," he groaned. "If you keep touching me, this is all going to be over too soon."

"I can't take any more," she panted.

With a great effort he pulled away from her. "Oh, yes, you can. I'm going to show you just how much."

And he did. By the time he positioned himself over her, he had kissed every square inch of her body, caressing it lovingly and tenderly. He kissed her as if they had the rest of their lives to make love, and he wanted to take all the time in the world to show her how much she was cherished.

She was a boneless, quivering mass when he finally surged into her. Wrapping herself around him, she felt the tension gathering again, low in her belly. Her eyes flew open. "Connor!"

He smiled against her cheek. "I told you we hadn't even begun yet."

Then he took her mouth as he thrust into her, joining them body and soul. When she flew over the edge one final time, she took him with her. And as they lay on the bed, arms and legs entwined, slick with sweat and panting, she knew that nothing would ever be the same for her again. Connor owned her heart and her soul, and no matter what happened, she could never get them back.

Suddenly he rolled over, taking her with him. She opened her eyes and looked into his bright blue ones. He was staring at her with tenderness and what might have been wonder, and she snuggled into the hollow of his shoulder with a little smile on her face. Apparently he'd been just as jolted as she by their lovemaking.

As if he'd read her mind and needed to deny it, his arms tightened around her then lifted her away. "Don't you want to hear what I found out in Glenwood Springs today?"

"I thought we were taking care of the important things first," she murmured, skimming her hand down his chest.

Grabbing her hand before she could dip below his waist, he tangled his fingers with hers and brought their joined hands to his mouth. "Absolutely. And I hope all the important things were taken care of to your satisfaction."

He raised up on one elbow to look at her, and she felt the hot color flood her cheeks. It was one thing to be bold and mouthy in the darkness. It was quite another to say those sexy things to him while he watched her.

"You know they were." She had to force herself to look at him while she answered. Then she closed her eyes as she cuddled against him. "Tell me about Glenwood Springs."

He hesitated for a minute, his arms tightening around her. Finally he said gently, "Your uncle is in a lot of trouble, Sarah. Maybe your cousin, too. That pond up at the top of the mountain is an illegal heap-leaching operation, and the EPA is going to be all over them like a cheap suit."

Leaning away from him, she looked at his grim face and frowned. "What's heap leaching?"

"It's a way of removing very small amounts of gold from large amounts of rock. Remember how Richard went ballistic when I asked him why there weren't any piles of rocks at the mine? It was because they'd hauled them up to the top of the mountain to leach out the tiny bits of gold left in them."

She sat up slowly, pushing her hair out of her face. "I don't understand. Why is heap leaching illegal? And what does the EPA have to do with it?"

"Heap leaching itself isn't illegal. But the process is tricky, and the chemicals it uses are very dangerous. They have to get permits, file environmental impact statements, and it's regulated by the EPA. Your uncle hasn't done any of that. He's just gone ahead and set up his own operation, trying to save some money by avoiding the regulations and inspections that are necessary."

She stared at him, dread coiling in her gut. "What has he done?"

Connor sat up and pulled her to him, holding her against his heart. "The main chemical used in the operation is cyanide." He eased her away from him and watched her face. "You know how dangerous that is."

She nodded, fear clutching her chest. All she could do was hold onto him more tightly.

"The first time I was up on the mountain, the time someone used my head for batting practice, I noticed that there were no fish in the stream. There wasn't anything in that stream besides water. No plants, no bugs, nothing."

He pulled her close again and continued, "They diverted the stream to make their leaching pool. Apparently they weren't careful enough, because some of the cyanide they put in the pool must have gotten into the stream and killed off everything there."

"What about our drinking water?" she asked, pulling away from him and staring, appalled. "Are we all drinking cyanide?"

"I hope not," he said grimly. "But the EPA will find out quickly enough."

"And you think that's how your father died." It wasn't a question, and he nodded.

"Cyanide poisoning can mimic a heart attack, and I think that's just what happened to my father. Since only a few people knew what really happened, it would be easy enough to cover it up."

"Is there any way you can prove it?"

"I doubt it, after so many years." He smoothed his hand down her hair, and she felt the tension running through his body. "I don't think it was deliberate, anyway. The last thing the Wesleys would want to do is call attention to what they were doing."

"But they killed your father," she cried. "You can't let that go unpunished."

"It's my word against theirs," he answered, and she heard the futility in his voice. "After eighteen years, nobody is going to get real excited about the death of an immigrant no one in this town had any use for, anyway."

"You're wrong, Connor." She spoke with absolute conviction. "If that's what happened, my uncle should be punished. Surely *someone* will be interested."

"We'll see." His voice was carefully neutral, but she heard the bitterness beneath his words. "Right now, the most important thing is stopping the leaching and getting the cyanide cleaned up."

He pulled her down onto the bed and drew the covers over them. Snuggling into him, wrapping her arms around him, she ached to take away some of his pain. "What are you going to do now?"

"I talked to the EPA yesterday in Glenwood Springs. Tomorrow I'm going to pay a visit to your uncle."

She shot upright in the bed. "You don't have to talk to him again. Let the EPA take care of him."

She heard his sigh in the darkness. "The EPA is part of the government. They're pretty good when it comes to an emergency, but it may take them awhile to get to Pine Butte. I want to make sure that heap-leaching operation stops tomorrow." He leaned against the headboard, and she felt his smile. "And besides, I'm human enough to want to be the one to tell old Ralph that his little game is up."

"Please, Connor, let it be," she begged. "I don't want anything to happen to you."

He laughed. "Your uncle is an old man, honey. There's nothing he can do to me."

"What about Richard? It'll be two against one."

"Whatever else they are, the Wesleys aren't stupid," he said gently. "They would gain nothing by hurting me. I'll be fine."

She stared at him for a moment and a chill shivered up her spine. "I hope you're right," she said softly.

Sliding down into the bed, she curled around him and held him next to her. She felt him relax as he fell asleep, but she lay staring out the window for a long time.

When the alarm clock trilled the next morning Sarah groaned and burrowed deeper into her pillow. She was sore and stiff, just what she'd expect after spending the last hours laying rigidly in bed, too worried to fall asleep. She couldn't face the morning yet.

Connor stirred next to her, and the alarm was suddenly silent. Even without looking she could feel him watching her. After a long moment he reached over and cupped his hand around the back of her neck.

"I didn't realize I'd tired you out so much last night."

His voice was warm and laughing, and she raised her head with a groan. "I hate people who are cheerful first thing in the morning, MacCormac. You might as well know that right now."

Grinning, he reached over and kissed her, then stood up. "And here I thought you were little Mary Sunshine in the morning."

"Not after a week of sleepless nights, I'm not." Pushing the hair off her face, she sat up in bed. Belatedly realizing she was naked, she snatched the sheet to cover herself.

Connor sat on the bed and ran his hand lightly down her back. "I bet I know a way to brighten your outlook on life."

She smiled in spite of herself. "You'd be a miracle worker, then."

His eyes darkened and he leaned closer. "Is that a dare? I can never resist a dare."

He'd just pulled her to him when the telephone rang. With a snarl of frustration, she broke away from Connor and picked up the receiver. "Hello." *This better be good,* she fumed to herself.

"Sarah?" The voice was high-pitched and unmistakable, the whine just below the surface. "This is Melanie." Her cousin Richard's wife. Trust a Wesley to have such impeccable timing.

"Hello, Melanie. What can I do for you?"

"I want to know what is going on, Sarah. Since that . . . that person is staying with you, I assume you will be able to tell me."

Her hand tightened on the phone. "What do you mean?" she asked carefully.

"I want to know why Richard's father called at such an ungodly hour this morning and scared Richard so much. I want to know why he had to go running off to that mine just now without explaining anything to me." Her voice rose until she was screeching over the phone. "I want to know what's been going on in Pine Butte ever since that Mac-Cormac boy came back to town."

Sarah held the phone away from her ear. "If Richard is upset about something, I have no idea why you should think I would know anything about it." Her voice was low and deadly. "You know I have nothing to do with the mine. Why didn't you ask your husband?"

"He won't tell me a thing," she complained, the familiar whine of discontent in her voice.

"I'm sorry, Melanie, I don't know what to tell you. I guess you'll just have to wait for Richard to get home."

After listening to her cousin's wife complain for a while longer, she gently interrupted. "I have to go now, Melanie. I'll talk to you some other time."

Hanging up the receiver, she turned to look at Connor, a rueful expression on her face. "I guess I don't even have the luxury of sulking this morning. That delightful conversation was with Richard's wife. It seems that Uncle Ralph called him early this morning and said something that got Richard all worked up. He took off for the mine in a dither."

Connor jumped off the bed and reached for his clothes. "Then I'm going out there, too. If I know the Wesleys, they're out there trying to destroy any evidence they can. I may not be able to nail them for killing my father, but I sure as hell can nail them for what they're doing to the environment."

Sarah yanked open a drawer and pulled out a clean pair of jeans and a T-shirt. "I'm coming with you."

"Sarah—"

"Don't bother," she interrupted. She whirled on him fiercely. "If you're going to take risks for this town, I'm going to be with you."

"You don't get it, do you, Sarah? It's not for the town, it's for me. This is the only way I can get any small measure of revenge for my father. Hell, if it was just the cyanide, they could pour gallons right into the town reservoir and I wouldn't care. No, this is the only way I can make your uncle and cousin pay, and pay they will. So don't go getting all misty-eyed about my good intentions."

He stood in the doorway, his face set and his eyes hard. If she didn't know him so well she might actually believe him. He wanted her to think he was a selfish bastard, interested only in his own revenge. She knew better. Beneath the hard shell around his heart, he cared about this town and he cared about her. She had to believe that.

"I'm still coming with you," she said firmly. "If you don't let me ride with you, I'll just follow in my truck."

He shook his head. "You are one stubborn woman, Sarah Wesley." His eyes softened as he looked at her. "All right, I'd rather have you with me than in that truck by yourself."

Jamming on her shoes, she ran down the stairs after him. Just as she reached the bottom she heard a frantic pounding on the front door of the clinic.

She stopped, staring at the door with panic and fear. What had happened? Had there been a confrontation out at the mine already? Had somebody had another accident, trying to cover up what had been going on?

She looked at Connor and he looked back. Finally nodding, he said, "Go ahead. I'll wait."

She rushed to open the door and found Tom Johnson and his wife, Mary, standing there. Mary had one arm wrapped around her abdomen and was leaning against her husband.

"We got a problem, Sarah," Tom said.

Chapter 15

Mary's gray face was sheened with sweat. Dread stirred in the pit of Sarah's stomach as she drew the couple into the clinic.

"What's wrong?"

"My water broke a couple of hours ago," Mary answered, her voice high-pitched with fear and panic. "The contractions are getting worse now."

"Why aren't you in Glenwood Springs?" Sarah cried, urging them toward an exam room.

"My mother got here last night. We were going to go today." Mary sounded defensive, and Sarah told herself to calm down. She'd be no help to Mary if she panicked, too.

"Maybe everything's all right," Sarah soothed. "Let's take a look."

Helping Mary onto an exam table, she wrapped the blood pressure cuff around the pregnant woman's arm. Pumping up the little bulb, she felt her heart plunge when she saw the reading. She unwrapped the cuff slowly, waiting until she could speak without her voice giving away her fear.

"Your pressure is too high, Mary. We're going to have to get the evacuation helicopter in from Glenwood."

Mary's gray face became even paler. "Will they be able to get here in time?" she whispered.

Sarah would have given anything to be able to tell her friend that everything would be all right. But she couldn't lie to her. "I don't know, Mary. I hope so. I'll do everything I can until the helicopter gets here."

Out of the corner of her eye she saw Connor standing in the waiting room, watching the three of them. Walking slowly out of the exam room, she shoved her hands in her pockets to hide their trembling.

"Mary's in labor, and her blood pressure is way too high." Her voice cracked with strain. "I'm going to get the evacuation helicopter in here, but it may take a while. You go ahead. There's no way I can go with you."

An odd look flickered across his face, a mixture of apology and regret. "Maybe I can help, Sarah." He paused, and she thought he flushed slightly. "I'm a doctor."

She felt as if she'd been punched in the stomach. Shocked, she could only stare at him.

"You're a doctor?" she finally repeated numbly.

He nodded. "I'm in a family practice in Denver. I've delivered my share of babies, and I can do a Caesarean if it's necessary."

His gaze shifted past her to the woman who waited in the exam room, and Sarah felt her heart begin to crack. *He was a doctor.* One of the most vital parts of his life, and he hadn't wanted to share it with her. The only reason he had mentioned it now was that he couldn't stand by and endanger two lives. It would be against his Hippocratic oath, she thought bitterly.

Turning away from him, she gestured toward the couple in the other room. "I'm sure they would appreciate your help. I don't think Mary can wait until the helicopter gets here."

She turned to go to the exam room, not looking to see if Connor followed. When she felt his hand on her shoulder, she stopped abruptly.

"Sarah, I'm sorry." His low voice was pitched to reach her ears only, and she could almost fool herself into thinking it was filled with regret.

She spun around and faced him, determined not to let him see the hurt. "Why are you sorry?" she demanded. "A doctor is just what Mary needs right now. In fact, a person could almost say you were the answer to a prayer." She didn't even try to keep the bitterness out of her voice.

"I'm sorry I didn't tell you earlier."

"You never made any promises to me, Connor," she said, fighting to keep her voice steady. "Right from the start, you warned me how it was going to be. You never gave me the right to expect anything more from you." She would never let him see that she had expected it anyway. She couldn't bear it if he knew what kind of fool she'd been.

"Sarah," he began, but Mary's small cry, quickly smothered, jerked his attention to the urgency of the situation. "We don't have time to talk about this now," he muttered, taking a step toward the exam room. "Why don't you ask her if she wants me to examine her?"

Hearing an unfamiliar note in his voice, she finally looked at him. Realization struck like a thunderbolt as she stared at the tense planes of his face. He was scared. Could he possibly be worried that Mary wouldn't want him to examine her? Could he really think that the townspeople still hated him so much they would refuse his help?

In spite of the pain that was tearing her apart inside, she wanted to reach out to him, to reassure him that his help would be more than welcomed. Her bruised heart ached for him, for the pain and hurt he had suffered as a child. Clenching her hands into fists to prevent her from making a fool of herself, she nodded.

Without a backward glance, she strode to the room where Mary sat on the exam table, leaning against her husband. Taking Mary's hand, she squatted next to her.

"Mary, Connor is a doctor. Would you like him to examine you and see if he can help you?"

Both Tom and Mary looked toward Connor, startled. Then, slowly, hope replaced the sick fear on their faces. "A doctor!" Mary stared at him as if he was her salvation. "Does he think he can do anything?"

"He doesn't know. He'll have to examine you first." Taking a deep breath, she added, "He's in family practice, so he's delivered lots of babies. But it's up to you."

Mary looked at Sarah with confusion. "Why wouldn't I want his help?"

"I can't think of a single reason." Looking up, she called, "Connor? Could you come take a look at Mary?"

He strode into the room and took Mary's hand. "I'll need to know how dilated you are. Do you understand what I'll have to do?"

Mary looked even more confused. "Of course I do. Why are you asking?"

Connor stood by the exam table, holding Mary's hand, and something shifted in his face. The bitterness she'd seen when he'd talked about Pine Butte, the anger and remembered pain from his childhood, all of it slipped away. All she saw now was compassion for the woman in front of him, and a fierce determination.

"All right, then. Johnson, you'll need to help your wife. This can be painful." He got everything ready, then waited until a contraction passed and examined her gently.

Standing up straight, he stripped off the rubber gloves and watched the woman in front of him. "Sarah, call the helicopter," he said without looking at her.

Taking Mary's hand, he waited until Sarah had tersely ordered the helicopter to get there as soon as possible, then said, "I don't think you can wait until the helicopter gets you to Glenwood Springs and the hospital. You're going to have this baby too damned soon, and your blood pressure is already far too high."

"What can we do?" Mary asked faintly, fear in her eyes.

"I can do a Caesarean section," Connor answered abruptly. "Circumstances aren't ideal, but I think it would give you and the baby the best chance."

"Then do it." Mary's eyes closed as another contraction overwhelmed her.

Connor watched her for a moment. "Don't you have any questions?"

"What kind of questions would I need to ask? I already know that Sarah trusts you, and that's good enough for me. Besides, what other choice do we have?"

"Not much." Still he hesitated. "Are you sure you wouldn't rather wait for the helicopter?"

"Would you?" Tom asked, watching Connor with fear and bewilderment mixed in his eyes.

"No, I wouldn't. Mary's blood pressure is climbing by the minute. We have to get that baby out of there."

"Then what are you waiting for?" Mary's voice was high and thin as another contraction gripped her.

"Nothing." Connor turned to Sarah. "We'll need to start an IV and get an anesthetic into her."

"I've got it ready," she answered, amazed that her voice was even but determined to keep it that way. She had to forget about her own pain until Mary's baby had been delivered. "Here you are."

Twenty-five minutes later Connor held up a squalling baby and smiled at Tom and Mary. "Well, his lungs certainly sound fine." He reached for the towel that Sarah held out to him and carefully wrapped the baby in it, then handed the baby to Sarah. "You have a good-looking son here, Mary."

She smiled weakly. "Is he all right, Mr. MacCormac?"

"I'll let the pediatrician in Glenwood give you the definitive answer, but he looks great to me."

"And how about Mary? Is she going to be all right?" Tom asked.

Connor looked at the sheriff. "Now that the baby is delivered, her blood pressure should come back down. She'll have to be watched carefully for a few days, and she's not out of the woods yet, but I think she'll be fine."

Tom smoothed the hair away from his wife's face, gazing at her with adoration. "She will be," he answered fiercely.

Ten minutes later, Connor stripped off his gloves and took the baby from Sarah. Handing him to his mother, he squatted down next to her. "I hear the helicopter now," he said gruffly. "You keep that baby next to you all the way to Glenwood Springs. Make sure he stays warm."

"How can I thank you for what you did, Mr. Mac-Cormac?" Mary asked softly, then blushed. "I guess I should say Dr. MacCormac, shouldn't I?"

"You should say Connor," he replied with a tender smile that transformed his face. "And you don't need to thank me. You gave me something almost as precious earlier this morning." He stood up as the paramedics came into the clinic. After a few minutes of consultation about what to do for Mary on the way to Glenwood, he stood back and watched as they carried Mary out the door on a stretcher, the baby clutched in her arms.

The door had barely closed when they heard the helicopter take off again. Sarah slowly turned to Connor.

"Thank you," she said, feeling her eyes fill with tears. "Mary's a good friend."

"Nothing to thank me for." He stepped over to her as if to take her in his arms, then stopped abruptly. "I'm glad I was here."

"So am I, Connor." *But why couldn't you have told me earlier?* she cried silently.

"I wanted to tell you, Sarah," he said as if he could read her mind. "I almost did, that day when I told you about Perry Cummings."

"But you didn't," she pointed out sadly, turning to go to her office. She had paperwork to do because of Mary's evacuation. And she needed to get away from Connor. She wasn't sure which was worse, her feelings of betrayal or her doubts about her own judgment. She'd fallen in love with a man who didn't trust her enough to tell her the most basic facts about himself.

"Sarah, please don't go. I can't bear to have you turn away from me."

"Why not, Connor? It's what you've been doing all along."

"I never meant to hurt you," he said, sounding desperate.

Still she wouldn't turn around. "But you did. You slept with me, but you didn't trust me enough to share that part of yourself."

"I couldn't," he cried, and the anguish in his voice almost made her go to him. "As much as I wanted to tell you, to share myself with you, I just couldn't." His voice dropped so low that she could barely hear him. "The only way I survived my childhood in Pine Butte was by keeping my feelings a secret, and old habits are hard to break. I let my bitterness toward this town blind me to your needs. I'll never forgive myself for that."

She turned to face him, forcing herself to stand still. The pain in his eyes reached out to her, trying to pull her closer.

"I thought I'd fallen in love with you, Connor," she whispered, whipping herself with her lack of judgment, feeling the pain of it cut into her heart. "But it was all a fantasy, wasn't it, a fling with a man I'd created in my imagination. I never knew the real Connor MacCormac, never knew what had happened in the twelve years since you left. You never let me see the real person underneath your skin. And what hurts the most is that I fell in love with you anyway."

She turned away, unwilling to let him see her cry. It would be a long time before she trusted her own judgment again.

The front door of the clinic opened and Josie walked in. "'Morning, Sarah. Hi, Connor." She breezed past them and into the next room, closing the door behind her.

Sarah froze, swallowing hard against the lump of tears in her throat. "It's late," she muttered to Connor. "You wanted to get right out to the mine. Look what time it is."

"It's okay, Sarah."

"I don't want you to miss your chance to find out what happened to your father."

"Two lives were saved," he said gently. "I think it's a fair exchange. Besides, they're not going to clean up that heap in just a couple of hours."

"Why don't we leave right now?" she asked, groping in her pocket for a tissue to blow her nose.

"You don't want to come with me now, Sarah," he said, his voice flat.

No, she didn't want to go with him. She wanted to crawl into the nearest hole and curl up in a ball until the pain went away. And if she had any sense at all, that's just what she would do.

But sense had nothing to do with it. In spite of the ache in her soul, she wasn't about to let him walk into a dangerous situation by himself. "I'm not letting you go alone. They're my uncle and cousin, and I'm going up there, even if I have to drive there myself."

He didn't say anything for a long time. She felt his hot gaze on her, although she wouldn't meet his eyes. Finally he said, "Did anyone ever tell you that you were damned stubborn?" She heard a note of wonder in his voice, but instead of looking at him she shoved her hands in her pockets and pushed past him, going into the next room to talk to Josie.

After leaving instructions about rescheduling her patients, Sarah followed him to the truck. As they bumped along the now-familiar road to the mine, she searched frantically for something to say to him. Silence hung between them, thick and heavy with pain and guilt. If she didn't say something soon, she would embarrass herself. She couldn't bear for him to see how vulnerable she was to him.

"Can I ask a question?" she said in a shaky voice. She hurried on before he could answer. "Why did you decide to become a doctor?"

She could feel him relax slightly next to her, but she didn't look at him. He glanced at her, then turned and looked out the window.

"When I left Pine Butte, I was just running. Barb..." He paused, then said carefully, "I couldn't stay here. I had to leave, but I had no plans, no money, nowhere to go. I got as far as a little town called Rio Bianco and got hungry."

She glanced at him and saw his mouth twist. "What happened?" she asked.

"I stole a car."

Her face must have expressed her shock, because he smiled grimly. "Yeah, I went from a wild kid to a criminal in about ten minutes. But I was a damned lucky stiff. The car happened to belong to the town doctor, and he caught me in the act. He saw something in me, and to this day I don't know what it was, but he didn't call the cops. Instead, he sentenced me himself.

"My punishment, he said, was going to be to ride with him for the next two weeks. He told me that he wanted me to learn the consequences of my actions."

He smiled softly. "I learned, all right. I saw exactly what would have happened if I'd been successful in stealing his car. I saw all the people that would have been in real trouble if Doc Webster hadn't been able to get out to treat them. I saw babies born, old people sick with pneumonia, children that needed their knees sutured after they fell out of a tree. It didn't take more than a couple of days for me to stop sulking and realize what I'd almost done. Before the two weeks were up, I knew there was nothing else in the world I wanted to do but become a doctor."

She blinked furiously to clear her eyes. "Your Doc Webster sounds like a wonderful man."

"The best," he said simply. "I stayed with him for the rest of the summer, then he helped me get financial aid to go to college. I spent all my vacations with him." He paused, then continued in a low voice, "He was my family, especially after my mother died."

He doesn't have to be your only family, she cried silently. She glanced at him. He stared out the window, obviously lost in memories of the man who'd taken his father's place.

Noticing the scenery, she realized they were getting close to the mine. A knot of fear began to replace the pain in her gut. They were on their way to confront the man who was responsible for his father's death. This wasn't just a little game they were playing, nipping at Ralph Wesley's ankles like a couple of persistent and annoying small dogs. This was deadly serious.

Connor knew exactly what had been going on at the Wesley mine. He had proof, and he intended to confront her uncle and cousin with that proof. She'd told him that her uncle was no murderer, but what would Ralph do when faced by a man who swore that justice would be done?

Ralph Wesley was a man determined to have his own way. He'd *had* things his own way in Pine Butte for as long as anyone could remember. No one stood up to Ralph Wesley, let alone accused him of a crime like murder.

They were walking, unarmed, into the lion's den. The road swam in front of Sarah as fear washed over her again. The entrance to the mine suddenly appeared in the road ahead, and she gripped the steering wheel more tightly. The coming confrontation would be ugly, and she wished passionately that it didn't have to happen.

She glanced at Connor again. His face was set in stone, hard and unyielding. There would be no dissuading him from facing her uncle, she knew. This was the reason he'd come back to Pine Butte, after all. So all she could do was stay with him and hope that somehow her presence would keep tempers from flaring out of control.

They pulled into the parking lot at the mine and saw the men at work on the ore cars. On the surface, everything seemed the same as the last time they were at the mine. But as they stepped out of the truck, she felt the tension in the air. It was there in the furtive way the men in the yard stared at them. It was there in the unnatural silence that fell over the yard when the men realized who was in the truck. Even the windows of the shabby office building seemed filled with menace.

"Stop it," she muttered to herself. This was no time for her imagination to kick in.

"Did you say something?" Connor asked quietly.

"No. I guess I'm just nervous."

A quick smile flitted across his face. "I thought you were the one so determined to come with me."

Straightening her spine, she said, "I was. I mean, I am. Let's go see who's in the office."

No one stopped them as they approached the building. She half expected her cousin to come running out, yelling at them to leave, but they walked into the dingy structure without seeing a soul.

"Where's your uncle's office?" Connor asked, his voice loud in the unnatural quiet.

She nodded toward the stairs, licking her suddenly dry lips. "On the second floor. This way."

When they reached the door, it was firmly closed, but the murmur of voices behind the door told them the office was occupied. And, judging from the rising pitch of at least one voice, someone was scared.

Connor cocked one eyebrow at her. "I think it's time to make a dramatic entrance, don't you?" Without waiting for an answer, he opened the door and walked in.

Dead silence greeted them. There were three men standing around a desk—her uncle, her cousin and Harley Harrison, the foreman. Their faces were frozen in expressions of incredulity. Apparently they hadn't thought that Connor would be brave enough to beard them on their own territory.

"MacCormac!" Her cousin Richard's face turned an ugly shade of purple. "I thought I told you once before to stay away from here."

Connor's eyes flickered over him and dismissed him, then fixed on her uncle. "I think we need to talk, Wesley. Tell your...son to back off." He spoke without taking his eyes off the elder Wesley, and Sarah saw her cousin flush at the insult. Rage spread on his face, and Sarah saw her uncle reach out and put a hand in front of his son.

"I want to hear what MacCormac seems to think is so important."

Connor let his eyes move from one man to the other, and Sarah saw the utter contempt in them. Only Harley seemed even a little uncomfortable. Richard seethed with anger, and Ralph looked faintly bored.

"I know what's going on, Wesley. Up on the mountain. I know all about the heap leaching, and diverting the water from the stream to make your pool. I know about the cyanide, and so does the EPA."

For the first time Sarah saw a flicker of expression in her uncle's eyes, and she didn't like what she saw. She'd seen that expression before, on the rare occasions when someone had tried to stand up to Ralph Wesley.

It didn't seem to bother Connor a bit. He smiled, but there wasn't a trace of humor in his eyes.

"And I know what happened to my father." His voice was so soft that she wasn't sure if the other men in the room

could hear him. "But then, all of you have known all along
what happened to him, haven't you?"

Ralph Wesley spoke. "Your father died of a heart attack, MacCormac. That's what his death certificate shows,
and there's no reason to think otherwise." He straightened
and waved toward the door. "Now I have a business to
run, and you've interrupted an important meeting. I'll
thank you to leave."

"Not a chance, Wesley. Not until I get what I came here
for."

Ralph sighed and reached into his desk. Sarah felt Connor tense next to her, and he reached out and pushed her
behind him. *He expects Uncle Ralph to pull a gun,* she realized with sudden, blinding fear.

But instead her uncle pulled out his checkbook. "I suppose you want some money." There was nothing in his voice
but contempt. "I can't afford for you to make these rash,
unsubstantiated statements. How much?"

"Are you offering me money to keep my mouth shut,
Wesley?"

Sarah heard the menace in his voice, felt the tension coiling in his muscles. "Connor," she murmured, but he didn't
appear to hear her.

"Just like you paid my mother to keep her mouth shut?"
His voice was so soft now that she had to strain to hear him.
"You'll find I'm not quite as easy a mark. I'm not a widow
trying to raise a child on a pitiful pension from Wesley
Mining."

"Your mother got her pension from the mine and nothing more," Ralph said flatly. "There was no reason to pay
her any additional money. Your father had a heart attack,
plain and simple."

"You're wrong, Uncle Ralph." Sarah stepped next to
Connor and faced her uncle. "Connor's father died from
cyanide poisoning. From the illegal heap-leaching operation you have on the top of the mountain."

"Rubbish. I may have an illegal heap leach, but no one's
ever died because of it."

He believed that, Sarah realized with a shock. She looked
from her uncle to her cousin. There in Richard's eyes was

the answer. He knew. He knew all about Connor's father and the cyanide. And he knew just what had happened.

Richard's gaze met hers. He knew she understood.

As Connor turned to face him, Richard yanked open a desk drawer and scrabbled around in it. Pulling out a gun, he held it in a shaky hand. The huge, deadly-looking barrel was pointed right at Connor.

"You didn't learn, did you, MacCormac? You couldn't take a hint." His voice was shrill and high-pitched, and Sarah watched, appalled. She couldn't have moved if she'd wanted to.

"I thought things were going my way when I recognized you on Eagle Ridge Road. You shouldn't have stopped and taken your helmet off. I'd never forget your face, and when I saw you I knew it was my chance to take care of you once and for all. But that do-gooder sheriff we have found you, and *she* managed to save your worthless life."

He pointed the gun in Sarah's direction, and Connor drew her behind him again.

"I even followed you that first day you went up the mountain. I was sure you were headed for the heap. You've been damned hard to get rid of, MacCormac." His mouth twisted into a sneer. "At least up until now. Let's see what kind of luck you have against a gun."

Sarah looked at her uncle. For the first time that she could remember, her uncle looked confused. Confused and frightened.

"Uncle Ralph never knew about any of this, did he, Richard?" She tried to keep her voice soft and soothing, to distract him from the gun he held in his hand.

"I don't need my father telling me every move to make," he said shrilly. "I don't have to get his approval for everything I do. And I don't have to wait until he tells me it's okay before I get rid of you, MacCormac."

He raised the gun, and Connor shoved her to the floor before lunging at Richard. He was too late. Harley Harrison was already wrestling with him.

Connor, Sarah and Ralph watched for a moment in stunned silence as the two men rolled around on the floor. Then Connor leaped around the desk and put his foot on

Richard's wrist. Sarah heard a sickening crack as a bone snapped, and with a thin scream, Richard dropped the gun.

Harley hauled Richard to his feet, and the younger man hunched over, cradling his injured wrist in his other hand. Connor stepped away from him.

"It's broken," he said shortly to the whimpering Richard. "But it'll mend." He turned to Harley. "You knew what was going on."

It was a statement, not a question, and Harley nodded, refusing to meet Connor's eyes. "The old man didn't know anything about your father," he said, nodding in Ralph's direction.

Sarah looked at her uncle. For the first time, he did look like an old man. Fear and uncertainty lined his face. He looked as if he'd shrunk several inches in the last few minutes.

Connor's face hardened. "Don't tell me he knew nothing about the heap leaching. I won't buy it."

"No, he knew about that. Hell, it was his idea. But he made one mistake. He put Junior in charge." He jerked his head in Richard's direction. "And Junior screwed up."

"He screwed up big-time," Connor said softly. "What happened?"

"He mixed the cyanide solution wrong. Made it way too strong. When your old man picked it up, some of it slopped on his hands and into his face." Harley stopped and looked at Connor with sympathy. "He dropped dead. It looked just like a heart attack, and that's what we told the doc from Glenwood." He shrugged. "They didn't look any further. There wouldn't be any reason to check for cyanide."

Sarah could only imagine Connor's pain at hearing his father's death described so callously. A place deep in her heart urged her to go to Connor and comfort him, but she held herself stiffly in place. She needed some comfort herself.

"So who paid off my mother?" Connor's voice was hard and completely without mercy.

"Richard did." Harley looked at the whimpering man and contempt flickered in his eyes. "He wanted to be sure she didn't ask any awkward questions."

Connor fixed Harley with a piercing look. "You sent me that anonymous note, didn't you?"

Harley shifted uncomfortably. "Yeah," he finally admitted. "My wife works at the bank. It wasn't too tough for her to get the address from Goodman."

"But she didn't want you to write to me, did she?" he asked softly.

Harley shifted again, then looked directly at Connor. Sarah saw regret and a glimmer of the old defiance in the foreman's eyes. "No, she didn't. She didn't want the gravy train to stop." He glanced at Ralph. "Mr. Wesley pays me well to keep the heap running smoothly. Thelma was afraid that if you came back to town and figured out what was going on, the money would stop." Shame flickered in his eyes, and he looked away.

"She was right," Connor said grimly. "As of right now, that heap-leaching operation is shut down." He stared at Harley. "I just have one more question. Why did you write to me? You must have known what would happen if I came back to town, looking for answers."

"Yeah, I guess I did know." Harley ran his hand over the dark stubble of beard on his chin. "I supppose that's why I wrote to you." He paused, and his gaze rested on Richard. "He was making mistakes, and sooner or later there was going to be another accident like your father's."

Harley watched Richard for a moment, then looked at Connor. "I knew I'd be blamed for the next one," he said bluntly. "No way was I going to take the rap for his mistakes. I guess I thought that if you came back to town, I'd be off the hook one way or another. Either you'd figure out what was going on, or I'd figure out a way to make you look responsible for any accidents up there on the mountain." He stared at Connor, defiance mixed with shame in his eyes.

Connor stared back for a while, until suddenly his face relaxed just a bit. "At least you're honest about it, Harrison." His gaze flickered from Ralph to Richard. "I guess you were in a hell of a bind."

"Yeah," the foreman muttered, not looking at anyone.

Connor's gaze shifted to Ralph. He stared at him for a long moment, until Ralph looked away. Amazingly, Sarah saw a dull red color mottle his cheeks.

"I didn't know, MacCormac."

Connor's face hardened again, and a muscle in his jaw twitched. "You might not have known how my father was killed, but that doesn't lessen your responsibility. That was *your* heap up there. You put your son in charge, knowing what a screw-up he was. No, *you* might not have known, but I blame you as much as Richard."

For the first time Sarah saw fear in her uncle's eyes. "What do you want from me, MacCormac? I can't bring your father back. I already offered you money. What more do you want?"

"I want the heap cleaned up, Wesley." Connor's voice was a whisper, soft and deadly. "I want every bit of cyanide off that mountain, I want the wall that's diverting the stream torn down, and I want the stream restored to its previous cleanliness." His lips compressed as he stared at the elder Wesley. "I want to see fish in that stream again, and birds living in the trees above it. And I want you to make sure the drinking water for Pine Butte is completely clean and safe."

"That would cost a fortune!"

Connor smiled thinly. "Exactly. But I suspect you'll find it preferable to jail. Which is your only alternative."

"I may have bent some of the EPA's regulations, but I won't get thrown into jail for that." Some of Ralph's old bluster was back, awakened, no doubt, by the thought of having to spend some money. Sarah watched him, the tiny glimmer of sympathy she'd felt for the old man quickly disappearing.

"Not only have you broken the law, Wesley, you've killed a man because of your greed. Most courts tend to frown on that."

Ralph opened his mouth to argue again, and Connor silenced him with a slash of his hand. "The EPA has already been notified, so don't bother trying to bribe me again. You're caught, Wesley, and there's no way you can squirm out of it this time."

Connor stepped back and surveyed the three men standing in front of him. "You boys have a lot of work to do. I suggest you get started." Turning on his heel, Connor walked out of the room without a backward glance.

Sarah looked at Richard, who was leaning against the wall, holding his broken wrist. "You'd better come into the clinic and let me set that for you, Richard." Without waiting for an answer, she followed Connor out of the building.

He was waiting for her next to the truck. The men unloading the ore cars still watched them furtively, waiting, no doubt, for the explosion from Ralph or Richard. When he saw her walking toward him, Connor got into the driver's side of the truck. She got in and silently handed him the keys.

Neither of them spoke until they were on the road to town, the mine out of sight behind them. It was over, everything was over, and dread settled in Sarah's chest like a leaden weight. She bit her tongue, willing the words away. She didn't want to ask what came next. She was horribly afraid that she already knew.

The silence became so thick and tense that she had to say something. Glancing at Connor, she saw him staring grimly at the road in front of him. She licked her lips. "What do we do now?"

He looked at her, and a grim smile washed over his face. Some of the strain disappeared, and he said, "Now we wait for the EPA to show up on their white horses."

Chapter 16

Sarah tried to swallow the lump in her throat. "Of course," she muttered. She couldn't meet his eyes. "I mean, after that."

"I'm afraid your cousin Richard will be spending some time in jail. As far as the heap-leaching operation, it'll take them a while to assess the situation and figure out exactly what has to be done. When I talked to the EPA yesterday in Glenwood, they told me it could take a year or more to get the heap completely cleaned up."

Was he being deliberately thickheaded? Or maybe, she thought with a chill, it hadn't even occurred to him that there was anything more important to talk about than the mine. After all, he hadn't thought it necessary to tell her about his life. An icicle pierced her chest as she clung to the armrest.

"Everyone in Pine Butte is going to be very grateful to you." She forced the words through numb lips and stared out the windshield. Trees and rocks flashed past, the colors blurring and running together. *You will not cry,* she told herself fiercely.

"The people of Pine Butte should be damned ashamed of themselves. They let Ralph Wesley bully them for the past twenty-five years, and this is their reward. I hope they've learned a lesson."

She'd thought his bitterness had disappeared this morning after he'd treated Mary Johnson. Apparently she'd been wrong. She kept her head averted so he couldn't see the tears that threatened to overflow. "I suspect they've learned a lot of lessons in the past couple of weeks," she whispered, the last ember of hope quietly flickering out.

"I hope so," he grunted, swerving to avoid a pothole in the road. "The people here—" she felt his eyes on her but refused to turn and look at him "—shouldn't have to live in fear of Ralph Wesley."

There was no time to respond to him. Before the last words were out of his mouth, he turned the truck sharply and they were in back of the clinic again.

Maybe it was best that their conversation ended when it did, she told herself, getting out of the truck and hurrying for the door. She didn't want to embarrass herself and make Connor uncomfortable by pleading with him to stay, and if she'd stayed in the truck with him for much longer, that's just what would have happened.

He'd told her all along that he wasn't going to stay. He'd warned her, and she'd gone and fallen in love with him anyway. Now she would just have to pay the piper.

The back door of the clinic banged behind her as she hurried in, not looking to see if Connor was following her. There were probably at least a dozen people waiting for her in the front of the clinic. Maybe if she kept busy, she wouldn't think about Connor packing his things in the bedroom just around the corner from her.

The waiting room was, indeed, full, and she stopped in the doorway and drew a deep breath. Connor came up behind her. He didn't make a sound but she knew he was there. Straightening her back, she stepped into the room and walked over to the desk.

"I'm back, Josie. Go ahead and put the first person in an exam room."

Josie nodded her head toward one corner. "The sheriff's been waiting for you and Mr. MacCormac. You'd better talk to him first."

Sarah spun around and saw Tom Johnson sitting on the edge of one of their hard plastic chairs. Fear spilled over her and she sucked in a breath.

"What's wrong?" she cried. "What happened?"

Tom rose from the chair and walked toward her. His face was gray and set in stone. "I need to talk to you, Sarah, and MacCormac, too. Can we go into one of the exam rooms?"

Sarah glanced at Connor. He looked sick with worry as he watched Tom Johnson walk to the first room. He followed her into the room and closed the door quietly.

"Is Mary all right?" he asked as soon as the door was shut.

Tom nodded jerkily. "Mary's fine. I talked to her on the phone from Glenwood just a little while ago. Her blood pressure has come down a little and the doctor said it should keep coming down. The baby's fine, too." He looked at Connor, and a strange look passed over his face, shame, regret and sorrow all rolled into one. "He said you did a great job."

"Then what are you doing here?" Sarah asked sharply. "Why didn't you go to Glenwood with Mary?"

"I couldn't. I had to make sure everything was set with Mary's mom and the kids first." His gaze slid away from her as he added, "And I couldn't leave without talking to MacCormac."

"What is it, Sheriff?" Connor's voice sounded wary.

Tom took a deep breath and turned to face Connor. "I couldn't leave town without straightening something out. Especially since you might not be here when Mary and I come home." He took another breath and shoved his hands into his pockets. "I know you weren't the father of Barb Wesley's baby. I was."

"What?" Sarah gasped. "How could you be? You didn't even live here then."

"I was on the police force in Meeker. We met at a party there."

Sarah looked at Connor. His face had frozen in a mask of anger. Pain flickered deep in his eyes.

"I thought you looked familiar. I must have seen you with her." His voice hardened, sounding implacable and unforgiving. "You were the one who abandoned her to die by herself, then."

"I didn't mean for that to happen," Tom said softly, and Sarah saw ancient sorrow in his eyes. "She went into labor early. If her pregnancy had gone full term, I would have been divorced and with her." He turned away, but not before Sarah saw the regret in his eyes. "Maybe she still would have died, but at least I would have been with her."

Connor looked at Tom with contempt. "Let me get this straight. You were married, but you got a teenage girl pregnant and then abandoned her to endure her pregnancy alone. And you say you didn't mean to."

"I couldn't do anything about it," Tom cried, his voice filled with wrenching anguish. "I was already in the middle of a divorce when we met. I knew if my wife found out about Barb and me she would never let the divorce go through. I thought the best thing for us was for me to stay away from Barb until the divorce was final. I was going to marry her the next day."

In spite of herself, Sarah could sympathize with his predicament. Tom must have suffered over that decision every day of his life. There was one thing, though, that she couldn't forgive him for. "Why did you let everyone, including me, go on thinking that Connor was the father of Barb's baby after you got your divorce? Surely then you could have told me."

Tom's face turned a dull red and he looked at the floor. "MacCormac was gone, and nobody ever heard from him. I figured he wasn't ever coming back. By the time I moved here and met Mary, it was ancient history. I didn't figure there was any reason to bring it up."

"You stand for justice, Tom," Sarah cried passionately. "How could you put on that badge every day, knowing what you had done to someone's reputation?"

Connor looked at her and raised his hand, as if to touch her shoulder. After a moment he let it drop. Jamming his hands into his pockets, he sighed. "He's right, Sarah. It's ancient history. It wouldn't have made any difference if people knew the truth. They've thought of me one way for the past twelve years, and it's going to take more than Tom confessing to make them change their opinions."

"It would be a start." She turned on him fiercely. "People here don't want to think badly of you, Connor. They just haven't had any reason not to. You left town at eighteen, with everyone thinking you'd gotten Barb pregnant and then abandoned her. Let them see the real you. Let them know what you've become." Her voice softened. "The people in Pine Butte want to forgive you and admit they were wrong. But in order to do that, you have to forgive them first."

Connor's head jerked in her direction. "*I* have to forgive *them?*"

"Yes, you do," she answered softly. "You have to forgive them for the way they treated you when you were a child, and for not believing you when Barb accused you of being the father of her baby. You have to let go of your anger. You can't let what happened here twelve years ago poison your life anymore."

"It doesn't even affect my life anymore, let alone poison it," he said harshly.

"I think you're wrong. You said you loved Barb. Have you ever loved anyone since?"

She watched as he flinched, his face turning even harder and colder, and she nodded, feeling her heart slowly beginning to crumble. "I didn't think so. You'll never be able to love anyone unless you forgive the people here for what they did and put it behind you."

"Now you're a psychiatrist, too?" Connor snarled at her. "My life is just fine the way it is. I don't need any small-town do-gooder nurse telling me what to do to have a fulfilling life."

"I'm going to tell everyone in Pine Butte the truth, MacCormac," Tom interrupted. "That's why I stayed here rather than going to Glenwood Springs with Mary. I wanted you to know that it may have taken twelve years, but I'm going to put the record straight."

Tom's words fell into the charged silence as Connor and Sarah stared at each other. A painful hand squeezed Sarah's heart, breaking it into smaller bits. She told herself that Connor was hurting and that's why he said such cruel things. She even told herself she believed it. But inside, she felt herself withering as she acknowledged that there wasn't any way Connor was going to stay in Pine Butte. And even if she could leave, Connor had demonstrated just how important she was to him. She wasn't about to beg for love from a man who didn't trust her enough to tell her about himself.

She saw Connor wrench his gaze away from her and look at Tom again. "You go ahead and do whatever you like. It doesn't affect me in any way."

Tom's eyes slid from Connor to Sarah. "Somehow I thought that maybe you were going to stay here in Pine Butte. We can sure use a good doctor."

"I said from day one that I wasn't staying. And I meant it."

"It doesn't matter. Whether you go or stay, I'm going to make sure that everyone in town knows the truth."

Connor shrugged. "If you want to play the martyr, that's okay with me. Just don't think it'll make me change my mind."

"I'm not trying to change your mind, MacCormac. I just want to do the right thing. It's taken me far too long already." Without another word, Tom turned and walked out the door.

Connor turned to Sarah, but she couldn't meet his eyes. Her throat was thick and full of tears. She would *not* beg him to change his mind, she told herself, looking everywhere but at him. Some things had to be given freely. And so far, he hadn't given her much of himself.

"I can't stay, Sarah." His voice pleaded with her to understand and agree. "This town took things from me that I can never get back. If I stayed here, I would constantly be reliving my past. I can't do that."

"Isn't it time to put the past behind you?" she asked gently. "Forgiving isn't as hard as you think it is."

He paused, then said in a low voice, "If I could do it at all, it would be for you, Sarah." He looked at her with haunted, pain-filled eyes.

"It has to be for yourself, Connor." The fist tightened around her heart.

"Sarah, come with me. Please." His voice thickened and he took a step toward her.

Slowly she shook her head. "I can't do that. You know I have to stay. I can't leave the people I love without medical care."

He stared at her, pain and anguish in his eyes. If he raised his hand or took a step toward her, she would be lost. She'd cling to him and beg shamelessly for him to stay.

But he stood rooted to the floor, hands clenched into fists at his sides, until he finally closed his eyes.

"Sarah."

It sounded as if her name had been torn out of him. She waited, but he didn't say anything more. Her heart shriveled painfully and crumbled in her chest.

"There really isn't anything left to say, is there, Connor? You've made your choices and your feelings very clear." She turned away, clutching the doorknob so hard her knuckles turned white. "I've got a waiting room full of people," she whispered, hating the thickness in her voice and refusing to meet his eyes. "And I know you must have a lot to do. I won't keep you."

She moved slowly to the door, but couldn't bear to walk away without one last look at him. "Goodbye, Connor. Thank you for everything."

He stood staring at her, tenderness fighting with the hardness in his eyes. The hardness won, and she closed the door quietly behind her.

Connor stood rooted to the floor for a long time, watching the place where Sarah had disappeared. Her goodbye had sounded awfully final.

But then why wouldn't it, he asked himself bitterly. He'd made it pretty plain that he wasn't interested in anything Sarah Wesley had to offer.

His lips thinned as he remembered her asking him if he'd been in love since he left Pine Butte and Barb. What the hell did she know about love, stuck here in this hick town all her life? She'd told him she hadn't been involved with anyone since she came back to Pine Butte six years ago. She had no idea how much it could hurt to love someone.

It took him only a few minutes to pack his belongings. A half hour later, everything was loaded onto his motorcycle and he was ready to go. All he had to do, he told himself, was get on the bike, start it up and ride away.

He'd leave Pine Butte, Colorado, and everything it stood for behind him. It would never have any power over him again. He'd finally defeated Ralph Wesley and learned the truth about his father, and now he could get on with the rest of his life.

A life that would be sterile and empty without Sarah, a small voice reminded him, and he tightened his grip on the leather backpack. There was no way anything could work out between him and Sarah. The harsh truth made his chest tighten, but he ignored the pain. She couldn't leave, and he wasn't about to stay. There was no place for him here in Pine Butte. His memories, and those of the rest of the townspeople, went too deep. And besides, Sarah had never asked him to stay.

Taking one last look around the bedroom, he slung the pack over his shoulder and walked out the door. He stood in the hallway and looked toward the clinic, longing for just one more glimpse of Sarah.

It would have to last a lifetime.

He heard Josie talking to someone in the waiting room, and the soft murmur of voices from one exam room told him that Sarah was with a patient.

After standing for a long minute, staring at the closed door of the exam room, he turned and walked out the back door. Maybe it was better this way. A clean break would avoid teary scenes and painful goodbyes. Besides, he acknowledged bleakly, she'd already said goodbye to him. It would be a long time before he forgot the pain in her eyes as she'd said, "Thank you for everything."

His motorcycle roared to life, and he turned the bike and headed toward Eagle Ridge Road. He didn't look back until he got to the place on the switchback where he'd stopped nine days before, driving into town. Easing the throttle down to idle, he slowed and lifted the visor of his helmet.

Pine Butte looked the same as it had nine short days ago. The houses were still dusty, the sign that welcomed visitors still looked shabby and decrepit. But *he* had changed, he realized slowly as he looked at the town where he'd grown up.

The words Sarah had spoken about forgiveness floated through his mind, and he knew with a shock of certainty that they weren't necessary anymore. Twelve years of hatred, and as many more years of torment before he'd finally left Pine Butte, vanished in the blink of an eye.

Now, when it was too late, he realized the past wasn't important. He looked at the roofs of the houses below him, and his bitterness toward the town crumpled into dust. The town of Pine Butte faded into insignificance. Now, when it was too late, he realized that Sarah was all that mattered. And Sarah hadn't asked him to stay.

Where there was no trust there couldn't be love.

Snapping the visor down, he revved his motorcycle and roared toward Denver. He didn't look back again.

Sarah paused in the exam room as she heard Connor's motorcycle sputter to life behind the clinic. She drew in a deep breath, waiting for the sudden silence that would mean he'd changed his mind and was coming back into the clinic to tell her he was staying. The motorcycle just roared louder as he put it in gear and then the noise gradually faded as he drove away from Pine Butte.

Carefully she let out the breath she hadn't realized she'd been holding. Looking at the floor, she blinked several times and swallowed the hard, bitter lump in her throat. After what seemed like an eternity, she looked up at the child's face that swam before her.

"I'm sorry, Billy. What were you saying? I couldn't hear you there for a moment."

As the child chattered away to her, she felt the last of her hope slipping away, like the last leaves that fall from the trees in the winter.

Chapter 17

Connor rubbed his face wearily and leaned against the counter in the Denver hospital, staring at the chart with bleary eyes. His day had started here twenty hours earlier, and it would be another hour before he could get home. At least, he told himself, he wouldn't lay in bed tonight staring at the ceiling, seeing Sarah's face everywhere. With any luck at all, by the time he got home he'd be too tired to even brush his teeth, let alone lay awake brooding about Sarah Wesley.

Pushing himself away from the counter, he stared at the chart in his hands. He had to write instructions for the child he'd just admitted to the hospital. *Pull it together,* he told himself savagely. He had to think about his patient, not Sarah.

Except not an hour went by that he didn't think about Sarah. And it was even harder to keep her out of his mind when he was tired. He slammed the chart onto the counter, making the night-duty nurses jump in their seats. He'd been home from Pine Butte for a month, and the longing for her got worse every day.

"Why don't you go home, Dr. MacCormac?" he heard one of the nurses say. "You've been here an awfully long time."

"I have to get orders set up for Christy Kining." His voice hardly sounded like his own. Hoarse and harsh, it sounded as if he'd been up and talking for at least forty-eight hours.

"You don't have to do it tonight," the nurse answered gently. "Go home and get some rest."

"In a minute," he answered irritably. He stared at the chart as the lines became wavy and blurry. Finally, sighing with resignation, he shoved it into the rack at the nurse's station. "All right," he snarled. "I'll be back at seven o'clock."

Running one hand through his hair, he walked down the hall toward the elevator. Just before he pushed the call button, he heard someone behind him.

"Dr. MacCormac?" a vaguely familiar voice said.

He turned around reluctantly. Whoever it was, he didn't want to talk to them at two o'clock in the morning.

The woman who hurried toward him looked familiar, but it took a moment to place her. When he finally realized who she was, his face relaxed into a smile that quickly turned into a worried frown.

"Mary Johnson! What are you doing here? Is something wrong with the baby?"

"No, the baby's fine. It's our daughter, Jenny." She paused, and he saw the fear on her face and her struggle to control it. "She's here for heart surgery. Sarah's been telling us for a couple of years that we have to get it done, and after what happened with the baby, we didn't want to take any chances by putting it off."

"I remember Sarah mentioned it once," he said softly. Even speaking her name made his heart ache.

"She arranged everything for us," Mary told him, the fear and anxiety in her eyes momentarily replaced by a smile as she spoke of her friend. "She even called the Parent's Place house so we would have a place to stay."

Connor stared at her for a moment, not seeing the worried woman who stood in front of him. All he could see was Sarah's luminous face, shining with love. A love that he had refused, pushing her away and grinding her precious gift into the dirt.

He forced his attention to the woman who watched him. "When is your daughter's surgery scheduled?" he forced himself to ask. All he really wanted to know about was Sarah.

Mary licked her lips. "Tomorrow morning. The doctor told us it should be routine, and that afterward Jenny'll be as good as new." She looked down. "But I worry," she added in a low voice.

Taking her arm, Connor led the woman to her daughter's room. Every pediatric room was a single, equipped with a chair that folded out into a bed. Her child slept peacefully in the semidark of the room. "You have to get some sleep, Mary. You don't want to scare Jenny in the morning when you're so tired you can't keep your eyes open, do you?"

"I know," she sighed. "I just can't convince my mind to slow down enough to sleep, though."

"You need to think about something else," Connor said firmly. He paused and watched Mary settle herself in the chair. He tried to think of something else to ask her, but he couldn't think of anything but Sarah. "How's Sarah?" he finally asked.

Mary froze and looked at him. "What difference does it make to you?" she questioned carefully.

"I care about her." He sounded as if the admission had been torn out of him, and he forced himself to continue. "I want her to be happy."

Mary stared at him for a long time. "If that's true, you sure have a funny way of showing it," she finally said. "She's been desperately unhappy since you left, but you know Sarah. She's working harder than ever to try to cover it up. She's going to make herself sick if she keeps it up."

Connor compressed his lips into a thin line. "And that bastard Ralph Wesley still won't pay to hire a doctor for the town?" Maybe the anger could keep him from thinking about Sarah being unhappy.

Mary's eyes glinted with humor. "Ralph has other things to worry about right now. The EPA came down on him with both feet right after you left. He's so busy tap-dancing for them he hasn't shown his face in town for a couple of weeks."

Connor made a noncommittal noise and stood to leave. Hearing about Sarah only made his loneliness and pain worse, and he wasn't in the mood right now to offer sympathy to Mary. "Good luck with Jenny's surgery tomorrow. I'm sure everything'll turn out fine."

He almost made it to the door before Mary stopped him. "Just a minute, Dr. MacCormac...I mean, Connor."

He didn't know Mary Johnson could sound so commanding, and he stopped and turned around. "Is there something I can do for you, Mary?"

"Yes, there is. Why did you leave Pine Butte?"

He stared at her for a minute and she stared right back, her gaze not wavering. A smile finally curved the corners of his mouth in spite of himself. "You don't beat around the bush, do you?"

"I learned not to," she said frankly. "The baby and I both had a close call. It does kind of put things into perspective. I know it sounds corny, but you never know how much time you have. It seems pretty silly to waste it over something that was over and done with years ago."

"It's not that simple, Mary."

"Isn't it? What's going to seem more important twenty years from now, your quarrel with Pine Butte or having a life with Sarah?" Mary watched him steadily, her eyes calm and direct. "You think about that, Connor."

"It isn't as simple as that," he repeated. "I let Sarah down. I didn't tell her the truth about myself. She gave everything to me, and I gave her nothing in return. She's better off without me." He paused, then added carefully, "And she didn't ask me to stay."

"Did you let her think you'd want to?"

"I didn't have to. She couldn't still want me after the way I treated her. She couldn't possibly forgive me."

"Why don't you give her a chance to tell you that herself? Don't you think you owe her that much?" Mary watched him with wise eyes. "And don't worry about what the town thinks."

"I don't give a damn about Pine Butte. All I care about is Sarah."

"Then maybe you're using it as an excuse not to take a chance with Sarah."

"I don't need any excuses." But he knew she was right. He'd spent a lifetime protecting himself from pain.

Mary watched him for a moment, then smiled. "I think you'd be surprised about how the town feels about you."

"No, I wouldn't. I know exactly how they feel. I just don't care anymore."

"They're awfully proud that someone from Pine Butte made something of himself," she said softly. "And I think they'd be even prouder if he came home."

"Bull," he snapped. "I'll always be that no-good MacCormac kid."

"You're wrong." Mary's quiet voice rang with certainty in the semi-darkness of the room. "What Ralph and Richard Wesley say doesn't reflect what the rest of the town thinks." She rose from the chair and came to stand in front of him, taking his hand. "Everyone wants to give you a chance, Connor. Our parents may have been bigoted when your father first came to town, but give us a little credit for being able to change." Her face reddened and she dropped his hand. "And Tom has made sure everyone in town knows the truth about him and Barb Wesley." She watched him steadily. "So the only thing stopping you is yourself. Are you sure you're not using what happened when you were a child as an excuse for not taking a chance now?"

The moment stretched out as he stood staring at Mary. She wasn't talking about the town and they both knew it. Finally he said softly, "I'm not sure of anything right now, Mary. But this isn't the time to discuss it. You have more important things to do. You need to get some rest." He bent over and kissed her cheek. "I'll be back in the morning to make sure everything is okay." He walked out of the hospital room, pausing to look back. Mary stood watching him, her expression impossible to read.

Jamming his hands into his pockets, Connor strode out of the hospital and found his motorcycle in the parking lot. He tried to concentrate on the light traffic, but Mary's words kept playing over and over in his head. When he finally got home, he lay in his bed and stared at the ceiling, thinking about Sarah and Pine Butte and the lost innocence of his youth.

Pine Butte had always stood for everything he hated about his childhood. It had been a symbol of every unjust thing that had happened to him as a child. But maybe Mary had been right, he thought slowly. Maybe he'd used the town as an excuse because he'd been afraid that Sarah couldn't forgive him for not trusting her. And instead of asking her and risking another rejection, he'd justified his refusal to stay in Pine Butte by saying the town wouldn't want him there.

If he was being honest, he'd admit the grudge he'd felt against the town had vanished sometime during the days he'd spent there with Sarah. It had disappeared when he'd discovered something far more worthwhile, something far more precious than his hatred for one small town. No, nothing mattered anymore besides Sarah.

And could what Mary said possibly be true? Could Sarah possibly forgive him for deceiving her? Could it really be as easy as Mary claimed? That all he had to do was talk to Sarah? He watched the flickering shadows on his wall from the car headlights below in the street, and wondered if he dared to take a chance.

He walked into the surgical waiting room the next morning at ten o'clock. Tom and Mary Johnson were both there, huddled together on a small love seat, their hands entwined and identical looks of sick worry on their faces. He dropped into the chair next to them.

"How're you doing?" he asked softly.

"It seems like it's taking forever," Tom answered in a low, tortured voice.

"It always does. It may be another hour at least before you hear anything," Connor warned.

Mary opened her mouth to say something, but at that moment the doors to the surgery area swung open and one of the heart surgeons came out, smiling broadly. Tom and Mary jumped up at the same time and rushed over to him.

"Your little girl is fine," he said, and Connor slumped in his chair. He saw the tension drain from Tom and Mary at the same time. "She's in recovery now. She'll be going to her room in another hour or so, and we'll get you up there as soon as she is."

The heart surgeon lowered his voice and told the Johnsons a few more details, and Connor stood up. Mary turned around to look at him, and he gave her a thumbs-up.

"You're all going to do great." He watched her for a moment, and slowly began to smile. "And I have something important to do, too." Slipping out of the room, he headed for the parking lot.

Sarah rolled over and fumbled with the alarm clock, falling back into bed when the shrill noise finally stopped. It was getting harder and harder to get up in the morning. Maybe because she spent too much time laying awake at night, thinking about things that couldn't be.

Pushing back the covers, she stepped out of bed and shivered. The air blowing through her open window was definitely chilly. Fall was coming to the mountains, and that meant winter wasn't far behind. That bleak season always made her feel especially claustrophobic, knowing that the mountain passes were covered with snow for days at a time and she was trapped in Pine Butte.

But everything made her feel that way nowadays, she thought bitterly, heading for the shower. Instead of being in the place she belonged, doing the kind of work she loved, Pine Butte and her job had become her penance. She was trapped here with no way out. Denver and Connor were only four hours away, but they might as well have been on another planet for all the good that did her.

Of course, Connor had demonstrated just how important she was to him when he'd left a month ago. She hadn't heard a word from him, and every day that passed made her die a little more inside. Finishing her shower, she dressed and ate her breakfast and went down to the clinic, operating on autopilot just as she had since the day Connor had left.

She glanced at the appointment book and saw it was full. That was good. The busier she was, the less time she had to think about what was missing from her life. A perfect day, as far as she was concerned, was twelve hours of patients followed by one or two emergency calls. By the time she fell into bed she felt like a zombie and slept like one, too.

Holding her cup of coffee, she moved into her office and sat down at her desk. All her records were up to date and there was no correspondence to fill the hour until 9 a.m. when her first patients would arrive. Listlessly she picked up a professional journal and began to read it.

She hadn't gotten more than a couple of paragraphs read before she heard an insistent knocking on the front door of the clinic. At least an emergency would give her something to do until the clinic opened. Throwing the magazine on her desk, she hurried to the door.

Connor stood in front of her, wearing his familiar black jeans and leather jacket. She just stood and stared at him, not sure whether he was real or just a wished-for specter of her imagination.

The specter cleared his throat. "May I come in?"

"Of course," she muttered, starting to life and moving to one side.

He closed the door behind him and stood watching her. For a moment neither of them moved, each watching the other. Then she saw the uncertainty in his eyes, the growing fear, and she couldn't hold back for another second. She took one step, and then threw herself into his arms.

"Connor," she whispered, her face buried in the leather jacket, her arms holding him close. "You're back." Her fists gripped harder on the smooth leather. "You don't know how much I've missed you."

"Yes, I do." His voice was fierce and his arms tightened painfully around her. "I've missed you just as much."

She leaned back, brought her hands up to his face. "What are you doing here?" she whispered.

He smiled, his face more tender than she'd ever seen it. "I couldn't stay away. There was too much I needed here." His eyes twinkling, he added, "Nobody in Denver makes a cup of coffee like Earlene."

She smiled slowly, joy filling her heart. "Do you think you could make do with mine, instead?"

"I think so," he whispered. Bending over her, he kissed her with a tenderness that quickly escalated into passion. By the time he raised his head, his face was flushed and she didn't want him to stop.

"Connor," she whispered, "we're standing in the waiting room. Let's go upstairs."

He smiled at her again and took her hand as he headed for the stairs. "All right, but anyone who looked in the windows would only see us talking. There's a lot I have to say to you, Sarah."

Her step faltered as she glanced at him. Had he come only to talk to her? Maybe he hadn't come back to stay, after all. Maybe he just hadn't liked the way they'd parted, and had come to make sure there were no hard feelings.

She followed him to her apartment, coloring faintly when she saw the mess she'd left in the kitchen. *Who cares,* she told herself fiercely. If all he'd come to do was talk, then leave, it didn't matter what her kitchen looked like.

He pulled her down on the couch and sat next to her. Holding on to her hand, he stared out the window for a long time, until finally her stomach began to roil and she couldn't take the waiting anymore.

"Why have you come back, Connor?"

He looked at her in surprise. "Because I couldn't stay away any longer." He must have seen the confusion in her eyes, because he dropped her hand and cupped her face. "There are a lot of things I could live without, Sarah, but you're not one of them. I've come back to see if you'll have me here in Pine Butte."

The fist around her heart began to loosen. "Of course I want you here, Connor. How could you doubt that for even a second?"

"I said some pretty horrible things before I left last time. And I know I hurt you terribly by not telling you about myself earlier. Maybe you changed your mind about me."

"Never. I love you, Connor. Nothing you could say would make me stop loving you."

He drew her into his arms. "I love you too, Sarah, and I'm so sorry for the way I hurt you. I've spent every second of every day this past month regretting what I said to you."

"It doesn't matter. You're here now, and that's what's important," she said, burrowing deeper into his embrace.

"No," he said, drawing away from her. "I have to tell you this. You were right, you know. About everything you said. I *was* afraid to love you, and I was using what happened here in Pine Butte twelve years ago as an excuse to run away. It just took me a while to figure that out."

She felt her lips curving in a smile as she leaned over to kiss his throat. "What made you realize that?"

"Mary Johnson, of all people. I ran into her at the hospital the day before yesterday. She said some things to me that made me realize what a jerk I was being. Once I came to my senses, I got here as soon as I could."

"So you're back to stay?" She held her breath, waiting for his answer.

"If you'll have me. I figure I can handle the clinic when you're gone, and when you're here we can do it together."

"What do you mean, when I'm gone? Where do you think I'll be going?"

He eased away from her and pulled an envelope out of his pocket. "Remember how you told me your dream was to travel? Here's your ticket to the world."

She stared at him. "Let me get this straight. You came back to Pine Butte so I could leave?"

"Isn't that what you want? You told me about all the places you want to see and all the things you want to do. I want you to be happy."

Something melted inside her as she looked at him. "You idiot," she said lovingly. "Do you really think I'd want to do all those things by myself? Do you honestly think I'd walk away from you just so I could travel?"

"You said it was your dream."

"That was before I knew you. *You* are my dream. All I want is to be with you. It doesn't matter if I don't see Europe or China or the pyramids in Egypt. If I do nothing but spend the rest of my life with you I'll have fulfilled every dream worth having."

"I thought you wanted your freedom."

"That was before I met you and realized that true freedom is spending your life with the man you love."

"Sarah," he whispered as he drew her closer. "Does that mean you'll marry me?"

"Yes, Connor. There's nothing I want more."

Their lips met, and passion blazed to life instantly. After a moment, he stood up and swung her into his arms and headed for the bedroom.

They melted together like fire and smoke, feeding off each other's passion and need until they were both frantic with desire.

"Sweet Sarah, I couldn't think of anything but you," he groaned, sliding his hands over her back and sides, trying to touch her everywhere at once.

She twined around him, her hands busy rediscovering him. "Oh, Connor, I've missed you so. Please don't ever leave me again."

"Never," he answered fiercely, claiming her mouth as he plunged into her.

She rose up to meet him, holding on as she crested and flew off the peak, gasping his name over and over. His arms tightened around her as he poured himself into her.

They lay together for a long time, holding each other too tightly, neither of them willing to let go. Murmuring endearments and words of love, they clung together as if they would never be parted again.

Finally she stirred and turned in his arms. Running her fingers over his chest, she tangled them in the soft mat of hair and murmured, "I probably have patients waiting downstairs."

"I think they'll be willing to wait a few more minutes." As he leaned against the back of the bed, he gazed at her, his eyes full of love. Slowly his mouth curved up in a grin. "Are you sure you won't reconsider about that trip? I'm afraid I'm going to get real lonely."

Before she could question him, he leaned over to rummage in the pile of clothes that had been hastily tossed to the floor. When he sat up, he held a second envelope in his hand. It was identical to the one she'd tossed on the floor.

"You didn't really think I was so unselfish that I'd let you get away from me, did you?" He leaned toward her, his eyes glittering. "Sarah, I couldn't bear to be away from you for a day, let alone for a couple of months."

"What's in that envelope?" she asked, her voice faint.

He grinned at her and tossed it in her lap. "Take a look."

She opened it slowly, her heart pounding. Inside was a sheaf of airline tickets stapled together. On top was an itinerary for a two-month trip.

"That other envelope on the living room floor is the other set of tickets."

"You know I can't leave, Connor." Anguish filled her voice and she refused to let herself hope.

"Sure you can. You didn't look at the letter."

"What letter?" Hands shaking, she opened the envelope again. Underneath the tickets was a single folded sheet of paper. She opened it slowly, holding her breath. It was from one of Connor's colleagues in the Denver hospital, stating that he was looking forward to taking over her practice in Pine Butte for two months.

"Is it true?" she whispered. "We can leave, together, for two whole months?"

"I thought a two-month honeymoon sounded good. What do you think?"

"I think I love you," she answered, dropping the envelope on the bed and throwing herself into his arms. "But you didn't have to do this. I meant it when I said I'd be happy just to be with you."

"I know you did." He smiled as his kiss trailed down her throat and found her ear. "But I can't wait to make love to you on a beach under a Mediterranean moon."

It was a long time later when they finally got out of bed and pulled their clothes on. "The waiting room is probably full of people," she said, knowing she should feel guilty but refusing to.

Pulling her close one last time, he gave her a very thorough kiss then let her go. "Well, then, let's get busy. I don't want them to get the wrong idea about their new doctor."

She watched him move around the room and thought it was very possible she was going to die of happiness. "Are you going to help me today, then?"

"Of course." He grinned at her. "You're stuck with me now, lady. And if you decide you don't like the way I practice medicine, that's just tough. So the sooner you get used to me, the better."

Laughing, she headed for the stairs, saying over her shoulder, "Somehow, I don't think that's going to be a problem. But if you think you can order me around, you'd better think again."

He caught her in his arms and smoothed back her hair. "Honey, I wouldn't even think of it." He kissed her again, a long, lingering kiss that promised a future bright with love and happiness.

Then, hand in hand, they walked down the stairs. Connor MacCormac was home at last.

* * * * *

Silhouette celebrates motherhood in May with...

Debbie Macomber
Jill Marie Landis
Gina Ferris Wilkins

in

Three Mothers & a Cradle

Join three award-winning authors in this beautiful collection you'll treasure forever. The same antique, hand-crafted cradle connects these three heartwarming romances, which celebrate the joys and excitement of motherhood. Makes the perfect gift for yourself or a loved one!

A special celebration of love,

Only from

▼ *Silhouette*®
™

—where passion lives.

Take 4 bestselling love stories FREE

Plus get a FREE surprise gift!

Special Limited-time Offer

Mail to Silhouette Reader Service™

3010 Walden Avenue
P.O. Box 1867
Buffalo, N.Y. 14269-1867

YES! Please send me 4 free Silhouette Intimate Moments® novels and my free surprise gift. Then send me 6 brand-new novels every month, which I will receive months before they appear in bookstores. Bill me at the low price of $2.89 each plus 25¢ delivery and applicable sales tax, if any.* That's the complete price and a savings of over 10% off the cover prices—quite a bargain! I understand that accepting the books and gift places me under no obligation ever to buy any books. I can always return a shipment and cancel at any time. Even if I never buy another book from Silhouette, the 4 free books and the surprise gift are mine to keep forever.

245 BPA ANRR

Name	(PLEASE PRINT)	
Address		Apt. No.
City	State	Zip

This offer is limited to one order per household and not valid to present Silhouette Intimate Moments® subscribers. *Terms and prices are subject to change without notice. Sales tax applicable in N.Y.

UMOM-9295   ©1990 Harlequin Enterprises Limited

HEARTBREAKERS

Hot on the heels of **American Heroes** comes Silhouette Intimate Moments' latest and greatest lineup of men: **Heartbreakers.** They know who they are—and *who* they want. And they're out to steal your heart.

RITA award-winning author Emilie Richards kicks off the series in March 1995 with *Duncan's Lady,* IM #625. Duncan Sinclair believed in hard facts, cold reality and his daughter's love. Then sprightly Mara MacTavish challenged his beliefs—and hardened heart—with her magical allure.

In April *New York Times* bestseller Nora Roberts sends hell-raiser Rafe MacKade home in *The Return of Rafe MacKade,* IM #631. Rafe had always gotten what he wanted—until Regan Bishop came to town. She resisted his rugged charm and seething sensuality, but it was only a matter of time....

Don't miss these first two **Heartbreakers,** from two stellar authors, found only in—

Patricia Coughlin

Graces the ROMANTIC TRADITIONS lineup in April 1995 with *Love in the First Degree*, IM #632, her sexy spin on the "wrongly convicted" plot line.

Luke Cabrio needed a lawyer, but high-powered attorney Claire Mackenzie was the last person he wanted representing him. For Claire alone was able to raise his pulse while lowering his defenses...and discovering the truth behind a vicious murder.

ROMANTIC TRADITIONS: *Classic tales, freshly told. Let them touch your heart with the power of love*, only in—

SIMRT7

THE MACKADE BROTHERS

the exciting new series by
New York Times bestselling author

Nora Roberts

The MacKade Brothers—looking for trouble,
and always finding it. Now they're on a collision
course with love. And it all begins with

**THE RETURN OF RAFE MACKADE
(Intimate Moments #631, April 1995)**

The whole town was buzzing. Rafe MacKade
was back in Antietam, and that meant only one
thing—there was bound to be trouble....

Be on the lookout for the next book in the
series, **THE PRIDE OF JARED MACKADE—
Silhouette Special Edition's 1000th Book!**
It's an extraspecial event not to be missed,
coming your way in December 1995!

THE MACKADE BROTHERS—these sexy, trouble-
loving men will be heading out to you in alter-
nate books from Silhouette Intimate Moments
and Silhouette Special Edition.
Watch out for them!

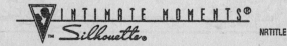

INTIMATE MOMENTS®
™ *Silhouette*®

**Five unforgettable
couples say "I Do"...
with a little help
from their friends**

*Always a
Bridesmaid!*

Always a bridesmaid, never a bride...that's
me, Katie Jones--a woman with more taffeta
bridesmaid dresses than dates! I'm just one of
the continuing characters you'll get to know in
ALWAYS A BRIDESMAID!--Silhouette's new
across-the-lines series about the lives, loves...and
weddings--of five couples here in Clover, South
Carolina. Share in all our celebrations! (With so
many events to attend, I'm sure to get my own
groom!)

In June, **Desire** hosts
THE ENGAGEMENT PARTY by Barbara Boswell

In July, **Romance** holds
THE BRIDAL SHOWER by Elizabeth August

In August, **Intimate Moments** gives
THE BACHELOR PARTY by Paula Detmer Riggs

In September, **Shadows** showcases
THE ABANDONED BRIDE by Jane Toombs

In October, **Special Edition** introduces
FINALLY A BRIDE by Sherryl Woods

Don't miss a single one--wherever
Silhouette books are sold.

Silhouette®

AAB-G